MOTHER LAND

Mother Land

DMETRI KAKMI

London

First published in 2008 for the
Writing & Society Research Group
at the University of Western Sydney
by the Giramondo Publishing Company

First published in Great Britain by Eland Publishing Ltd
61 Exmouth Market, London EC1R 4QL in October 2009

Cover design by Nick Randall
Cover image: *On the bow of a Caique* © Robert A. McCabe
from *Greece: Images of an Enchanted Land 1945–1965*,
published by Patakis Publishers and Quantuck Lane Press
Map © Reginald Piggott

To the memory of
Kaliopi Kakmi (1939–1993)

CONTENTS

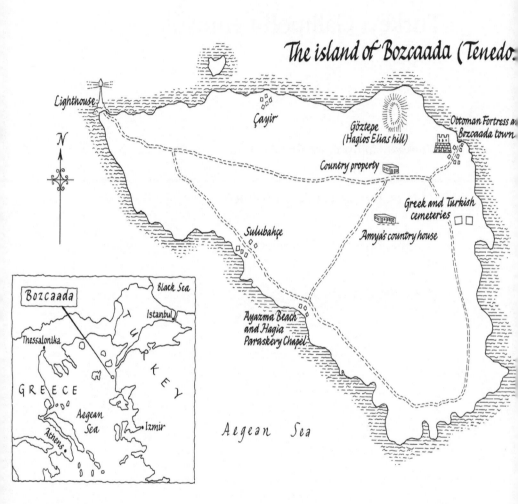

The island of Bozcaada (Tenedo[

Lighthouse

Çayır

Göztepe
(Hagios Elias hill)

Ottoman Fortress an
Bozcaada town

Country property

Greek and Turkish
cemeteries

Sulubahçe

Amya's country house

Ayazma Beach
and Hagia
Paraskevy Chapel

N

Aegean Sea

Bozcaada

Black Sea

Istanbul

T U R K E Y

Thessalonika

GREECE

Aegean
Sea

Izmir

Athens

Turkey, Gallipoli Peninsula
2002

Candidate to exile, whatever your destination, one day or other you will return to your starting point.

DAHMANE EL HARRACHI

I STAND at land's end, gazing at the Aegean Sea. The day is stifling. There is not a breath of wind. Far beneath, waves lick the base of the cliffs. But there is no heart to their effort. They froth and dissipate. Even the gulls have given up and drift in wide, lazy circles against the pale sky. On the opposite shore of the Dardanelle Straits, the ruin of Troy is a pimple on the fertile plain.

'Here, I brought these for you,' says my friend Sinan, handing me a pair of binoculars. 'I thought you might want to see the island from here.'

I take them, touched and grateful for his thoughtfulness. He is kind and sensitive, and I do not know if I would have ventured this far had it not been for him. I turn to face the open sea and adjust the binoculars until murky distance leaps into sharp focus. Sitting on the southwest horizon is an island. Its lavender hump trails a lumpy tail on the ultimate cliché: Homer's 'wine-dark sea'. All the same, there they are, the narrows that inspired the fabulist historian to such rapturous declamations; wine dark, indeed. There too is the place he wrote about when time still followed a pagan rhythm: Tenedos, or Bozcaada as it is known today. In the haze, it resembles a prehistoric beast stretched out and lazing in the setting sun. As my eyes linger on its curves and indentations, something else steps forward to claim the stage – something I have not seen or thought of in many years.

Three islets sit low on the water. I hold my breath. As a boy, I used to be captivated by their aloofness and solitude. When

I'd had enough of people, I yearned to build a hut and live on one of them, alone, separate and untouched by a world that, even at that age, seemed capricious and delinquent beyond reckoning. Back then the islets seemed like sailors, braving the immense savagery of the sea that darkened and swelled in winter, battering, overwhelming everything, sending thick sheens of spray into the air and threatening to tear down the foundations of the land, and rake out to the depths the thin soil, the grasses and the yellow cat's ear flowers that sprouted in warmer months. But that was in another time, another place. Before the tide of history and politics compelled my family to abandon our homeland and to settle in Australia, a voluminous, yet no less insular island on the other side of the world. And here am I now, gazing from across the water at Tenedos, the birthplace I have not set foot on for more than three decades. Strange how the line never really breaks; strange how one is reeled back, easy as fish.

When Greeks lived on Tenedos in greater numbers, they called the biggest islet Mavriya. At its centre stood a lighthouse. Beneath it sat a whitewashed chapel dedicated to Saint Nicholas. For some reason, the villagers thought it a suitable place to graze their donkeys during the summer months, which accounts for why the more literal-minded Turks called it Donkey Island. Alongside is Snake Island, so called because it was said to be, and perhaps still is, teeming with serpents; and because of its crescent-moon shape, the third islet is known as Sickle Island. Though it could as easily have been named Goat Island, since the islanders used to bring their goats to fatten themselves on the lush grasses that sprouted after the spring rains. At least that's how I remember it . . .

My binoculars seek the once familiar sights of Mavriya. I work my fingers to sharpen the focus. For a moment the world refuses to be corralled inside the lens. It flies out in alarm on both sides. Then two different times, two worlds, waver and fight for supremacy before my eyes. Past and present, super-imposed over one another, merge, separate and melt. What I want to see, and what is actually there, grapple and fight a desperate battle. When the victor finally raises his arm, the ruins, lying close to the soil, reveal themselves. The lighthouse is a mottled stump. The chapel is no more than a low crumbling wall. I linger for a moment, searching for signs of life. Nothing stirs. Not even a blade of grass. My eyes fly across the island of snakes to settle on the westernmost peninsula. Where there was once nothing but wilderness, there now turns a regiment of wind turbines. They march across the strip of land in single file; their great white blades slice the air in ghostly silence, as if rock and soil were a fantastical vessel destined for unknown shores. It could not have been a more incongruous sight had a craft landed from outer space.

Modernity has obviously made inroads here as well. As late as 1971, there was no electricity or running water on Tenedos – at least not in most private homes. Automobiles were a rarity, perplexing and alarming symbols of a world beyond reach or even imagining. Islanders used to get about on horse, mule and donkey; kerosene lamps illuminated the majority of homes, and water was brought from the numerous fountains scattered about the village. Most of the inhabitants were peasants in every sense of that anachronistic term, and eked out a living by attempting to tame sea and soil.

As I watch, a ferryboat detaches itself from the Anatolian mainland, heading for the island. It is weighed down with vehicles. Once, Captain Yakar's boat had taken passengers back and forth, and that only in calm weather. In winter, we were mostly cut off. Sometimes even the phone in the post office died and no news was to be had. Now technology has pulled the island closer to the world. Most inhabitants probably have cell phones and western-style flushing toilets – unheard-of luxuries in our day.

Sinan tells me that it is time to leave. I nod absent-mindedly. The sun licks the horizon, painting the sea a misty mauve on which sparkles an oily gold suffused with shades of oyster pink and bronze. Reluctant to let go the vision, I lift the seeing glasses again and train them on Tenedos. If only I could catch a glimpse of our house, the old neighbourhood, the church. If I could establish their veracity, I would sleep well tonight; but, in the profusion of dwellings, old and new, only a minaret stands out. As darkness falls, a gloom rolls from the foot of the hill. It stretches and enfolds the village. I imagine that my eyes can actually see, from this distance, a string of fairy lights flicker round the base of the fortress on the shore, knowing that the café will be about to open for the nightly trade. I thought I heard, coming from across the water, the evening call to prayer. *Allahu ekber*, God is great, surely the most piercing lullaby in the world. For a moment I glimpse a gangly boy with close-cropped hair running beneath the linden trees, heading with great urgency for the pier. For a second, he is almost real. For the blink of an eye, he looks across the wastes of time, straight into my eyes, and we almost recognise one another. Then he too falls into the obscurity that devours all, and Tenedos melts into darkness as if it had never existed.

Strange to think that Sinan and I will be on the island the next day; it feels as if I am returning to a place that is mythical, a figment of an overheated imagination.

In my breast pocket, I have a black-and-white photograph of my mother taken in the late 1950s. It shows a striking young woman, composed, self-assured, a Mona Lisa smile on her painted lips. She must have been sixteen, seventeen at most when the likeness was taken. Before flying out of Australia, I had vowed to bury the photograph on Tenedos. It is where the young girl ought to rest now that she is no more. Just as I hope that, when my time comes, someone will bring my ashes here, too.

Sinan rests a hand on my shoulder. 'It is time to go back,' he whispers. His thick eyebrows meet over the bridge of his nose, making him look like a prince out of an Ottoman miniature. I smile and nod, fighting back the urge to clasp his hand – a common enough Turkish affectation that does not meet with his approval.

As I stand at land's end, two paths uncoil above me in the form of twined serpents. In their immense bodies are images of a lifetime. A great exhibition presents itself, and I wonder what it means and where it has come from. It tangles with the knotted roots of sea grasses, and gently rolls across the seabed forgotten amphorae, coins, bejewelled crowns, the empty shells of crabs and limpets and the skulls of soldiers. The serpents form a tendril song that links blood and tendon, bone and marrow, sky to earth, and to the many strata of rock, fossil, mud and clay, all the way down to the core of the earth. Here time does not exist. Life, death, creation, destruction, past, present, future have yet to find a name; and that which has been lost is still playing out its final act.

Turkey, Bozcaada (Tenedos) 1969–1971

And the god created Tenedos so that people can live longer.

HERODOTUS

'BEFORE recorded time, when the world was younger than it is today, a mighty people lived on the opposite shore. They were called the Aeolians.' That's Grandfather Dimitro speaking. Listen because he knows a lot, and he does not take kindly to repeating himself. I am sitting with him on the peak of Saint Elias's hill behind our country house, gazing across the narrows toward the mainland. It is the highest spot on the island and the view is spectacular. Byron, my white West Highland terrier, busily sniffs zigzags into the ground with his wet nose. For once the wind is holding its breath. A few miles across the sea, Anatolia wavers through the milky haze. 'That's where the Aeolian coastal towns used to be,' Grandfather continues, pointing. His fisherman's finger rakes the land from south to north, trembling. The wrinkled skin hangs loose on the bone. 'In their time, before they were wiped out by the Persians, the Aeolians caused to be built two round hollow towers on the shores of the Marmara Sea, which were played like pipes when the wind blew, now plaintively whispering, and now wailing as if in sorrow, or again bursting forth in a joyous anthem.' Grandfather falls silent. A ship's horn reverberates across the landscape, booming in the vast sky. As if prompted, Grandfather goes on with the story. 'The years passed without anyone noticing them. When the name of the Aeolians was but dust in people's mouths and there was nothing left standing of the two round hollow towers, the wind could still be heard up and down the coast, playing its ghostly tune. These sounds that seemed to emanate from the bowels of the earth, and from the sky all at once, confused and frightened people. They chanted spells, burned incense and performed ceremonies until they drove Aeolus' music across the channel to our tiny island. Aeolus is the god of the winds. When he set foot on Tenedos, the goddess Hymethea kindly allowed him to live in one of her many splendid caverns, beneath this very hill.' Grandfather pats the earth beside him and smiles. Dust puffs up from the dry grasses, coating his fingers. 'So the story goes,' he says. 'On windy days, you can still hear Aeolus and Hymethea sing the sad songs the islanders like to hear.' I turn to face him. 'Why do we like sad songs?' I ask, perplexed. 'It's how we are,' he answers, scratching his close-cropped white beard. A sound in the meadow far below claims his attention. He angles his head as if listening to a faint call. 'It's your mother,' he says, his voice softening. 'She needs your help. Go, because she has nobody else.' I leap up and whistle for Byron. Grandpa swats my backside as I dash off. Remembering that I had to ask Grandfather in which cove to find the sea urchins, I turn round. But he has vanished, gone back to his resting place.

When I arrive at our country house, my mother is in a mood. She's thirty, of medium height, and very pretty, with a full head of mahogany hair and intense eyes. 'Where have you been?' she snaps. 'I've been calling for ages.' She's wearing a loose house dress and is short of breath. 'On the hill,' I tell her, 'with Grandfather Dimitro.' Mama presses her lips together. 'Are you still on about that?' she says. 'It's time you let the poor man's soul rest in peace.' The sun has burned her forehead and smooth cheeks. 'You're like your father. Never around when I need you,' she complains. 'Come on. Help me load up Train. I want to be back in town before dusk.' Train is the name of our donkey. He's a nervous, skittish beast. I help Mama pack. When I approach Train with something or other in my arms, he watches me with wild, suspicious eyes and bares his yellow teeth. He doesn't trust me, or anyone else for that matter. Mama is the only one who can approach him without risking his flinty hoofs. 'Give me that.' She grabs a bundle of blankets and pillows from my arms. 'You bring the stuff and I'll load him up. Scaredy cat.' I walk to the kitchen. Byron tangles up in my feet and I kick him aside, taking my frustrations out on him. He cowers for a moment but comes back again. I hate it when Mama calls me names. I do my best to care for her and my younger sister Electra when my father is at sea. No matter how hard I try, it's never enough for her. She has to stick in the dagger. I return with the mortar and pestle and some pots and pans. 'Where's Electra?' I ask, looking round for her. 'She went back to town with your Aunt Irene,' Mama replies. 'She's too little to be out in this heat. Give me those.' She takes the kitchen utensils. 'And go lock the chapel.' I dash to the house of worship that sits in a field of asphodel. It's a tiny structure made of rendered stone and a pitched roof. One by one, I blow out the candles and make sure that there are no oil lamps left burning. I close the shutters on the two windows and secure them. The light fades from the glinting dome and bare iconostasis. The precious icons were taken to town yesterday. At the entrance, I turn to face the sanctuary. I cross myself and bid the two saints who live here farewell. Then I turn the heavy key and lock the door. My mother is outside with the donkey. She's wrapped a lavender scarf round her head to keep off the sun. Hopefully she will also fool the military police that patrol the island into thinking we're Turks. 'Get on,' she orders. 'It's too far to walk in this heat.' I click my tongue against the roof of my mouth and tilt back my head. 'No, it's all right. You can ride him. You're more tired than I am.' Mama won't hear of it. 'Get on,' she says again, impatient. 'We can take it in turns.' She holds the donkey by the halter and brings him close to the steps. I climb on his back and grab the reins. 'Come on, Byron,' I call to the dog. 'Be careful he doesn't get under the donkey's hoofs,' my mother warns. 'You know what happened to the last one.' How can I forget! Black-hearted Train kicked my other terrier and broke his spine. The poor thing twitched and howled until my father put him out of his misery.

Now that it's autumn, people are locking their country houses and moving back to town. The landscape is sad and empty. The soil knows it's time to sleep. When next it wakes, in six or seven months, it will be fresh as a baby's smile. At the end of every May, my father says, 'Time to open the country house.' And the packing begins. Now that it's the beginning of September, the reverse is happening. The road to town is a snake coiling in the dust. It's trafficky with men, women and children. All are trudging tiredly beside donkeys and mules loaded with wooden crates. Those travelling in the same direction as us, they're carrying the grape harvest to the wineries. Those going in the opposite direction have already been and are returning to the vineyards with lighter burdens. 'Hey!' they shout. 'Hey!' as they pass. 'You all right?' 'Yep, all right, and you?' 'Good. Good. Can't complain . . . ' They flog their beasts of burden and, in a welter of noise and dust, move on.

In town, my mother and my sister Electra unload Train and put everything away. I tie Byron in the backyard and head for the hill that's behind the Greek Quarter. My cousin Timon and the other guys are up there, waiting. As soon as I leave the last house behind and step onto the incline, I sense it: the ever-present wind. It shoulders its way over the crest and round the coves, restless and sighing. It is late afternoon and the weather has cooled somewhat. I walk further up the hillside and open my lungs. I breathe in deep. I take another breath and kneel.

I touch the earth with the palm of my hand, like my grand-father did, and listen through my fingers. Here is a learning I made: when our Greek ancestors first settled on Tenedos they could not have known about the north-easterly wind. They could not have guessed that these blasts from the Asian steppes would carve a highway on the seas, bringing ideas that weren't native to our island. Nor could they have known that the winds would eventually cleave the island in two: upper and lower, Greek and Turkish, Christian and Muslim, love and hate, and something else – something that's like the uneasy truce between an island and the sea. The drunks in the tavern reckon that it's impossible for Greeks and Turks to live together. These cynics exist on both sides. Far as I can tell, Greek and Turk, Christian and Muslim, they're one and the same; differences are skin deep. 'We're all Allah's people, aren't we?' says my father's Turkish friend Ezet, and I trust him. 'Scratch a Greek and you'll find a Turk under the skin. Gaze into a Turk's eyes and a Greek will look back at you,' he's in the habit of saying. 'We've lived together so long we can't distinguish one from the other.' Hereabouts, they call the north-easterly wind *poyraz*. It's a Turkish word. *Poyraz* is everywhere. It gets in the water you drink and the food you eat. It gets under your skin and inflates it like a bladder. I've lived with the island's fierce and unpredictable winds for so long, I wouldn't be able to breathe any other air if I tried. That's how it is. Tenedos gets in the blood and the sea-breeze becomes part of you. You breathe it and you swim in it. After a while, it begins to sing in your lungs and speak through your mouth. 'One day,' my mother once said, 'this wind will carry us away.'

'Are you coming or not?' It's Cousin Timon. He's tired of waiting for me. The other gang members – Apostoli, Yerasimo and Aristo – have gone ahead. The rocks have swallowed them up. Timon looks a lot like me. He's gangly and thin as a switch, with a crop of dark brown hair. I usually know what he is thinking. Right now what's going through his sharp brain is this: I shouldn't have brought him along. He's too young. He's not up to this. 'Come on,' he insists, holding out his hand. He doesn't give up easily and will persist until he gets his way. 'You go ahead,' I tell him. 'I'm tired. This wind is giving me a head-ache. I'll join you later.' He's standing further up, looking down at me. Behind him the narrow path coils round the shoulder of the hill. The wind causes the clothes to ripple round his body. Timon knows I'm fibbing. He knows that I have no intention of joining the gang later; I just wanted to see him. I'm not one for boisterous games and snake hunting in the old castle. He knows that too. Timon and I, we've been tied together since birth. Because we're virtually twins, people think we're brothers. We're nothing of the sort. He's two years older than me, the son of my mother's older sister Irene. Timon touches the scar above his right eyebrow and dashes off, agile as a goat. 'Wait for me,' he yells to the others, waving his arms over his head. 'I'm coming!' Up high three dark dots are drawing closer to the castle that is a black tooth in the otherwise empty landscape. They stop briefly; then start moving again. Halfway between heaven and earth, beneath a pile of slow-moving clouds, another dot appears, closing the gap. I rest on a rock and sulk. I've let go my big chance. More than anything, I want to prove to the others that I am worthy of joining the gang. They're all two to three years older than me. My legs aren't as fast, nor my heart as brave. To them, I'm a pipsqueak and a nuisance; someone that holds them back from pushing their growing bodies to the limit.

Thunder growls behind the clouds. The breeze picks up. It's making earth music in the wild sage and thyme and oregano bushes. Timon, Apostoli, Aristo and Yerasimo descend the hill. They are walking single file, like the Indians in the *Tom Mix* comics we read. Aristo is swinging a dead snake in great loops over his head. He is the oldest in the group and furtive as a fart. His father has a vile temper and his older brother is simple. They say that Aristo is touched with both afflictions and that, one day, he will end up in big trouble. There's usually tension between Aristo and Timon, because my cousin is the leader of the gang and Aristo doesn't like playing second fiddle. He wants to take over. Thankfully, the other two guys won't vote him in. If I were allowed to vote, I wouldn't back him either. He's an ox, with legs that are too short for his long torso and arms that dangle low. When they are close, I walk part way to meet them. Aristo is ahead of the rest. He scowls at me. 'This is for you, shrimp,' he says, swinging back and whipping me in the face with the dead snake. It hits me across my left cheek and the back of the neck. I reel, holding my face. Aristo lets off a mean laugh. Timon immediately pounces on him. They roll in the grass, their arms a windmill of punches. A boulder stops them from rolling all the way into the village. Timon sits on Aristo and grabs him by the throat, swearing. They're both covered in dust. Grass tangles in hair that's grown long during the school summer break. Apostoli and Yerasimo make half-hearted attempts to separate them. When that fails, they stand back to enjoy the punch-up. 'He had it coming,' mutters Apostoli, rubbing his backside through the worn shorts. He's probably been playing the mare for them again.

When they exhaust themselves, Timon and Aristo stand up and smack the dust off their clothes. 'Apologise,' Timon says. He's breathless and red in the face. I don't want an apology from Aristo. It wouldn't mean anything. Besides Aristo is not the sort to apologise. 'He has to learn to fight,' he yells, pointing at me.

'He's piss weak. He cries like a girl. He doesn't belong with us.'
Gentle Apostoli puts his arm round my shoulders. Timon
keeps a sullen distance. When he's in a black mood, which
isn't often, it's best to leave him alone. Besides, he knows Aristo
is telling the truth. We descend in silence. The first house in
the village, or maybe it's the last, depending on which direction
you're coming from, belongs to Kokona. She's a widow that
lives alone beside the ravine. Her two sons are in America.
They never write. Kokona hasn't heard from them in years.
Her only company is an old mule, which she showers with
affection. The gang splits up. Yerasimo and Apostoli live next
to each other, so they go one way. Aristo goes off on his own,
whistling belligerently. I'm tempted to throw a rock at his fat
head, but Timon does not approve of such behaviour. Before
Timon leaves, he tells me to go straight home. 'Don't hang
around,' he says. 'It's not safe.' Hands in pockets, he's already
a miniature man dispensing comfort and protection. 'I want
to look in on Train,' I tell him. 'I've got to feed and water him.
Then I'll go home.' Timon nods and goes off. When we live in
town, Train shelters in a derelict house that my father inherited
from his father. It's a stone's throw from Kokona's place and
commands views of the harbour. We should be living up here,
instead of our dark place in the village proper.

'Baba's home,' my little sister shouts as I turn into our street.
Electra is a plump six year old, a fuzzy peach with tawny hair.
Even though her presence has not had an impact on me yet, her
dark, startled eyes often cause me to worry on her behalf. When
we go inside, Father is at the table in the front room, smoking.
A glass of cloudy *rakı* sits at his elbow. He's freshly bathed and
smells of *eau de cologne*. All the same, you can still catch a whiff
of the sea salt on his skin. One side of his face is in darkness and
the other in light. As always when he returns from a fishing trip,

he is pale and withdrawn, with a far-away look in his eyes. Mama is making cooking noises in the kitchen. 'Ah, my son, well met,' Baba says, scooping me in his arms. He kisses my cheek. His whiskers need a shave. Smoke rises from his mouth and nostrils. Before I can say anything, Mama calls from the kitchen. 'Where the devil have you been? I needed help to unpack and you disappear. Is this what we can expect from you?' When I don't reply, she adds, 'Well is it? Tell us now so that we can at least know where we stand.' No one replies. It's best to let her get it off her chest. My father puffs on his cigarette and sips the *rakı*. 'How many times do I have to tell you?' my mother calls again. 'It's not safe any more. You can't wander round like the old days. Tell him,' she commands my father. Baba's eyes see through the opposite wall and far away. It's hard to know what's in his head. 'Come get your dinner,' Mama calls. 'Quickly. We're going to Aunt Vasiliki's.' I hop off Baba's lap and we all gather in the kitchen.

While I mop up the chickpea, rice and yoghurt soup with crusty bread, Baba crushes his cigarette in the glass ashtray and lights another. 'Your mother's right,' he says. 'It isn't safe to wander the streets by yourself.' I ask him why not. 'I've told you a hundred times. Don't you listen? The government's turned the island into an open prison.' His long fingers hook the tip of his sharp nose when he plucks the cigarette from his lips. 'Do you know what that means?' he asks. I nod. 'Well, that's what Tenedos is now – an open prison.' He gets angry, blasphemes. Then he continues in a defeated voice. 'They've shipped criminals and mad people here. They're living in the houses that were abandoned by Greeks, free to wander round and do as they please.' I ask him why the government would do such a thing. It doesn't make sense. 'Because they hate Greeks.' My mother raises her voice. 'Be quiet, wife,' my father says. He tells Electra to close the front door. She slides off the chair and does as she's told. 'They want to drive us out,' my mother continues, undeterred. 'They want us to go. What better way to get rid of us than to fill the neighbourhood with cutthroats and maniacs? How quickly they forget what their precious Atatürk said. "You don't have to be a Muslim to be a Turk." That's what he said. A shared language, culture, tradition and connections to the land, that's enough to make a Turk of anyone. But these nationalists won't rest until we're all Muslims or dead, God forbid.' She goes quiet, as if a great bird has swooped in and carried her away.

When Baba returns from the sea, the first thing he wants to do is gather his wife and kids and visit the old family home in the Cauldron District. He was born in that house. It's by the water, at the end of a narrow street that opens onto a square. His younger sister Vasiliki lives there with her husband Yanni and their teenage daughter Zoe. Baba does not have other family. It's just him and his sister. The others are dead or in America; and since the living are as quiet as those that passed away it amounts to the same thing. When visiting his sister, Baba sits quietly in the guest room and, over the space of two or three hours, he knits his body back together again. Minute by minute, the flesh and bone that on the wave became gauzy as cheesecloth turns thick as a woollen jumper, regaining its vitality and substance. After a cup of Turkish coffee and a healthy dose of *rakı*, he's whole again and can get on with life. The visits are carbon copies of each other. Nothing changes. If someone in the street peeked in the window, they'd think we'd all been sitting on the spot, forever unmoving. Almost as soon as we arrive, Aunt Vasiliki serves coffee and water to the adults. Doe-eyed Zoe keeps Electra and me amused with sweets and her mandolin. Usually, local news is exchanged: who said or did what to whom, a curse on their lineage; may their scrotum or womb dry up; may their house fall down and the ground on which it stood be sown with salt. The depth of the curse alters depending on the severity of the case and the degree of displeasure elicited by the spoken-of individual. Aunt Vasiliki is a seamstress and therefore the hub of the island's news. Tonight, though, everyone talks about the bad words coming out of Cyprus. Things are getting worse down south and the ripples are beginning to impact our northern shores. Makarios, the bastard priest, they say, is stirring up more trouble. He's allied himself with Greek nationalists and that's making the Turks nervous. It's just like a churchman to stir up trouble. They are not happy with doing God's work; they have to get involved in politics, too. There is no telling what might happen next, or how events will affect us. Everybody fears a repeat of the exodus of 1964, but no one is brave enough to say so – they allude to it with a nod or a pointed exchange. To change the subject, my father and his sister start bickering. Because of her esteemed position as a seamstress, she likes to lord it over him, and everybody else come to think of it. 'You're a brick,' Vasiliki tells her brother, while showing my mother how to accomplish a tricky stitch on her gleaming Singer sewing machine. 'You'll never amount to anything.' Baba shrugs, resigned. 'What can I do about it,' he says, feebly. 'I'm illiterate.' 'And whose fault is that?' Vasiliki throws at him, 'yours or mine?' While they worry one another, Uncle Yanni sits serene as a vigil lamp. Calm and reflective, with a soft but firm voice, he is my favourite uncle. As the clock ticks away the hours, his amber-coloured worry beads fall gently one by one – click, click, click – through his fingers. Her eyes sparkling, Zoe picks up her adored mandolin and gently strums a melody. She loves that musical instrument more than life itself. You can tell by the way she buffs it with a touch of olive oil and a soft cloth that it's her entire world.

When it's time to leave, I plead with my mother to let me stay the night. Electra is already asleep. My father drapes her over his shoulder and off they go. When they are almost at the end of the street, Uncle Yanni shuts the door and turns the key in the lock. 'To bed,' he says, removing the cloth cap from his head. He has lustrous black hair, grown longer than is usual for a man, to hide the seven carbuncles on his skull.

I wake up. It's dark; there's nothing to see. I'm lying in a single bed. Zoe is pressed against me, wrapped tight under the covers. 'What is it?' she whispers. Her breath is moist against my ear. The wind is pacing round the house, keening. That's not what woke me up. I listen hard. I prick up my ears and close my eyes, the better to hear. 'I heard something,' I whisper back. Uncle Yanni is snoring in the next room. He's louder than the pounding sea that's shaking the foundations. How can Aunt Vasiliki sleep beside him? There it is again: footsteps on the landing. A floorboard creaks and then another. The footsteps stop outside the bedroom door. I open my eyes and stare, horrified, into darkness. My heart's hammering in my chest. I dare not breathe. A yellow light flickers round the edges of the door. 'Zoe,' I dare to whisper again, 'someone's on the landing.' She throws an arm round me and pulls me closer. I can feel her budding breasts push against my back. 'Don't worry,' she answers. 'It's only Saint Yorgos. He visits every night.'

I know she's trying to comfort me, but she's not doing a very good job. My heart stops. There's a saint in the house? Now we're done for! 'He'll go away soon,' Zoe reassures me. 'If you open the door, you'll see him. I wouldn't recommend it though. I peeked once and there he was, staring at me with his black-olive eyes.' I almost scream down the house; instead, I bite my tongue and pray for morning to come. When I close my eyes, I see the saint, walking up and down the passage. In the icon, he's a warrior on horseback. His lance pierces a dragon's flanks and blood squirts out. But, for some reason, in my head I see a stern, black-garbed priest with stovepipe hat. 'What does he want?' I ask, scared of the answer. 'He comes to make sure that your Aunt Vasiliki is keeping her promise,' Zoe replies. 'After she recovered from her illness, she promised to light the vigil lamp in his honour for the remainder of her days.' Zoe rubs my feet with hers. I calm down a little. 'Shush, now. If he hears you, he'll come in and stand by the bed until you fall asleep.'

I close my eyes and think of Grandfather Dimitro to calm me down. He inherited this house from his parents. They left it to him when the last sultan was still living in Istanbul. When he was a young man, Grandfather lost his first wife and two daughters to typhoid. He was so grief-stricken that, overnight, he lost his sight. Because there was no one to care for him, he was shipped off to the nuns on Tinos Island. Within the week, Grandfather was living at the Church of the Annunciation. They say that he lived there for eight years. Every day, a nun stood him before the icon of the Annunciation of the Archangel Gabriel. 'Do you see anything?' the nun would ask. Always the answer was in the negative. The years flew by. Across the water, Turkey changed. The sultan's reign ended. The Young Turks took over the running of the country, and sent our enemies, the English, the French, the Russians, and the Italians, scurrying back to their holes. The vultures that wanted to slice up our country and share the spoils. When Turkey turned into a republic, people became Europeans. They dressed in modern clothes and Romanised the alphabet. Back on Tinos, one blessed day, the nun stood Grandfather Dimitro before the icon and asked the question she had been asking these many years. He was in his early forties by this stage. 'What, if anything, do you see?' the ever-patient nun asked. My grandfather let out a wail and fell to his knees. He had not only seen through the murk that veiled his eyes, but he'd also had a vision: the Mother of Jesus herself, suffused in golden light. 'Go back to Tenedos,' she instructed in a sparkling voice. 'There a woman waits for you. She will give you a son and a daughter.' Grandfather quickly returned to Tenedos and married Electra Manolidis. She gave birth to two children, my father and his sister Vasiliki, in the room that's now a snoring chamber for Uncle Yanni. All of that happened between the two Great Wars.

Falling asleep inside this house is like sipping mint tea. It brings life to my body in the same way that it revives my father. The knowledge that my grandfather's people took their first and last breaths inside this house binds me to a line of fishermen, goatherds, and, if the rumours are to be believed, fierce strong-men and ruthless bandits, some Christian, others Muslim, and others from further afield: Russia and Poland. When I close my eyes, I become the heartbeat inside my grandfather's body. Though I speak to my grandfather all the time, he and Grand-mother Electra died before my parents made me. Even so, Grandfather Dimitro visits me from beyond life's borders. He's never really gone away. I was still in my crib when he paid his first visit. One day, when I was four, I spied him through a fog of incense smoke outside this bedroom door, where the saint is now. Grandfather was sitting by the bookshelf with the glass doors. 'Shush,' he said, finger to his lips, 'don't tell anyone.' He removed a book from the shelf. 'Come sit by me,' he said, beckoning. 'I'll read you a story from Homer. Before I do that, I want you to listen carefully. I have something very important to tell you.' He took a deep breath. 'Read. Read everything you can,' he instructed. 'Reading and writing are humanity's salvation.' When I didn't say anything, he added, 'Promise me you'll always put knowledge first. Question everything. Don't take anything at face value. They are the principles on which ancient Greece was built.' His slate-coloured eyes pulled the answer from me. I promised, kissing the back of his hand and touching it to my forehead as a sign of respect. Grandfather was a religious man who did not utter a word of Turkish as long as he lived. In his youth, the Greeks of Asia Minor rarely spoke the language of the Ottomans. Most lived in self-contained communities and hardly mixed, except through go-betweens. If anything, it was the representatives of the Ottoman court that learned to speak Greek to communicate with their subjects. Even though Turkish runs off my tongue easy as water, when I speak to Grandfather, it's in Greek.

The following morning, Uncle Yanni and I walk with the sea at our backs, but on Tenedos the sea is never behind you. It's in front, behind, and at your side. Its secret currents run in a circle, above and below. On Tenedos, the Aegean rules and all are subservient to her needs. The layout of the village sets up a kind of oppositional order to the sea's shifting chaos. The water that laps at our doorstep has the temperament of a thirteen-year-old – unpredictable and perverse. By contrast, the streets are predictable and knowable, if none too wide, and they criss-cross one another, good as worshippers in church. Three main streets begin in the heart of the village and run parallel until they dwindle in the countryside, while innumerable others pour down the surrounding slopes to wet their feet in the harbour. Aside from that, the town is split into districts, each with a name that reflects a unique quality of that area. Thus you have Almond Tree District, Fig Tree District, and so on. To reach our neighbourhood from where my aunt and uncle live in the Cauldron District, the streets wend up the gentle incline. At the

Church of the Annunciation of the Mother of God, Uncle
Yanni's mule knows to turn its flanks to the sun. Our house is
almost on the edge of the village, close to one of the three
schools. This time of the morning everything, even the ruined
houses and garbage-strewn lots, seems fresh and clean as a
just-picked melon. Uncle is not a seaman; he's headed for the
fields. He kisses the top of my head and leaves me on our
doorstep.

The minute I step into the living room, it's in the air. Or rather,
it's not. Yesterday evening, when I came home after feeding
Train, I could smell the sea in the sitting room. It had followed
my deep-sea diving father home and slithered under the divan.
Baba had to sit in a hot tub and scrub the salt off his skin. Even
then the *eau de cologne* couldn't hide the smell of brine. This
morning, he's already left on another fishing expedition and
the fishy smell has gone with him. First things first: I feed Byron.
I pet him and go back into the kitchen. Electra is eating breakfast, a huge white bow atop her head. She's small for her age
and is dwarfed by commonplace objects. In her hand is a slice
of buttered bread slathered in mulberry jam. The bread is so
large it could feed a pack of starving dogs. It's her first day of
school and she doesn't look happy about it. 'Don't worry,' I say,
rubbing her back. 'Evangelia is in the same class as you and I'll
be along the corridor.' That's the best I can manage. Nevertheless, she starts blubbering into her bread. Evangelia is Cousin
Timon's younger sister, and Electra's best friend. My mother
has her back turned. She's leaning into the washing trough, up
to her elbows in soapsuds. The window in front of her is foggy.
Steam rises from the trough and beads of condensation stream
down the glass. '*Haydi*,' she throws at me over her shoulder,
'get into your uniform. Eat something. It's time for school. And
you,' she says to Electra, 'stop crying or I'll give you something

to really cry about.' On the last word, she turns and locks eyes with me. With the milky window softening the early morning light from behind, she could be the film stars Figen Say or Hülya Koçiyit. Her full hair almost manages to draw attention away from a swollen lip and the purple ridge that runs down the left side of her face. Her expression dares me to say something. My eyes turn away, shamed. She has misbehaved again.

Amya is leaning on the stoop next door, a coffee cup in hand. Soft tendrils of steam make a ladder to heaven. She is my maternal grandmother's sister. As it is early, her hair hangs loose and wispy down her back. Electra and I walk past, hand in hand. 'Good luck my little angels,' Amya calls, 'learn plenty.' She waves. Her cheeks inflate like happy balloons and sink her eyes in fleshy folds of skin. In a while, her golden-haired daughter Athena will come out. They will sit in wicker chairs and the daughter will brush her mother's long grey hair, and coil it into a grizzled braid. While Athena lifts the brush and pulls it down again, a breeze will catch a stray strand and lift it over the rooftops to the sky. When it gets too close to the sun, it will burn and fall to earth. Mixed with the fertile soil, it will grow into a daffodil.

'Because you're not a Turk, may the bread you eat be poisonous.' That's how grade three at Independence Primary School started, first thing in the morning, before the class had its regulation bread roll and milk at ten. With these thirteen words, my appetite flew out the window. 'Because you're not a Turk, may the bread you eat be poisonous.' It's a shame because until then, I thought she was going to be a good teacher, this blonde tall-as-a-poplar woman. A bit pallid and thin-lipped, but you can't blame her for that. It stayed with me, what she said. I thought about it for the rest of the day, between breaking into a sweat

over sums and sticking the correct suffix on a root word. Half
the kids in class are Greek, the other half Turkish. The school
uniform is a black tunic with a starched white collar. The boys
have number-one buzz haircuts, on account of lice, and the girls
tie back their hair with a white ribbon. During Monday morning
assembly we all salute the white and red Turkish flag and sing
the national anthem. Our fingernails must be sparkling clean
and shoes polished to a shine. The Turkish boys are circumcised
and the Greek boys aren't. Aside from that, there's no difference
between us that I can see. But that means nothing to this sow
from the mainland. Half her students are Greek. So they deserve
to die. They're lower than dogs. Loathing has settled in her eyes.
She has a rock where her heart ought to be. I'd go home, except
I'll be beaten and sent back again. I've got no say in anything.
My mother believes in a good education. She's literate in Greek
and Turkish, and she's a miracle at sums. My father, on the
other hand, he can barely write his own name, poor thing – in
either language. He puts a cross where his signature ought to be,
cancelling himself out, or maybe he's trying to multiply himself.
I don't know. Things turned out that way because he left school
before his voice broke. First, he herded goats. Then, when he
was old enough, he went to sea. 'Don't be like him,' my mother
is in the habit of saying. 'A piece of wood.' My father speaks
islander Greek and Turkish, crackly as a thyme bush and full of
rocky landslides. When you live in a place, you stop seeing it.
Your thoughts take on the shape of the landscape. Your vowels
become round as the hills and your consonants jagged as the
coastline. Behind each sentence is the gurgle of the sea. Baba
says Greeks from Istanbul look down their noses when islanders
open their mouths. Mama reckons he doesn't know what he's
talking about. 'People from the city are civilised,' she sniffs. 'Not
barbarians.' Educated people intimidate Baba. Since there aren't
too many of them on Tenedos, he can relax. My mother, on the

other hand, must be gaunt for lack of sustenance. Her flower blooms round toffs that keep facial expression and gesture to a minimum. Rather than pick up food with their fingers, they use knives and forks. They cut their meat into tiny morsels and place it in their mouths, careful not to touch their lips. When relatives visit from Istanbul, Mama brings out the mannerisms she usually keeps in the bottom drawer with naphthalene flakes.

At recess I sit on the low wall beneath the poplars. Kids are running round the schoolyard, screaming their heads off. I pay them no mind. Across the road is the Dadaoğlu property. Behind high walls and covering the entire last block of the village, it's a triangular oasis of greenery on the edge of the Greek Quarter. The family is orthodox Muslim. They don't mix with anyone and you only see the men that work in the bakery on Republic Street. The neighbourhood gossips say that the Dadaoğlu fear contact with Christians. That's why they sneak out at night to collect water from the public fountain. Or they send their servant in the daytime. They obviously don't place too high a price on her soul, poor scurrying thing. Because the school is built into the base of the hill, on slightly higher ground, it's easy to spy on the Dadaoğlu property. I'm so busy mulling over the twisted logic handed out by the teacher that I barely notice the covered woman, sitting under the arbour with a book. What the teacher said, it's made my temples throb and my eyeballs ache. That's been happening a lot lately. 'She doesn't know what she's talking about,' says my friend Refik, a sage sprig between his teeth. His eyes are the same colour as the leaf. 'Come play.' He pulls me up by the hand and tucks the chewed up bit of sage behind my ear. 'Tell him the teacher's talking rubbish,' he says to his sister Deniz. She is older than us. Her eyes are so dark they could be the shell of a sea urchin. And she's just as prickly. She shrugs, not particularly interested.

'Don't take it to heart,' she replies. 'The teacher is from somewhere inland.' She flicks her wrist disdainfully. 'My father says it's difficult for people like her to understand what it's like for people that live on the Aegean.' Refik and Deniz are Turks. They reckon that their ancestors settled on Tenedos when Ahmet III was sultan, in the eighteenth century. They've been breathing Aegean air for so long, they're almost one of us. The school bell rings. Break is over. 'Come on,' says Refik, wrapping his arm round my shoulder. 'Don't let it get you down.' He gives me an encouraging squeeze. I want to tell him it's easier said than done. Instead, we both freeze. There's a ruckus in the Dadaoğlu garden. A man is standing in the dappled sunlight. He's looking in our direction, pointing and yelling. He says something incomprehensible. Then he turns and pulls the woman roughly to her feet. He slaps her hard across the face. She stumbles. The book falls from her hand. She runs indoors, holding her cheek. 'What are you waiting for?' pleads Deniz. 'Hurry. Get away from there before the madman comes after us.' She runs off, pulling her brother along by the hand. The man picks up the book, dusts it off, and places it reverently on the bench.

That night I tell Timon what the teacher said. We are sitting side by side on the stone seat outside our house. The evening is warm and buzzing with insects. When I finish, Timon bites his lip and trembles with rage. 'The cow,' he says, punching the palm of his hand. 'She can't do that. It's illegal to say such a thing. Doesn't she know the law?' His chest rises and falls rapidly. He runs a hand through his hair and stands up. 'Fuck her,' he shouts. His entire body vibrates. I've never seen him like this. 'We should report her.' 'Who to?' I ask, wishing I had not opened my mouth. He shrugs and yells, 'Fuck the whore.' Gorgeous Athena pokes her head out of the window next door and my heart melts. This is her spot. She sits here most evenings, sewing in the last light. 'Keep your voice down, dirty dog, and go wash your mouth with soap,' she yelps. 'That's no way to speak.' She is at least fifteen years older than Timon and he does not dare talk back. He stalks off instead, a trembling leaf before the storm. 'I'm going to tell your mother what you said,' Athena calls after him. When he is gone her gaze shifts to me. 'I heard what you told him,' she says, dropping her voice. 'I wouldn't talk so much if I were you. Words are like a branch stuck in a viper's nest. You don't know what you're stirring up until it's too late.' She glances behind her. When she's satisfied that no one's listening, she pins me with her violet eyes again. 'Especially don't tell your mother,' she whispers. 'The woman's mad as a wasp. There's no telling what she'll do to that teacher.' She drops the curtain. Her silhouette puts a match to the kerosene lamp and the room behind her blazes with light.

When the men are at sea, Tenedos becomes an island of women. Only the old men are left behind and the too young. Some things you learn at school. Others you learn in the streets. A learning I made in the streets is this: women keep going, same as always, dawn till dusk. They put their backs into everything they do, whether they're doubled-up crones or fresh as a May plum. And then they curl up and die. It's not like that with the men. If they can put their feet up and have a snooze, they will. Baba is out there, fishing and diving for sponge. When he grows old, he'll join the men in the *kafenio*, fiddling his worry beads and getting drawn into card games he could do without. The caique that employs him is in the Dardanelle Straits or maybe the Marmara Sea. Grandfather Dimitro reckons that in the old days, one of the many mouths leading to Hades was in the Straits. I believe him. Before I was born, my father says he saw his mother's ghost thereabouts. This is how the story goes: Grandmother Electra had been sick with cancer for a year and was on her last legs. They'd tried everything to save her, even consulting a blind Muslim holy man from the mainland. In the end, it was too late. God was calling Grandmother and there was no denying His will. Aunt Vasiliki was a young girl then. She did what she could, caring for her parents and making a living as a seamstress. Baba went to sea to help make ends meet. One evening the *Buğday* was moored in the Marmara Sea, round Sarköy. Paşalimani, I think. The sea was made of glass, reflecting the stars and moon. Baba was on deck alone when his mother's ghost appeared before him. He would have been twenty-six at the time. Grandmother, he said, was bathed in a phosphorescent light and her voice sounded distant, as if it was coming from another world. 'Stamo,' she said, 'when you return to Tenedos, don't cry. I'm no longer there.' Her words were still ringing in his ears when she leaped into the sea. The water claimed her without so much as parting or making a sound. The *Buğday* returned to Tenedos at first light. On the way, Baba said, they encountered another boat coming from the opposite direction. 'Stamo,' the men cried, 'Where have you been? Your poor mother died last night. Hurry up and get back home where you belong.' It was summer. Grandmother Electra was interred as soon as her soul freed itself from the body and returned to its source. Grandfather Dimitro joined her four years later.

Mama is keen to swim. 'This,' she says, 'will be the last fine day we'll have in a long time. We must make the most of it.' It's Saturday afternoon. The wind has dropped and the sun, high in the sky, has licked away the shadows. Wearing a one-piece swimsuit beneath her dress, Mama grabs my sister and me by the hand and heads to the beach in the Cauldron District. Byron takes up the rear. Unlike most islanders, Mama likes to immerse herself in water. It's a habit she picked up in Istanbul. 'In summer,' she says, 'we used to take the ferryboat to the islands in the Marmara Sea and swim all day.' I'm not on good terms with the sea. It's too unpredictable and it makes me suspicious. Baba says the sea has two faces. One minute it's your best friend, the next your worst enemy. You can only trust it to cradle your bones. He says the people who think it's a playground are foreigners from cities. 'Tourists don't know the sea's true nature,' he insists. 'They're weekend sailors. They go out in their yachts, get caught in a storm and when they sink, they're mystified. They want to know what happened and why. They launch useless inquests when the answer's right there before their eyes. Nature is not a playground. It's serious business.' He ought to know. He's seen workmates diving for sponge swell up and die because of a careless error. 'The head grows so big they have to weld the diving helmet off,' Baba insisted. 'Inside they're like a puffer fish, unrecognisable.' While Mama swims, I look after Electra and watch the sea change expressions to entice the light. It's true to no one. It lies to everyone. Me baptise myself in it? Never. My kingdom is solid ground beneath my feet. Scaling rocks and climbing trees. That's for me. Watching Mama in her one-piece with the modesty flap, my heart's in my mouth. I stand on the shore, glued to the head that's floating way past the fortress. Even brave Byron is fretfully scampering at the water's edge. When I turn my head, I see Turkish men sitting in the fortress battlements. They spy on the Greek women and play with themselves. Mama couldn't care less what the dirty dogs do. She swims out and paddles water. One day, she won't come back. Then she'll learn. Sometimes I think that's what she wants, my mother: to be borne away and never return.

Baba is back. He's been gone a long time. When he steps ashore, gaunt and gangly and flapping in his unwashed clothes, he brings gifts from the sea. 'They're from Poseidon,' he declares, handing them out to us. There's a pink-as-a-baby's tongue conch for me, a fancy twist of a shell for Electra; and Mama's palms froth with a frilly brown sponge. Baba acts as though he's given her something truly special. He laughs and smiles. One time, he dredged up three old coins from the seabed. On one side they showed the first king and queen of Tenedos: Tenes and his sister Hymethea. The back of their heads was a tangle of hair. Brother and sister welded together. On the flip side the coin showed a double-headed axe, symbol of the unyielding nature of the ancient Tenedians. The coins are nothing special; they doze under the soil right across the island, waiting to be plucked up. All you have to do is dig and there they are. They're so happy to be rescued, they settle into your palm like birdlings in a nest. A plastic bag is on the floor. Baba reaches into it and pulls out a two-handled jar with a narrow neck and a pointy base. It's mottled with age and crusty with shells. 'It's been on the seabed for who knows how long,' he says, studying it. Mama has trouble getting it to stand on the table. 'It needs supports,' Baba points out. 'That's how they made them stand up in ancient times. Captain Starenios says they used to hold oil and wine.' Mama is not impressed. She hates it when he tells her things she believes she ought to know. Baba stands back, admiring the vase through the smoke pouring out of his nostrils and mouth. 'There's enough rubbish in the house,' Mama says. After dinner, she tosses out the jar with the vegetable scraps. It smashes against the far wall in the yard, sending Byron into a flurry of barks.

After church the following Sunday, Baba and I go to the country property; there is work to do. Throughout summer he collects manure and breaks it down in troughs filled with water from the wells that dot the property. Before winter, he digs the loamy earth in the ruin between the main house and the kitchen and mixes in the manure. With thumb and forefinger he pushes in rows of tomato plants and covers them with a plastic sheet. 'The walls will shelter the plants from the cold,' he tells me. 'Come spring, they'll be as tall as you and we'll have tomatoes before anyone else.' He smiles, ruffling my hair. I look round. The world has pulled a blanket up to its chin. Soon it will be covered over the head, first with frost and then, if we're lucky, with snow. What was emerald and sparkling several months ago is now bronze. Life is withdrawing under the soil. The trees are shedding their leaves. The shorn grape vines crouch low on the ground and a sudden squall blows from Saint Elias's hill. It sweeps everything before it, causing the poplars to hiss and the bamboo to clatter in their own tongue. Leaves are tossed through the air like brimstone butterflies. In the cold months, I don't spare a thought for the country house. It ceases to exist. Come spring, Baba will put me on Train's back. Together we'll come to see the ruby-red tomatoes clustered beneath the fragrant leaves.

Before returning to town, I want to pay my respects to Grandfather Dimitro. His grave is in the olive grove, against the wall that separates our property from its neighbour. It is covered in moss and scratchy lichen. 'Hurry up, then,' my father says. 'Do what you have to do.' I run beneath the cherry trees, through the now-dozing vegetable garden, toward the olive grove. I place a myrtle branch at the head of the grave and bid my grandfather farewell. Then I kneel and put my eye to a low gap in the stone structure. Deep inside the maggoty darkness, I see his dead eye turn to regard me with affection. Typically, his head is resting on a fat, mouldy tome. 'See you next summer,' I say. 'Be a good boy,' he replies.

It's night. Mama is sitting on the divan, with her legs curled

under her. She is listening to the world seep out of the sparkly
gold cloth that covers the radio speakers. I'm helping Electra
learn the alphabet. Baba is gone again. Because of the fine
weather, the fishing season has been extended. Mama's hands
are always working, knitting, crocheting or shelling peas. She's
incapable of doing one thing for too long. She gets bored and
skips from one task to the next, a regular wagtail. The volume
on the radio is low so as not to disturb Amya's husband, Uncle
Haralambos, next door. The radio is my mother's prize possession. 'If we are to be rescued from our isolation,' she declares,
'we must make the affairs of the world our own.' Her eyes
flash and her hands disturb the air when she speaks. When the
batteries start to fade, she calls out, 'Dimitro, the world is
departing. Batteries, we must have batteries.' If I don't hurry
and the radio stops broadcasting in the middle of a programme,
she calls out, 'Dimitro, the radio's died. Quickly, put on your
shoes and go to the grocer. Here's some money. Two batteries.'
First Mama listens to the Greek news from across the border:
Makarios and his nationalists are still stirring up trouble in
Cyprus. 'In nineteen sixty-four,' Mama reminisces, 'when you
were smaller than you are now, and your sister was only three
months old, Greek Cypriots killed many Turkish Cypriots.
Since then Ankara has been looking at the Greeks that live in
Turkey with a jaundiced eye. We didn't do anything wrong.
What happened in Cyprus had nothing to do with us. Still, we
had to pay for the sins of others, like we always do.' She sounds
like our donkey Train, weary but outraged after a beating.
Thousands of Greeks were deported, she continues. Once
again, only Greeks with Turkish citizenship were allowed to
remain. The government confiscated properties and closed
down businesses that belonged to Greeks. Ethnic schools ceased
to exist and it became compulsory for Greek children to attend
Turkish schools. Mama huffs and puffs, pulling her collar as if

she's suffocating. 'It's going to happen again,' she says, shaking that insolent head of hers. 'I can smell it in the air. They're either going to kill us, or ship us all off.' She changes stations in the scant light, Greek from over the border one minute, Turkish from Anatolia the next. When Electra and I go to bed, sounds rise through the floorboards. The barely audible click of knitting needles, the delicate sound of a tulip tea glass returning to its saucer, the Turkish melodies that tangle with our dreams. When commercials interrupt the programme, Mama impatiently changes stations. (She has no time for people who want to sell her things.) For a second the sound of static and garbled noise pours forth, as if the spheres are communicating with her. Then, seemingly from another planet, or even from beyond life's borders, distant music insinuates itself. As the sounds waver and grow bold, assertive, Mama settles, for a time, on a station. Outside dogs bark. The sirocco moans in the eaves. Mama adjusts the dial and another tongue pours forth, different yet familiar. It's Greek, the mother tongue. Yet it lacks the yearning qualities of Turkish that carries in every note the music of the steppes.

I can't read or write Greek. I simply open my mouth and out comes the talk. Only it's not proper Greek; it's *Rumce*, a mixture of Greek and Turkish, dovetailing into one another. By the time a word or phrase leaves my mouth, it's done a complete about face. Greek turns to Turkish. Turkish turns to Greek. The words copulating on my tongue make my mouth fizzy. That's why I say that the language I speak does not have an alphabet. Don't ask me how, but I was fluent in Turkish before going to school. 'My son is smart,' my mother says, leaving it at that. Unlike her, my father is awed. He tells how I'd pick up discarded news-papers and magazines in the street and read, even before I started school. 'He takes after my father, may he rest in peace,' he tells everyone, whether they want to hear it or not. 'He was an educated man, my father. He read Odysseus' story, and many other books. He knew a lot. A book once told him that there was going to be a great war in this region. According to this book, the Arabs will rise up to eat the world. The only people they won't touch are the Greeks.' When the men at the *kafenio* ask him why Arabs will spare Greeks, Baba replies, 'My father said it's because Greece doesn't acknowledge Israel.' I don't know where Israel is, or if Greece's approval or otherwise means anything to it. All I know is that there is nothing unusual about Greece not acknowledging something that does not meet with its approval. Greece doesn't recognise us, its own people. As far as the stinking Greek government is concerned, Greeks that live in Asia Minor don't exist. Uncle Yanni once told me that when the junta took over in Greece, they wanted nothing more to do with us. They cut off the piddling stipend they used to send and recalled the peacekeeping police from the islands. To them we're traitors. They call us 'half-Turks' before spitting in the dust. I've seen them, gentlemen in ties and white shirts, spitting. They've left us at the mercy of Turkish nationalists, come what may. Turkish is nothing like Greek, though sometimes the same words crop up in both languages. Speaking Turkish is like sticking your feet in the sea that surrounds Tenedos. There's soft sand, sharp rock and spiny sea urchin. Though why the Turks changed the name of the island is beyond me. The island has been called Tenedos since antiquity. It means 'the place of Tenes'. He was the island's first king when Troy shone bright on the opposite shore. Bozcaada is the new Turkish name. It means 'Barren Island'. I can't tell a lie. Except for the needle-pine forests that give the island its wild melodious tone, there aren't too many trees hereabouts. But look around. Tenedos is piled high with watermelon, grape, apricot, almond, quince, cherry and mulberry. You can see for yourself that water virtually bubbles out of the ground. Springs and wells are everywhere. Calling Tenes' kingdom 'Barren Island' is insulting.

I am in Amya's house, peeking out of the window on the first floor. The faint crescent moon hinges in a powdery sky. It's very early Saturday morning. An unmoving mist hangs over everything. A rooster crows and another answers him. 'Are you ready?' asks Athena, coming into the room. The weather has turned and she is dressed accordingly. With her hair hidden under a pale yellow scarf, she looks angelic, full of smiles and optimism. Even her breath smells sweet to me. I tell her that I am ready. It's cold and gloomy inside Amya's house. Some of these rooms have probably never seen the sun. They smell damp and musty. Athena's father, Haralambos, sleeps in an alcove in the corridor, the floor of which juts into part of our house. When I walk past the alcove, the smell of stale piss clogs my nose. Sometimes, in the night, Haralambos misses his chamber pot or spills its contents and his urine trickles through the floorboards into our living room next door, adding to my mother's fury. 'Let's go,' Athena murmurs, taking my hand. 'I've lots to do today and you've got school in a couple of hours.' With a basket swinging from her slender arm, we set off toward the hill. Despite all the work she does, her hand is smooth and soft. It's brisk out. She lets go of my hand. We hug ourselves and stamp our feet as she closes the door. 'I know a place behind the house that used to belong to your Aunt Olga and Uncle Theophanou,' she says. 'There's a small depression above the quarry. This time of year it's full of wild lupin and holy thistle because it retains water.' A coil of blonde hair falls across her face and she blows it out of the way. In the upper reaches of the village, the streets are steep. I run ahead, skipping from stone to stone, and wait for Athena to catch up. Red-faced and out of breath, she struggles to make it to the top. When she bends over, her wide hips flare out beneath her coat, and her backside wags from side to side. I catch Barba Lefteri casting his eye over her. He's leaning out the window, enjoying his first smoke for the day. His eyes build dreams on Athena's posterior and he shakes his head to clear it from tainted thoughts. I almost shout at him: cut it out, old man. She's mine. Athena does not notice a thing. Her head is always in the clouds. She's so quiet, sometimes you forget she's there and get startled when, out of the shadows, a small voice pipes up. She has dreamy eyes. When you speak to her, she looks through a curtain of hair that sparkles like corn in the sun. Everyone knows I'm taken with her and they tease me about it. Once we walk past the pistachio tree and the evergreen carob, we're in the open. From here, the hill shoots up to the clouds. In bad weather, gale force winds rush down it like an uninterrupted river, battering the backs of houses and causing their spines to shiver.

Önce Vatan, everything for the Motherland. It's written in Turkish on the escarpment behind the village. The letters are so big they are visible from far out at sea. *Önce Vatan*. A giant soldier, also made of limestone, is built into the hillside to guard the proclamation. One hand grips a rifle, while the other points eastward. He's indomitable, heroic; he has only one thing in his sights: the day Turkey will pull herself out of the mire and rise shining to the surface. 'This way,' cries Athena, panting. She drags me by the elbow. 'It's down here. See?' The gully is not too far beneath the letter N. It's a long narrow crack in the earth, brimming with tiny yellow flowers. The smell of fennel rises up. Unless you are standing right at the lip of the depression, you wouldn't know it's there. The sides are steep and crumbly. It looks like the kind of place the goddess Hymethea would live in. I tell Athena to be careful. She drops the basket on a rock and climbs carefully down, hitching up her dress to show milky thighs. I stand by and play the guard. 'You put this in soups and stews,' Athena says, bringing over a luscious bunch of greenery. It resembles spinach leaves, dripping with dew. 'And this is very good for stomach aches or if you've got the farts,' she says, stuffing lupin in the basket. 'Allah created weeds for use,' says a male voice in Turkish. We are both startled. It's still very early and there is no one about. Athena cries out and spins round too quickly. She slips and tips over. The man is like a scythe. He cuts a swath through the flowers and catches her in his arms before she tumbles to the ground. For a second they are frozen in an awkward embrace. The man smiles at her and shows perfect white teeth. Athena leaps out of his arms as if she's been stung. She scrambles out of the hole and grabs her basket. 'Come, quickly,' she says, taking my hand. I turn to get a decent look at the man. He's tall, swarthy. When he sees me studying him, he waves a long arm over his head. 'I sowed an "if" in the valley of "it has been", and there grew up an "I would it were",' he calls, laughing. Athena glares at him. '*Kerata*, dog,' she spits. 'You were supposed to be keeping an eye out.' She cuffs me behind the ear. 'How was I supposed to know he was hiding in there?' I tell her. 'Besides,' I add, 'you could do worse than him. He looks like he knows how to work and he's a born poet.' Athena can't believe her ears. 'He's a nomad worker, you idiot, from the mainland. What do you take me for? We haven't all become Turks yet, thanks be to God.' I don't know what her problem is. It's a well-known fact that she's past marrying age. If she doesn't grab someone soon, she'll be left on the shelf.

The following weekend, the gang is hanging round the hills. We are playing Tarkan the Tartar warrior. Most times we cleave to the two windmills above the Cauldron, wielding wooden swords and yelping as we chase each other. Today we're to the north, where the creek runs down the ravine behind the blacksmith's and through the village. That doesn't happen anymore, though. The creek floods because rain pelts down like buckets emptying in winter. And it's worse when the snow melts. Before I was born, they say that a boy fell in the creek and drowned. He was swept out to sea where the creek pumps out beside the fortress. After that, they dismantled the seven bridges and covered the creek with concrete. That became the first modern street in Bozcaada. Republic Street cuts the village in two: upper and lower. Greeks huddle on the rocky slopes, and Turks by the sea. That's where the mosque is. Glowering Timon says the military police would kick the life out of anyone hanging around the *Önce Vatan*. So we keep away. If they show up, we scatter like rabbits. 'You've got to be careful,' pessimistic Apostoli says. 'The military police have eyes in the back of their heads and they can smell a Greek from ten miles.' Which is a shame because that just about covers the entire island, and there's no getting away from anyone. 'If the military police latch on to you, your days are numbered. You might as well kiss life good-bye. Best to keep your head down and pretend you don't exist,' Apostoli goes on. No one pays attention. He likes a good whine. Things are always in a bad way with him. All the same, he has a point. That's why the church bells never ring. They're too scared to announce themselves. Even on Sunday, when Christians dress up and walk the long, straight road that cuts through the upper portion of town, the bells remain tongueless, frozen in the belfry. They believe that if they are silent, the mosque will forget its neighbour is Christian.

Aristo points. 'Look who's coming.' He's got fuzz growing under his chin and it is making him look more demented than usual. Down by Kokona's house, it's Hasan and Süleyman. Hasan is the policeman's son and Süleyman's family are new arrivals

who took over the caretaker's house outside the old Greek
cemetery. They're short boys with flat oval faces and straight
dark hair. Hasan, especially, is mad as a cut snake. What are
they doing on the Greek side of the village? They have the entire
hillside behind the Turkish Quarter for their games, and now
they want ours too. That's what the others are thinking as well.
I can tell by the storm clouds hovering round their eyes. 'We
need to teach them a lesson,' says Aristo, clenching his fists.
'Let's get 'em,' Timon whispers, palming a couple of stones.
'Let's give them a warning first,' suggests Apostoli. Sometimes I
think he's more timid than me. I'm surprised he's still in the
gang. But the others enjoy riding him so much they let him
stay. Yerasimo won't hear of it. 'Fuck that,' he says. 'Actions
speak louder than words, aye boys?' He sniggers, his fingers
clacking with stones the size of walnuts. 'Let's hide,' Aristo
suggests. 'I don't think they've seen us.' We do as he says. I'm
pressed flat against a boulder, my heart pounding. Beside me,
Timon is breathing heavily and scuffing his heel in the ground.
His eyes are shooting spears of light and his compact body is
tense. All the while I'm scared out of my wits. I'm thinking
this is not right. Grandfather Dimitro would not approve, nor
would good old Ezet, my father's Turkish friend. If I go ahead
with this, I won't be able to face them again. On the other hand,
if I don't, the boys will think I'm a coward and a Turk. Timon
pokes out his head and quickly pulls it back again. 'They're not
far now,' he says. 'When I give the word; are you ready?' The
others nod and weigh the stones they're holding. I reluctantly
pick up a couple of pebbles. Hasan and Süleyman's voices are
close now. 'I need a marble with a red eye to complete my
collection,' I hear Hasan say. Süleyman laughs and answers,
'I've given you lots, but you keep losing them. You're a bad
player . . . ' I know what they're talking about. In my pocket I've
got a marble just like the one Hasan covets. It's a treasure, deep

orangey-red with a black slit down the middle of the clear glass. He can have mine if he'd only go back where he came from. Timon steps out from behind the rock. 'What are you two doing here?' he says, sounding hoarse, like he needs to hawk some phlegm and clear his passageways. Hasan and Süleyman freeze. Now there's only the wind round the escarpment and a tern screeching high above. The four of us step into view. When he sees us, Hasan yells, 'Run.' There's panic in his voice. They flee, sliding down the slope, leaving a trail of dust. The stones fly out of our hands of their own accord and follow the two boys like starlings darting for a worm. But they miss their targets and fall harmlessly to the ground. 'From now on, keep to your side of the village,' yells Aristo, hopping from one stumpy leg to the other. 'Or next time we'll break your heads and feed what little brains you've got to the crows.'

My heart is heavy. What we did, it's not right. When I am certain Hasan and Süleyman are gone and I won't bump into them, I head home. I can feel my grandfather's eyes staring holes into the back of my head. It's late afternoon. A cold wind has sprung up and a luminous white cloud is slowly rolling in from the north. Before too long houses surround me. 'Pst, want to play?' It's Lelia, sitting at the start of the laneway that leads to her house. She's feeding the chickens, throwing the corn in wide, lazy semi-circles. The birds run round, pecking feverishly at the ground. When I don't play with the boys, I play with the girls in our street: Lelia and Acantha. They're in the same grade as me; together we've outgrown our baby clothes and are leggy as colts. I check to see if the front door to our house is closed. It is. 'Sure,' I say, lowering my voice so that my mother doesn't hear me. If she knew I was out here, she'd give me a job to do. I turn into the narrow dead-end lane. Lelia puts the bucket of chicken feed inside the barn and shuts the door. 'Let's go to the lane beside Pagona's house,' she whispers, taking my hand. 'So that my mother can't spy on us.' Lelia's eight years are more mature than mine. Beneath her bob cut, she has a face that resembles a golden apple. It's hard to resist her. She leads me as if I'm a blind man and she my guide. As soon as we step into the main thoroughfare, we turn left in front of Pagona's house. Another left turn and we're in a narrow corridor between the two houses. Instead of breaking heads, Lelia prefers to play doctors and nurses. Crouching on the ground, she lifts her tiny fingers and pretends to bathe my imaginary wounds with dirt. She scoops dust in her palm and rubs it into my arm. With a spotless white handkerchief she bandages my hand and takes my pulse. Done nursing, she places my fingers on her breast. 'I swear your life is safe in my hands,' she utters. Underneath the fabric, she is soft and warm. Her heart beats faster than mine. When light scuttles into our hiding place, her hair lifts and sparkles. She reminds me of apple chunks dipped in honey, and I want to eat her. Our other friend, Acantha, lives on the other side of the walkway. If she's not included in our games, she cries. Her nose turns into a river of snot that pours into her gaping mouth. Then her mother Eleni comes out to tell us off. When I play with the girls, Timon and the other boys make fun, their voices thick and ropey. They reckon I'm soft. When it's dark and everyone's indoors, Timon sits beside me in the street. His long legs are spread apart and his elbows rest on his knees. At ten he's already a mirror of his father, except that he's got hair. 'You've got to toughen up,' he says, turning to look at me. 'Otherwise you'll never survive.' I'm lost. 'Survive what?' I ask. He has no answer. As far as I'm concerned, it's a matter of deciding between playing roughhouse games with the boys and spending time in a nursery with the girls. When I can't decide, I invite the girls to tag along with the boys. That doesn't work though, because the boys drive the girls away with lewd remarks.

My other friend, Refik, lives in the Turkish Quarter. It won't do
to mix with him outside of school.

The sow sings. She stands on hefty legs and paces before the
frosty windowpanes. Walking between the rows of desks, she
sways her right hand like a conductor, the tip of the forefinger
touching the tip of the thumb. The class sings along, too. Her
voice is nothing special. Judging from the expression on her
face, though, she means every word that emerges from behind
her teeth. It's a patriotic song about Atatürk, our westward-
looking, blue-eyed hero. His picture is everywhere: in schools,
barbershops, cinemas, post offices and official buildings. His
image has replaced God and the saints as the new guardian of
the people, aloof, stern and, above all, disapproving of anything that does not benefit the state. The sow is consumed by
Atatürk's triumphs; he did give women the vote, after all. She
sees through her students, past the school walls, to a shining
future, stretching beyond the Toros Mountains. The class, boys
and girls, Greeks and Turks, a couple of Jews that keep to
themselves, and the two new Pontian arrivals from the Black
Sea, sing along. We're birds chirping to our own time. A picture
of our hero hangs above the blackboard. The racket is getting
on his nerves; he wants to be left alone to smoke cigars and
drink *rakı* in peace. Not listen to children sing. In dinner jacket
and bowtie, he's a magnet for our eyes. Even the chalk dust rises
to greet him. Then the weak sunlight comes in and polishes the
frame bright. The sow says we must store the words of the song
in our hearts. In time, the message it contains will become
second nature. It will make us the champions at the forefront of
our glorious nation. At the end of the song, all students rise
and shout, 'Long live Atatürk's republic!' except me. It isn't
deliberate; I am just daydreaming.

'And where is your mind, pray tell?' I snap out of my reverie. The sow is towering over me, her pale eyes blazing. I'm quaking so much my tongue won't work. 'Stand up,' she says, jerking her head. 'Put out your hand.' My legs have turned to jellyfish. I'm thinking any minute now I'm going to piss myself. She takes my ear lobe between her thumb and forefinger and pulls me up. Her fingernails are red talons. They dig into my flesh. 'Put out your hand.' My eyes grow wider. But my limbs remain frozen. 'You are disobedient as well, I see,' she snorts. 'You're laughing at me, is that it? Maybe you don't understand. Perhaps you would like me to speak your language.' Behind her I can see my friends, Acantha and Lelia, rigid at their desks. From the corner of my eye, I see the big thick ruler in the teacher's hand slice the air like the wing of an albatross. The flat of the wood connects with my head across my left ear. My head pivots to the right. For a minute, the world is a telephone ringing. Then someone cuts the line and there's a woolly silence. After a while, I hear a heart pumping, someone screaming down the line. He's far away, on the other side of the island. Or maybe he hasn't been born yet and the scream is coming from the future. Sound breaks. It's me that's calling out in that high-pitched voice. My palm is sweating red and my ear is a cataract. Blood turns the starched white collar round my neck into the Turkish flag. I dash out of the classroom and race across the empty playground, clutching my ear and screaming. The fallen leaves run after me. Overhead the sky moans. The spiky tips of the poplars whip back and forth in the breeze. My mother stands at the school gate, pale. She opens her arms and I fall into her. 'I could hear your screams from inside the house,' she utters. 'What happened? Who did this to you?' I tell her. 'Leave her to me,' she says, gritting her teeth.

'You're not going near that school until this is sorted,' my mother says, cleaning blood out of my ear and tying a bandage to my head. She asks Athena to sit with me; then she stomps off, arms stiff by her side. 'Galatea, take it easy,' Athena calls. 'Take it easy nothing. They're not getting away with this,' my mother yells over her shoulder. 'You call that an education? In the name of God, he's only a kid. What's he ever done to them?' Her face is a bruised mulberry, and her eyes shoot lightning bolts. Neighbours stick out their heads to see what's going on. Before you know it, they are chickens squawking at a feeding frenzy. Volcano-like, my mother's eruptions blanket the street, and the neighbours are keen to see what she will do next. In these narrow streets and alleyways, we live piled on top of each other. Your business is not your own. Even whispers have wings. Exhausted, I fall asleep with my head in Athena's lap. When I open my eyes, a man is bending over me. He's the teacher that takes the upper grades, a kind and gentle man. Athena gives him a wary look and leaves the room. 'Dimitri, how are you, *pehlivan*, wrestler?' he says, using the Turkish pronunciation for my name. With his pencil-thin moustache he could be a film star. 'You'll be fine,' he reassures, stroking my hair. 'You're a brave boy. I'm sorry for what happened. You must forgive your teacher. Sometimes people forget themselves.' His eyes are green olives floating in a swarthy head. Now they're cloudy with brine. He strokes my head and his words pump me up; make me cheerful. My mother brings coffee and water and they sit together to one side, talking in low voices. 'Levent Efendi,' she says, stricken. 'What's to become of us?' He has no answer; only stares at the floor. 'I don't know, *kyria*,' he replies, finally. 'What I do know is this: you should not have gone into that classroom and attacked the teacher in front of her pupils.' My mother points at me, tries to justify her actions. He holds up his hand and goes on. 'Pardon me for saying so, perhaps it is not my place, but it's unwise to cause trouble under the circum-stances. Nor is it right to behave like that in front of children. It does not set a good example.' My mother is shamed into fiddling with her coffee cup. 'The teacher was thinking of pressing charges but I think we managed to talk her out of it, given the inappropriateness of her behaviour . . . ' he trails off. When he leaves, I sleep as if I'll never wake. In my dreams, I hear my mother mutter, 'No one touches my children. If they do, I'll rip them apart.'

Baba has been away for a long time. That's it, I think. He's never coming back. The sea has finally claimed him, too. Then he pops up, a bottle of Pepsi and four bright yellow bananas in a string bag. The weather's closed in. It's been cold and rainy for days. 'Shut your eyes and put out your hands,' he says to Electra and me. We know what's coming. Still, Electra and I, we humour him. 'These are gifts from God,' he says, stooping. 'You must share them with your mother and father.' Electra closes her fingers round the bananas, and I grab the Pepsi. 'Relish them,' Baba instructs, 'because who knows when we'll see their like again.' He is suddenly sober and serious. It must have cost him a lot to buy these luxuries. The fragrant yellow fruit in Electra's hand is a boat. It makes me want to be a sailor, always on the move. Pepsi is another story altogether. In every drop, the liquid contains a promise of earthly paradise. One sip transports you to a land that has vanquished want. Pepsi is America, where they invent everything. Including Ava Gardner and Marlon Brando, what we see in the cinema on Saturday night. The people that dream of leaving the island call America 'the West'. They swell up and say 'the West', as if it's sent them a personal letter of invitation. They go away and come back rich, driving a Chevrolet. When the sun travels across the sky, that's where it's going in such a hurry: from the east to America. 'Give me some Coca-Cola, too,' says Athena. 'Quick, give me. Ah, how my heart yearns,' she says, throwing back her shining head. 'It's Pepsi,' I point out, hoping not to offend. 'Same old same old,' she replies, twirling the bracelets on her wrist. A day later, Baba is gone again. He didn't even mention my bandaged ear. 'Your father follows the sea,' Mama says, in a dreamy voice. 'The tides bring him home and the tides take him away again. Don't expect anything from men like that.' When he returns, it will be the end of the season. The *Buğday* won't go out again till late March.

Although there is nothing really wrong with me, my mother keeps me home from school. She hovers round all day, a crow protecting its young. When I venture out, she says, 'Don't go far. Where are you going? Come back. It's not safe.' Every day after school Levent Efendi drops in to leave lessons for me. I'm shy. I can't look him in the face. I rest my eyes on his large hands and thin wrists. There's no wedding band. Only glossy black hairs caress the long fingers. He says I excel at reading and writing but must harness my numbers. 'I recommend a private tutor,' he says, facing my mother. 'And where will the money come from, pray tell?' my mother asks, sharp as a knife. 'I hear Kyrios Mihalis is seeking work.' My mother rakes Levent Efendi's face with her eyes and tightens her eloquent lips. He turns away, the truth about our poverty dawning. When the government closed the ethnic schools, Greek teachers found themselves out of work. Those that weren't Turkish citizens left the country. One or two remained, unable or unwilling to leave. Kyrios Mihalis was one of them. A teacher without students is like an unopened book. It sits on the shelf, gathering dust. Its knowledge locked in. That's what's happening to Kyrios Mihalis; he's devouring himself from the inside out, waiting for someone to summon him back to life. He is a bitter and sad man. The women in the street are impressed by Levent Efendi's daily visits. His comings and goings have caused tongues to wag. 'Galatea's invited a Turkish gentleman into her house while her husband's away,' they chortle, casting meaningful glances from behind their eyelashes. Their life is a romantic novel. I can't deny that in his high-shouldered suit, Levent Efendi cuts a fine figure. He is a man in the prime of life. 'An educated gentleman; that's what I'd like to be,' I tell Athena. 'Then I'll marry you,' I tease. She laughs and laughs, cleaning okra, peeling potatoes, laughs and laughs. 'Let her laugh,' my mother says, scornful as ever. 'What would she know? I'll make something of you yet.'

On the street, my bandaged ear is a hero. 'You look like Lord Byron fighting for Greek independence,' the women squawk. 'Now it's your turn to break a Turkish head or two. Do it for us, lad. Make an omelette of their brains. Do it for all of us.' For a runt like me, that's something. I puff up and strut. Whenever Timon sees my bandaged head, he turns purple as an autumn grape and swears. 'I'm leaving as soon as I can,' he thunders. If I were a compass, Timon would be my north. If he went, I'd lose all sense of direction. Anyway, where's he going to go? He's resourceful but only ten years old. Besides, I tell him, not all Turks have it in for us. The ones causing trouble are the new arrivals: the people shipped in to live in the houses abandoned by our relatives and neighbours. 'That's what they want you to think,' Timon replies, thumping the wall behind him. 'They're all the same. First they win your trust; then they slit your throat while you're sleeping in your bed. Don't you get it? They want to do to us what they did to the Armenians and the Jews.' My opinion may not count for much, but I'm with Baba's pal Ezet. He says, 'The time for recriminations is over.' When I say this, Timon is outraged. His skylark's eyes turn black and he charges out of the house. 'What a sap you are. Wait till the others hear about this,' he bellows. 'They'll want to do something about it, even if you don't.'

While Mama tidies up the house, I gather Byron in my arms
and head for the hills. He snuggles under my chin and licks the
salty skin. Up here, I'm free and alone. There is no one to
meddle with my thoughts. The sky is vast and puffy with cloud.
The sea crinkled cellophane. The mainland is a misty mauve
ring round the world. Cargo ships go up and down, from the
Black Sea to the Mediterranean and further out. It's bitterly
cold; the smell of rain is on the marrow-freezing wind. It makes
my eyes sting and nose run. I spin on the spot, arms outstretched. The village is at my feet. I am Apollo's eye, above all
things. To one side, the houses, the fortress, the harbour. To the
other side, hills, knolls, cliffs and outcrops unfold. As far as the
eye can see: coves and jagged rocks. Seagulls are tossed like
scraps on the air currents. In this loneliness, nothing can touch
me. I scale the rocks. My feet turn to goats' hoofs, steady and
sure, my arms into wings, light and fluid. I want to fly in ever-
widening circles. Day by day, I feel the muscles in my legs and
thighs develop. My arms reach out, my fingers grab and hold,
and my toes dig in. Gazing out to sea, I understand how my
father could make a mistress of ferocious *thalassa*, the sea. She
is everywhere, the first and last love. When my mother came
along, the sea and my father must have resented her. When the
light starts to fade and my bones ache with the cold, I call Byron
and head for the village. On the way, I check on Train and pick
Jerusalem sage for making tea. At home, I give it to my mother.
'It's well past its time,' she says, flinging the twigs into the cesspit
at the back door.

My mother has gone out and left Electra and me in Athena's
care. As soon as Mama is out of sight, Athena picks up a
romanzo and flings it in my lap. We are in her house. 'Read this
to me,' she says. 'My hands are full. I've got to peel these
potatoes.' Athena is as beautiful as Helen of Troy, but she is

not too bright. She truly believes she can trick me into reading
the photo romances translated from the Italian. I give her a
sidelong glance. I'm no fool. I know she can't read or write.
'That way I can keep an eye on you, too. You're such a gad-
about,' she finishes, flicking a strand of hair behind her ear.
'All right,' I respond. 'But first you've got to let me touch your
hair.' 'What?' she shrieks with mock horror. 'Get away from
here, you devil. Where did you learn such things? Listen to
that, will you? Did you hear what he said?' she asks no one in
particular. Electra laughs, looking from one to the other as if
watching a play. The advantage lies with me and I push as far
as possible without causing offence. '*Aman*, you're going to be
the end of me,' Athena says, relenting. 'All right, you can touch
my hair, you pest. But don't tell anyone.' I run my hand down
the golden waterfall that is her hair, wishing I were brave
enough to bury my face in it. She pulls away. 'Now, please, I
can't wait any longer. Read . . . ' She points at the book,
desperate to find out what happened to the clandestine lovers
caught in an embrace. 'Read!'

I am walking to the cemetery with Mama. The weeds by the
roadside are dusted with early morning frost; the bare branches
of a fig tree sparkle silver in the early light. The cold snatches at
our clothes and makes them tremble on our meagre bones. The
blacksmith's hut on the edge of the town is a black cave made
of scrap metal, plastic sheets and discarded wood. There are
old wheels, rusty chains, piles of horseshoes, anvils, axes, and
hammers. Standing by the open door, the smithy looks to be
made of soot and flame. '*Kali mera*,' he shouts, lifting an arm
thick as a tree trunk. He's a Turk who greets the day in Greek.
When he speaks, his voice is clashing iron. His soiled apron
seems to be one with his skin. Behind the hut, water trickles
down from the hills without a sound. It's as if it's falling on soft

cushions. Mama holds my hand and mechanically puts one foot in front of the other. '*Kali mera* to you,' she mutters, flicking her eye in the man's direction. It's the first time she's spoken this morning. She looks at me with the eyes of a basilisk encountered on an empty road, distant and slightly hostile. At the crossroads, we veer toward the cemeteries. When we pass the army base, Mama lets go my hand and leaps a low wall into a field. When she clambers out again, she is holding a bunch of myrtle. Further on, a narrow track and high walls separate the Christian dead from the Muslim dead. Still, nature has found a way to bring the disintegrating bodies together. My father's Turkish friend Ezet says ants are busy carrying Greek hair across the road to play cards in Turkish graves. Likewise, worms roll Turkish eyeballs under the wall to challenge Greeks at backgammon. 'All day and all night,' he says, 'the dead are visiting one another in secret and in defiance of man's laws. Beneath our feet is a network of tunnels, a hive of activity, an entire city, as those who've passed on chortle at the folly of those above. In death,' he adds, tapping the side of his nose, 'we realise we're all alike.'

My mother pushes open the iron gates and heads past the ossuary, toward the far corner of the graveyard. Poplars murmur in the breeze and crows split the air in two with their cries. Beneath a bare stick of an almond tree is a tiny grave. The unmarked iron crucifix is tilted at an angle. My mother places the myrtle on the mound and straightens the cross. She pulls out weeds and pats the earth flat again, as if smoothing a blanket. Then she lights the incense in a brass censer she brought with her and waves it three times over the grave. Up, down, left to right. Smoke flies everywhere. She seems to be in a trance. 'He was your brother,' she says, her voice remote as thunder. 'The Lord, in his wisdom, lifted him to paradise when he was still a baby. His name was Dimitro, too. You are named after him and he lives on in you. When you drink a glass of water, drink two, one for you and one for him. When you take a morsel of food into your mouth, remember to always eat for him as well. No matter what you do in life, always do it twice, once in his name and once for yourself. If you don't, you betray your brother's memory. Commemorate him with your every breath and he will live forever. Remember. There are two people inside you.' She jabs me so hard in the chest that I stumble back. 'And it's up to you to keep the other one alive. He must never be forgotten, cast aside as if his life meant nothing.' Above her, the almond tree rattles its skeletal fingers as if it's agreeing with her. Her voice breaks and her facial muscles undulate beneath the skin. She is feverish and quietly moaning. 'He was meant for great things.' She studies me, her lips white. She's kneeling and for once, we're eye to eye. 'Don't disappoint me,' she says, rising. Later, on the road, she says, 'And let's keep this between us. Not a word to anyone.'

When we return to town, Mama marches straight into the house and slams the door behind her. She does not even acknowledge Athena, who is sitting on the steps of a neighbour's house; they are rich and have a flight of stairs that leads to an imposing entrance. Athena is peeling carrots and dropping them into a bucket of water. If that's all she does with her time, you can be sure I'll eat well when we marry. 'We've been to see my brother,' I tell her, nuzzling beside her for warmth. She nods. 'Lower your voice,' she says, crossing herself clumsily with the knife still in her hand. Then she changes the subject. 'Your father and Zotico are coming back soon, God willing.' Her older brother Zotico works with Baba on the *Buğday*. 'I know,' I say. 'I'm going to the pier first thing Monday morning.' Then we sit silent as two o'clock. Athena stretches her legs and flexes her bare toes. I'm glad to see that she does not feel the cold; a man needs a strong wife. It's so quiet you can hear a mouse whisper, the sands shift on the beach. Music tinkles deep inside the neighbour's house at our backs. A woman covered head to toe in white steps onto the balcony of the Dadaoğlu mansion. She throws a rug over the railing and starts beating it with a wooden paddle. Only the pale oval of her face is visible. The wooden paddle rises and falls. Dust billows down to the cobbles. 'I can't get used to seeing someone covered like that,' Athena murmurs. 'It must be so sad, like a ghost.' She shudders as though the cold has finally crept under her skirt and touched her secret places.

Dadaoğlu is an enemy of the people. He opposes the republic and wants Turkey to become an Islamic state. They say that in the 1950s, he was arrested for smashing a bust of Atatürk somewhere on the mainland. The authorities were going to lock him up when his older brother intervened. If Dadaoğlu junior went to prison, Dadaoğlu senior could be counted on to take every lira that he had invested in the country and go back to wherever it was he came from. Some said it was Iran. He was a wealthy man, so they made a deal and a compromise was reached. Dadaoğlu junior would be exiled to one of the islands, and since Turkey only possesses two islands in the Aegean, it ended up being Bozcaada. Get out of sight, they told him, and don't make a sound, or you'll be food for worms. This is a secular state, not a theocracy. Naturally, Dadaoğlu was captivated by the beauty of our island and settled here. At first, he rented the mansion from a Greek guy called Mihalis Christothoulo. (Athena and I are sitting in front of his house.) Later, Dadaoğlu purchased the property outright. Now he owns just about the entire island. Unfortunately, he is also buying the vineyards sold by the departing Greeks and allowing them to fall to ruin.

He opposes alcohol consumption and he's trying to discourage our heathen ways.

I picture Athena covered head to toe. But she and the *çarşaf* don't go together. She's too beautiful to cover up. Athena and her brother Zotico, they are very different. He's a glossy black rooster, and she a golden fleece. They're much older than me, but that doesn't stop me from putting them on a pedestal. Zotico is the man I want to be when I grow up; and his sister is the woman I want to marry. 'Poor thing, pretty as an angel but not too bright,' my mother says, tapping her temple. 'Don't speak ill of my wife, please,' I snap. My mother doesn't miss a beat. 'Well, I hope you teach her to read and write, then,' she snaps right back, 'because I'm not having another illiterate in the house. One's enough, thank *you* very much.' As soon as I can, I tell Amya what my mother said about Athena. Far from being offended, my grandmother's sister chortles and her hefty bosom jiggles up and down. 'Don't worry, *yavrum*, my little one,' she says, 'your mother doesn't mean it. But it's true. Like oil and water, Athena and learning do not mix. She floats on the surface while her deeper currents go unexplored. Now she's like her father and me – without letters. That's how things are. Besides, an education would be wasted on Athena. She'll marry and have her own family. What's a woman going to do with reading and writing? Knowledge will only get her into trouble. Look at your mother. What good did an education do for her? You, on the other hand,' she declares, pinching my cheek, 'you are meant for great things.'

My mother is making *yufka*. Her hands and forearms are covered in flour. Doughy balls sit to one side on the kitchen table. With a rolling pin, she works the dough until it's a round paper-thin sheet. She cuts it into small squares; sprinkles them

with flour and then sets them aside. When they're dry, they'll
be dropped into broth with egg and lemon juice. I close the
back door, as much to keep out the cold as the smell rising
from the cesspit. Electra is helping my mother, an exercise
book forgotten on the floor. Her reading has improved, but
you can tell learning is not a priority for her. She receives so
little encouragement. 'Pour the lemon juice over the *hortorizo*
and give it a stir,' my mother tells her. 'Be careful. Don't burn
yourself.' Electra carefully pours the lemon juice over a stew of
dandelion, docks, nettles and rice, and gives it a stir. At that
moment, the Muslim call to prayer floats above the rooftops. I
picture the *hoca* standing on the balcony at the pinnacle of the
spindly minaret, holding his hands behind his ears, palms to
the front and fingers up. '*Allahu ekber*; God is great; testify that
there is no God but Allah and Mohammad is his Prophet.
Come to prayer!' Slow and mournful, the voice harmonises
and blends, filling the air with yearning, pulling the clouds and
the birds closer to earth. Hearing it, I always forget to breathe.
I don't have a religious bone in my body. Still, I find it difficult
to ignore so beautiful a song. 'Mama,' I say, deliberately adopting
the lilting whine she hates, 'has the Greek God lost his voice?'
She gives me an exasperated glance. 'What are you talking
about?' Electra puts down the wooden spoon and returns to her
book on the floor. 'Well,' I try to explain, 'the Turkish God
reminds his worshippers to do *namaz*. But the Greek God is
always silent. Why doesn't He call to us, too? Doesn't He want
us to go to church and pray?' Mama flips her wrist dismissively.
'Oh, that,' she says. 'More like some nationalist pigs don't want
us to pray. When they closed the Greek schools, they also said it
was forbidden to ring the church bells.' When she sees that I am
puzzled, she adds, 'Prayers keep God alive. If people stop
praying, He will die. If you kill God, you also kill the will of the
people. Sooner or later, they'll fade as if they had never been.'

The *hoca*'s voice fills the space above the rooftops. Yet the call to prayer also sounds melancholy. As if a being higher than God was heartbroken. Darkness shrugs its pelt and covers the glass in the window frame. 'I guess,' my mother says after a little while, 'they were scared that the church bells drowned them out.' Here her voice deepens. She calls out like the *hoca* and utters a jaw-dropping blasphemy against the Muslim god. Had someone heard her, she would have been stoned to death. She complements the insult with a drawn-out, comic tremolo and smiles wickedly. Electra and me, we're stunned. Nevertheless, we giggle. It's good to see Mama being so playful. For a minute, her eyes spark. She smiles and flashes her straight, even teeth, looking a brighter person. I didn't know Mama had it in her to utter such profanities. 'You know nothing about me,' she says, arching her eyebrows.

While we feed our stomachs, Mama's heart flies to Istanbul. *Stin polis* she calls it in Greek. The city. 'Because,' she utters breathlessly, 'it's the queen of cities. The most beautiful, the most enchanted, the most exalted. It doesn't need a name. Everyone knows it. All you have to say is *stin polis* and people know what you mean. When the Russians came to Constantinople, they couldn't believe their eyes. They thought that if there was a heaven then the beauty of Constantinople must be proof of its existence. Right there and then, they converted to Christianity.' When Mama was eleven, she was sent to live in Istanbul. It was the thing to do for village girls in those days. Her mother had done it in the 1930s. Grandfather Elias found a post for Mama in the household of a well-to-do branch of his family. They taught her about the world and, to pay them back, she worked for them as a maid. The wealthy family lived in Arnavutköy, on the European side of the Bosphorus. 'Your grandfather Elias is from Maidos,' Mama says, fork halfway to her mouth. She often forgets to eat. 'One branch of his family was high up in the Greek Orthodox Patriarchate in Constantinople. Important guests and dignitaries visited the house in Arnavutköy. There were sumptuous dinners and drinks in the cool of the evening. The balcony doors were flung open to catch the sea breeze. We even had a beautiful fish tank, which was fashionable then. I was kept very busy, cooking, cleaning, serving, and more besides.' She gestures as if to say there was no end to the work. 'They got their pound of flesh out of me, that's for sure. Nevertheless, I saw things that will last me for the rest of my life.' She sighs deeply to let regret fly out of her mouth. 'I had lovely dresses. Mind you, they were hand-me-downs but that didn't bother me. I was taught how to behave in society, how to speak Greek properly. I even learned French and to appreciate American movies in the cinema houses of Beyoğlu. Fred Astaire, Ginger Rogers were my favourites.' Altogether, Mama lived eight years in Istanbul. In the sixth year, for reasons she won't divulge, she sought a more accommodating post in the house of a Greek merchant in Tarlabaşı. This time the house faced the old city from across the Golden Horn. Mama had the palaces, minarets, domes and the Spice Bazaar at her feet. During this time, she says, she was happiest. 'There was no back-biting, no bitching and jealousy in that house.' Fate intervened when she was nineteen. One day, without warning, she was yanked back to Tenedos. Before she could come to her senses, they married her off to my father. He was a thirty-one-year-old fisherman and they barely knew each other. 'We'd met once before, on the boat to Constantinople. He was going to serve in the army. And I, well, I was going to have my life turned upside down . . . ' No one could make head or tail of the cards dealt her, least of all my mother. 'All I was left with was a stack of useless good manners and a chest full of dresses I couldn't possibly wear in this backwater.'

When my mother's in this mood, she forgets everything. Her eyes see a distant city afloat on sweet waters. Noise assails her ears. She lives again the high life. The island, her husband, children, they cease to exist. They belong to someone else. Not her. When her eyes witness the calamity again, she forgets even to watch her tongue. 'Why did they bother sending me in the first place? What was the purpose?' She rails at no one in particular. She puts down the fork and leans her elbows on the table, weeps. 'What was the point if I'm to spend the rest of my life shitting in the open among people with dirt under their fingernails?'

Electra and I go to bed. Outside an owl hoots. The wind unfastens a tile on the roof and causes it to rattle. From upstairs, we hear Mama turn on the radio and put kindling in the woodstove. When she thinks we're asleep, out comes a shoe box from under the divan. I sit in the shadows at the top of the stairs and watch. In the lamplight, she lingers over trinkets, letters written on thin, crackly paper. From a round powder box she takes out a flick of hair, dark as coal. She twirls it in her fingers, sniffs, and returns it with reverence to its rightful place. With eager, practised fingers, she rakes through a stack of black-and-white photographs. Every now and then, she stops and touches with her fingertips the people whose images are imprinted there. She presses one special photograph to her breast and sighs. There is such sadness in it, such longing, that I almost scramble down the stairs to hug her. But she'd probably beat me and send me back to bed. One day, when she was out, I pulled the box out and had a look at that photograph. It shows two people: a man in a suit and tie, looking over the shoulder of a pretty woman in an off-the-shoulder gown. She is impersonating Ava Gardner, while the man with the Clark Gable moustache smiles sharp as a tack. Mama touches her lips to the image. Then scissors flash in the lamplight. She cuts out the man and consigns him to the flames. His fire lights up her cheeks.

In the morning, it's my job to go to the grocer opposite the church. I walk into the shop. '*Merhaba*, Osil.' My chime is as loud as the bell that hangs over the door. 'Call me *Theo*, Uncle,' he shoots back with a cackle. 'How many times do I have to tell you? Why stand on formalities when I see you every day?' Osil and me, we're not related. He's a Greek-speaking Turk from Mitilini, an island on the Greek side of the border. The Greek government ousted Osil and many Turks like him in fifty-five. Being an islander, portly Osil wanted to stay close to the sea; that's why he settled on Tenedos. He took charge of the grocer's shop when the Greek owner migrated to America. 'One day, this'll be over,' Osil remarks, making a sweeping gesture. I'm not sure if he means the troubles that surround us, or the world in general. 'Then I can go back to my grandfather's olive groves, may he forgive me for abandoning them.' Osil greets me in Greek and I answer in Turkish. It's a game we play. When my pockets are empty and I can't pay for the goods I buy with a *kuruş* or a lira, Osil takes a pencil from behind his ear, wets it on his tongue, and writes the amount in a spiral notebook. 'Pay next month,' he says, shrugging. It's nothing to him. It's not like we're going anywhere. 'Or better still, tell that good-hearted father of yours to remember me when he has half a dozen red mullet to spare, or an octopus. Now that would be nice grilled with a squeeze of lemon . . . ' He smacks his fleshy lips. He is a good man who likes his food. You can usually find him eating the produce in the store. If his wife catches him at it, she tells him off. On Tenedos no one's a stranger. Uncle, Aunty, that's an honorific we give to those who've earned our trust. 'Listen to me, Dimitri,' he says, adjusting the apron he wears. 'Greeks, Turks, we're in the same boat. We're all oppressed brothers.'

'Unroll your carpets and I shall see what's in your heart,' says Levent Efendi, reaching for my hand. He places it on the table-top and covers it with his own hand. 'That's what my father used to say when I was your age.' It's evening. Mama is leaning her elbow on the table, coffee cup beside her. Electra stares open-mouthed at Levent Efendi as if she's never seen anything like him before. She is awed by the fact that we have one of those scary teachers in our house. Levent Efendi lets go my hand and reads from a pocket-sized book. 'Rum or Rome was what the Ottomans called their newly established state in Anatolia after the defeat of the Byzantines.' He reads by the light of the kerosene lamp. 'Do you understand?' he asks. I nod. 'What do Turks call Greeks?' he asks, sharp as a teacher; I guess he can't help himself. '*Gavur*, infidel,' I answer immediately. 'No, the proper name,' he insists, his face contorting as if he's bitten into a lemon. 'They call us *Rum*.' 'That's right,' he whispers. 'And did you know that Turks also name all westerners *Rum*?' That's news to me. 'What does that tell you?' he asks, relentless. 'Think!' I make like smarty pants Costas Hrisostom, across the street; I narrow my eyes and furrow my brow. If Turks call Greeks and all westerners *Rum*, it means that Levantine Greeks are westerners. We are of the West. We are not of the East. That means I already carry the fabled West inside me. We've been American all along, without being aware of it. 'Sooner or later, we're all going to be Americans,' the teacher says, smiling ruefully. 'Greece and Turkey sit on the cusp. They don't belong to the east or the west. Greece is Narcissus gazing at his own reflection in the waters of the Aegean. What he sees staring back at him from the depths is Turkey. Narcissus is puzzled by what he sees. He's frightened. He believes that his reflection is more real than he is. He wants to have what his reflection has and yet still retain his essence. The truth is that he is neither one nor the other. He exists somewhere in between.

He must kiss his own reflection, bring together the two parts, in order to be truly whole, truly alive, to create something that hasn't existed before. That's what makes the Greeks and Turks that live close to the Aegean a singular people. You. Me. We're Levantines. The Levantines are the in-between people, trapped between Greece and Turkey.' He makes like a beanpole. 'Next time someone calls you *Rum*, or *gavur*,' he tells me, 'I give you permission to hold your head up high and say, "Yes, I am. What of it? I am Byzantine and Ottoman and I look to the future that is a marriage between East and West."' While he speaks, my mother listens intently. 'Why are you filling his head with this nonsense?' she asks, puzzled. 'This is dangerous talk for a child. He could get into serious trouble if he repeats it anywhere.' He turns to her. 'Nonetheless, he ought to know who and what he is,' Levent Efendi says. 'Without that he is lost.' When he leaves, I place my head on his cushion. Levent Efendi has the same body odour as my father: unfiltered cigarettes, *eau de cologne*, and a day's sweat trapped beneath synthetic fabric. I breathe deep, drawing it in through my nostrils and mouth. All that's missing is the smell of the sea, the salty tang of bonito and seaweed.

Athena and our neighbour Costas Hrisostom sit close together in a limpid patch of sunshine. Costas is reading from a Greek book. He is an undersized, frail fellow. As he reads, cottony vowels and lancing syllables chime in the air. Athena rests her chin in her palm and closes her eyes, enraptured. When I see them sitting together, my blood boils. I see red. I storm over and call Athena a whore. Then I turn on Costas. 'You're an ugly goblin,' I yell. 'What are those noises you're making? That's not reading, you simpleton. You monkey.' I make fluffing noises with my lips, imitating his speech. 'Go to the devil, you freak.' With that, I knock the book out of his hands. It falls to the ground. A pink, raw-looking cleft distorts Costas's upper lip and pushes back one of his nostrils. 'A donkey bit his mother when she was pregnant,' say the women in the street. And if they are without child, they quickly add, 'May misfortune look the other way when we have children.' When Costas is flustered the slightly pendulous tip of his upper lip rubs his bottom lip, distorting his speech. Like Athena, he lives in his head, never happier than when alone. He's not much of an athlete, but he has an ear for languages and the law. Behind his back, people say he's bound to go far, despite his unfortunate face. Without uttering a word, Costas picks up the book and strides indoors. 'You ought to be ashamed.' Athena's eyes are swimming with tears. 'What has he ever done but show you kindness? He's the gentlest soul. Go away, I don't love you any more. Wait until your mother finds out.' When I dare go indoors, my mother's waiting. 'You're out of control,' she says, not looking up from crocheting. A storm cloud swirls behind her teeth. 'Next week, it's back to school with you. It's time you learned a thing or two about manners.' She falls on me with the broom handle and beats me until my backside is raw. Amya barges in, shouting, 'Enough, Galatea. Enough. You'll break his bones. He's only a child, my daughter. Only a child.' She takes the broom from my mother and steps between us. My mother's face is black, her breathing laboured. That night, she sends me to bed on an empty stomach. Electra sleeps with her. Alone, I cry myself to sleep.

In the morning, the madwoman sends me to the Hrisostom house with a peace offering. She orders me to apologise. 'Make it good and mean it, or next time I skin you alive.' I dash through the drumming rain. Costas's mother Fotini opens the door. 'He's left for school,' she says when I ask for him. Shame-faced, I hand her a jar of homemade rose-petal jam. She takes it.

'He loves you like a brother,' she says, 'and that's how you treat him.' I race away on winged feet, terrified of her accusing eyes. There is an unfinished building on the far side of the school. The portico faces a muddy paddock. Beyond that is the black-smith's hut and the army base, now hidden from view by thick veils of rain. Soon after the Turks took over the Greek school, they started building new classrooms. Halfway through the job, money ran out and the construction was never finished. The concrete shell they erected now houses scorpions and sparrows. Students are warned to keep out, as if the building is haunted. I sit under the portico where it's dry. The field is soaked. Miserable grasses sag under the weight of the elemental pounding they are receiving. Further along the road, a bare fig tree struggles out of a ditch. When the wind changes direction and blows from behind me, it snags the pupils' voices in the school and brings them to my ears. 'If anyone comes near me,' I declare, 'I'll tear him to pieces.' I make a fist and shake it at the sky. Unimpressed, it pisses on my knuckles.

'Today's the day,' Timon says. It's Saturday afternoon. He and I are perched on the roof of the school toilet block. The yard is empty. The sky is slate. Puddles gleam like plates on the concrete band round the deserted building. 'The gang's coming,' Timon goes on. 'They'll be here as soon as they get out of their school uniforms and eat something. Ready . . . ' Timon is usually calm as the sea in August. Today, he's restless as the waves at Point Aeolus. He bounces on his toes, balances on his heels, teeters on the outer edges of his feet. 'Ready for what?' I ask, baffled. He spins round, wide-eyed. 'What do you think?' He slaps the palm of his hand on his forehead. '*Aman*, you're a blockhead. We're going to break some Turkish heads, idiot. It's all planned.' Timon wants to get back at them for what the sow did to me. When the other three arrive, I'm cast in the shade. They're big and gangly, with buzz-cuts and frosty eyes. For a time they make a ruckus, behaving like movie gangsters. I am tempted to snake down the poplar that grows by the side of the building and go home. Timon is running out of patience. He's keen to get going. He gives the word. The five of us swarm off the rooftop and rampage through the village, keeping to the heights. I rush to keep up. Süleyman lives outside the gates of the old Greek cemetery, in the Fig District. From a ledge a quarter of the way up the hill, five pairs of eyes spy on the clearing ringed with walnut trees. There's a two-storey house in the middle of it, shade-dappled and peaceful. A strong wind is blowing down the flanks of the rise, causing the broad leaves to shiver and hiss with discontent. A little girl is scratching in the dust with the chickens. A woman in baggy trousers and white scarf wrapped tight round her hair is walking in and out of the entrance to the house. Four window cases catch the light and throw it back at us. Süleyman is nowhere in sight. The five of us crouch low, weighing plump stones in our palms. There's an arsenal waiting by my side. I picture the sow hitting me with the ruler and my ear burns hot. I hear Levent Efendi say, 'Sometimes people forget themselves.' Süleyman comes out of the house, swinging a silver pail. 'When I give the word,' Timon whispers. 'One . . . two . . . three . . . Go!' Five pairs of lips kiss five stones and arc them through the air. 'Again,' Timon gives the order. 'Then take off.' Judgement rains on the house with the red-tiled roof. The woman screams and almost instantly the windows shatter. It's as if her voice can break glass. The little girl wails and Süleyman runs round like a headless chicken, flapping his arms. Pigeons clatter out of the trees. The woman hustles her children indoors. Then she charges out again, wielding a broom and berating the sky. A long scarf of wind snatches her cries and carries them to our ears. The gang of five take flight, some over the hill, others in the streets below. It's best not to be seen together. Pretend like nothing happened. Tomorrow is Sunday. We'll go to church, light a candle and kiss the icons. 'God will love us for doing his will,' says Aristo, patting me on the back. 'Now you're one of the gang.' He's breathless with accomplishment.

On the way home, I drop in on Grandmother Evangelia and Grandfather Elias. She is an older copy of her sister Amya; and he is regal in his contemptuous silence. They live at Latif's guesthouse. Latif is a rich Greek-Turk. Richer than most people round here anyway. He gives Grandmother and Grandfather free board. They, in turn, care for his establishment. That's what the rich do: pay somebody to do the hard work while they sit back and rake in the money. When I arrive, Grandmother is upstairs, cleaning rooms. Grandfather is downstairs in his room, and he's feeling fiery. 'The people that are being shipped in won't be happy until Greeks are wiped off the face of the earth.' He slaps the newspaper with the back of his hand. Scorn twists his face. 'Soon there will be so many of them that we'll be pushed into the sea,' he bellows. He's half deaf and thinks everybody else is too. Grandmother comes in and tells him to shut up. 'The whole street can hear you,' she yells. 'What are you shouting for?' He insults her and goes back to what he's saying. 'The only thing that will make them happy is streets washed with Greek blood.' I tell him that even the local Turks are unnerved by the new arrivals. 'Refik told me,' I add to give my words authority. Grandfather turns my words in his mind. 'If the Turks are worried,' he concludes, 'then there's good reason for us to be jittery. I'm telling you, if the Muslims take over the world we're done for.' His pendulous lower lip is trembling. He shifts his ebony worry beads to his left hand and slowly crosses himself with the right. In his clean, white shirt, vest and striped pants, Grandfather Elias is a gentleman. He returned from World War One with shattered eardrums and a gammy leg. I don't know which leg because I've never seen him walk. He's always sitting down. He is twenty years older than Grandmother. His family moved from Maidos to Tenedos shortly before the Greek-Turkish population exchanges in 1923, to escape the worst of the troubles. By the looks of things, he married Grandmother because he needed a servant. His hair is white and translucent as spider webs, but he still lavishes attention on his Hitler moustache. There's a pile of newspapers and magazines beside his chair. He pores through them dawn till dusk. While Grandmother looks after the hotel guests, and holds down two other jobs to make ends meet, Grandfather sits in his room, acquainting himself with news of the world that, from what Grandmother says, he despises and rejected long ago. He's so busy formulating opinions that he has no time for family. When his children visit, he treats them like they're something he stepped on in a back alley. 'Leave him be,' my grandmother shrugs. 'It's fate. What can I do? Fight the will of God?'

I still pray. Only when I kneel and hold my hands before me, my thoughts are directed toward the saints whose icons are in the shrine in the corner of the bedroom I share with Electra. There are the two saints Theodorei, and Saint Demetrios. All three are on horseback, spearing, lancing, killing. Their feet are drenched in blood. When my lips move, it's for them to hear. Sometimes, Saint Demetrios puts on Grandfather Dimitro's face and pretends to be him, bearded and hunched. He stands by my bedside, burning like a votive candle in the dark. Then peace descends and nothing dares disturb our sleep. The saints are sullen friends. I talk to them and argue and berate. When I was younger, I wanted to be a priest of the Greek Orthodox Church. Grandfather Elias was overjoyed. He sat me on his knee – a rare display of affection – and pinched my cheek. Now that I'm uncertain about the calling, he serves up contempt on a silver platter. 'How can you be Greek and not Orthodox?' he demands, puzzled. 'You can't have one without the other. If you count yourself among the Greeks, then you must be Orthodox. If you are not among the Orthodox flock, then you can't call yourself Greek. You're nothing but a Turk. A Muslim.' I can't figure out how he arrives at that conclusion. There's no logic to his words. It is possible to be one without the other. Sometimes I think I am a Muslim because I enjoy listening to the *hoca*'s call to prayer.

There are chapels dedicated to saints in the countryside – thirty-two in all. 'There are many chapels,' Grandfather Dimitro informs me, 'because Tenedos is and always has been a very holy place. The Tenedians were Christianised as early as the second century. By the fourth century we even had our own home-grown saint. His name was Abudimus. He was martyred under a Roman called Diocletian.' When you enter the country chapels, it's like stepping inside the saint's body. His or her presence permeates everything from the foundations to the ceiling. But I've never felt the presence of God inside the big church in town. He has washed His hands of us; He thinks people are a lost cause. He was never human to begin with. So He can't possibly understand what it feels like to have two legs and two arms, to sit in a bed of mint and take a draught of cooling water from a well. The saints, on the other hand, knew mortality before grace made them divine. If nothing else, God's smart enough to know that. That's why He allows the saints to stay on earth. To be close by, to hear our prayers, to help the Virgin with the chores. God knows the poor woman's got enough on her hands. She's like Grandmother Evangelia, orders coming out her backside. When I ask God to smooth things out between Greeks and Turks, He pretends He doesn't hear. That's when my ever-reliable Grandfather Dimitro leans out of the light. He puts his cool hand on my forehead and kisses my cheek. 'Our country is our body,' he whispers. 'Never forget that.'

Sunday morning, the church bells hang silent in the belfry. Nevertheless, the devout hear their peal in their hearts and souls. With sleep in their eyes and the night still rattling in their voice boxes, the people emerge on the street. As if summoned by a soundless call, the villagers wend their way to worship. The congregation has God well and truly in its sights. For fear of breaking our concentration, even a dog dare not bark or bird sing. Amya and Athena are trailing behind Mama, Electra and me. Uncle Haralambos leaves the house only for labour and drink, not necessarily in that order. He let it be known some time ago that the divinity had let him down once too often, and he wouldn't be fronting up to church again until He mended His ways. Timon and his family join the procession at the next block. Electra lets go my mother's hand and joins her friend Evangelia. I don't leave my mother's side. I am angry with Timon for making me break that Turkish woman's windows. Because of an Ottoman decree, the church was built sunk into the hillside so that it would not block the view of the mosque that used to be behind it. From street level, we have to descend the fifteen steps to the church courtyard. With each step down, the air grows frigid. Breath plumes hang before faces as if people are emitting clouds of incense smoke, releasing their pent-up holiness. Moss grows in the cracks on the marble stairs, and they're slippery with dampness. We enter the church. In the narthex, Mama donates a few bronze coins to the charity box, scoops up three butter-coloured candles and gives one each to Electra and me. 'Light the candle,' she orders. 'Cross yourselves and then kiss the icon. And don't forget to say a prayer for your father's safe return.' There's no need for instructions. By now, the ritual is second nature. Sometimes I think Mama talks to hear her own voice, to make sure she's alive and kicking, that she didn't fade away during the night. After I abase myself before the icon of The Mother of God, I settle between Uncle Yanni and Zoe. 'You're looking smart,' Zoe whispers, giving my hand a squeeze. 'But you should take that off inside the church.' She indicates the olive beret on my head. Aunt Vasiliki leans across her husband. 'Humble yourself before God,' she hisses, snatching the offending article off my head. 'He doesn't favour arrogance.' She tucks the beret in the black bag on her lap. 'I'll give it back to you outside, you cheeky boy.' She smiles and her sharp features soften. I hate to say it, but I feel safer, more comfortable and loved with them than I do with my parents. Uncle Yanni rests my hand in his cracked palm and gazes to the front. His thick glossy hair is swept back to cover the carbuncles on his head. In profile, he has the unruffled, angular features of a saint. The iconostasis, rising from floor to ceiling, is God's breastplate descended from heaven to illuminate the world. It is bristling with oil lamps and the icons of armoured saints, spearing dragons and assorted enemies of the faith. The priest emerges from the sanctuary, swinging a censer and chanting the liturgy. In full silver beard and stovepipe hat, he cuts a theatrical figure, festooned in crucifixes, gold and brocade. From where I'm sitting, he seems to be floating on a cloud of frankincense and myrrh. The congregation rises to its feet and crosses its united body as if it were a school of fish with a universal brain. Not for the first time, I regret not making more of an effort to join the priesthood. It would be nice to have this unfailing power and control over people.

The sun has gone down. Night is creeping over the village. Here and there, light refuses to let go, creating silver ridges on tiles and eaves. I left our house intending to visit Grandmother, but

I've ended up in the opposite direction, deep inside the Turkish Quarter. It's after evening *namaz* for Muslims, and there's no one about. Dogs bark behind high walls. Spritely Byron snaps and growls at them. Streetlights burn on corners. Otherwise, it's a long line of houses with barred windows in this dark and strange part of town. Even though it's only a ten minute walk from where we live, it might as well be another world. It's a surprisingly balmy evening and some doors are open to the street. The radio is on in most houses. When I walk by I see families, sitting round the table, a kerosene lamp burning high on a wall. The people appear to be floating in space inside a warm, golden bubble. The scenes are all the same. There's always a man and a woman, a girl and a boy. Sometimes there's a solitary child, swinging his or her legs beneath the table. They don't seem that different from Greek families, and I wonder why we're so scared of them. Exactly the same scenes are being played out on the other side of Republic Street. There are plates and cutlery on the table. The familiar sights and sounds. They make me feel lonely, yet somehow connected, in a loop. I keep walking. I'm not brave. I shouldn't be here. The sow lives nearby. And that gives my feet determination. I want to see how the slavering bitch lives. Where she sleeps at night. What her lair looks like. When I find it, the door is open. I kneel and take hold of Byron's collar. It would not go well for me if he ran inside. The sow is sitting at a bench with her back to the wall, her feet planted squarely on the floor. She's wearing white, and holding a spoon. Her hair is light, falling straight to her shoulders, lit from above by a bare bulb. So the teachers have electricity. They probably have running water, too. Her husband Ibrahim sits opposite her. He passes the bread. His wife takes a slice. She tears it and dips it into a bowl placed before her. She takes a timid bite and rests her forehead in the palm of her hand, as if her head's too heavy for her neck to support. Her husband's forearm falls across the table. It is glossy with black hairs. His hand strokes her pointy elbow. Lips move but the sounds don't reach outside. It's like watching the black-and-white silent film from a couple of years back, and I'm invisible in the dark. The teacher runs the tips of her fingers beneath her eyes. 'Are you looking for someone?' a kindly voice asks. I spin round, alarmed. It's a well-dressed man, holding Deniz's hand. Deniz's face is glowing with curiosity. Her hair is tied back and she's still wearing her school uniform. Only her hands and pale face float in the darkness. 'What are you doing here?' her eyes ask silently. 'Are you looking for Refik?' she says aloud. I blink. When my lids lift, Byron and I are scooting down an alley, panicked as rabbits.

It's Monday morning. Dawn. In the kitchen, I gulp a bowl of yesterday's bread soaked in scalding salty milk sprinkled with oregano. I button my coat and dash out. Byron wants to come with me, but I do not want the complication of having to look after him. The *Buğday* is due back soon. I'll greet my father and Zotico and then go to school. 'Don't dawdle. Head straight for the harbour,' my mother warns. It's still dark. The empty street echoes with my footsteps. One or two windows glow with light as people prepare for the day. It's been raining through the night and a south-westerly trimmed with barbed wire brings tears to my eyes. The *Buğday* will be having a hard time of it on the waves. Pulling the multicoloured beanie over my ears, I set off at a canter, glad of the mittens and scarf my mother knitted. When I reach the church, I stay on the opposite curb. What I did to Costas was beyond the pale and the divinities behind the wrought iron fence are expert at inflicting punishment for such callous behaviour. I've apologised to Costas. But that counts for little with the sadists from heaven. If they want a kidney, I'll hand it to them. All I want in return is to be on talking terms with Athena again. This business of not speaking to me and pretending to be fascinated by the hairs on an okra when she sees me is wearing thin. If she doesn't come to her senses soon, I'll start courting Lelia. I go past the Talay winery and the locked-up movie house, toward the square. Doorways are menacing with shadow. Anyone could be hiding in there. By the time I emerge from under the avenue of linden and plane trees on the waterfront, the sun is brushing the horizon with the downy feathers of newborn chicks.

There's no sign of the *Buğday*. The sea's a howling mammoth. It looks as if Poseidon is reaching up to grapple with his brother Zeus, and from their overexerted lungs escape the howls of a thousand beasts. The force of the wind almost picks me up and tosses me aside like scrap paper. Apart from two men tarring a docked boat, there's no one about. Boats and caiques lurch crazily in the water, their bells chiming with alarm. I wander along the causeway that skirts the fortress. Waves dash against the concrete and explode into a million freezing shards. Summer seems a long way off. At the halfway point, the path is under water. There's no way to reach the area where the outdoor cinema is set up in warmer months. I turn back and crouch by a cluster of overturned lobster baskets. A skin-and-bones dog sniffs my shoes. I shoo him off, wishing Byron was here. Dejected, the dog slinks away, tail pressed tightly to his rump. Surrounded by flying water and low clouds, I feel as if the island has plummeted off the edge of the world into a void from which even Atlas can't save it. It occurs to me that, despite living in a fishbowl between two continents, we're very isolated. I hadn't thought of it that way before. Finally, the *Buğday* appears on the crest of a wave. It resembles a piece of driftwood, heaving and tossing on the back of a giant serpent. I dash to the end of the pier and wait excitedly until it draws near enough for me to recognise the faces of the men on board. There's Captain Starenios, his son-in-law Anistas, the new occasional hand Usin, and good old Ezet. It's good to see him again; it has been too long. At starboard, Athena's brother Zotico stands steady as a mast beside my father. I wave, jumping up and down as much with excitement as to keep warm. I'm not sure which man gladdens my heart most: Zotico or my father. Unshaved and heavily clothed, they could be pirates. Zotico tosses two thick ropes overboard. 'Tie them round the bollards,' he yells above the roar of the storm. I do as he says. Then he extends his arms. 'Come on,' he calls out, wiggling his fingers. 'Come aboard.' I toss back my head, No. There's half a world between the pier and the boat. Water's frothing down there as if it's boiling in a cauldron. '*Haydi*, don't be scared. I'm right here. I'll catch you,' he calls again. 'Don't you trust me?' The other men gather to watch. This is a test. If I jump, it will prove that I am a man. On the other hand, if I jump and miss the boat, I'll fall in the drink and drown. '*Haydi*, Zotico, leave the boy alone,' Ezet says. 'Can't you see his legs aren't long enough?' He shakes his head, disgusted. 'Come on, coward,' Zotico calls again. 'Don't make me wait.' His teeth are chalk in his swarthy face. I can't resist him. 'Don't listen to him, *yavrum*. Follow your heart. Not what the devil tells you to do,' Ezet shouts back, giving Zotico a dirty look. My father's gone below deck so that he doesn't have to watch his only son drown. Tossed on the waves, the *Buğday* goes up and down. One minute it's high above, the next way below the frothing maw. If I'm to come out of this alive, I will have to time it to the second. I leap into the void. For what seems an eternity, I freeze in mid-air. Nothing exists but me with my arms and legs extended, even the water stops churning. My right hand is out, ready to grab life. When movement returns, I fly through the air. My hand closes round something. The tip of my boot makes contact with what I hope is wood and, as I'm about to give up hope, I fall into Zotico's arms. The men clap. '*Haydi,* he almost pissed himself,' Usin says. Everybody laughs. I grin into the smelly weave of Zotico's black jumper. My heart is hammering and my knees are wobbly. My father emerges to clap me on the back. 'Bravo,' he says. 'You did good.' Ezet clasps my hand in his paw. We shake hands. 'Don't ever do that again,' he mutters, bending down. 'Your mother would eat us alive if anything happened to you.' He too smells of fish and brine. Scales are embedded in the warp and weft of his jumper. They glint on his high rubber boots. 'I've got something for you,' he whispers, casting a glance over his shoulder. 'Can you guess what it is?' I nod, grinning. 'Keep it to yourself, then. Don't say a word. Here it is. Quick before anyone sees.' He pushes a comic book under my coat and steps back. 'It's a good one,' he murmurs, going back to work. Ezet keeps me supplied with Tarkan comics. My mother says Tarkan is a savage, and innocent children shouldn't be subjected to sex and violence. That's why Ezet passes them to me on the sly. Timon hides them under the floorboards in his bedroom. When no one's around, we sit cross-legged on the floor, and fly away to the distant mountains and valleys that were the original home of the Turks.

The caique continues to buck and toss in the storm. It reminds me of a mad mule, trying to dislodge its rider. The howling wind rises to a crescendo above the fortress. A loud clap of thunder follows and utter silence falls. Then fat raindrops splatter the deck. Almost instantly the rain stops and wind rams into the caique. It pitches to one side. Everything and everyone is thrown about. I fall down. Quick as lightning, Zotico dashes over. I think it's to make sure I'm unharmed. Instead, he slips a piece of paper into my fist. 'Take this to her as soon as you get

off the boat,' he mutters and dashes off again. I don't even
bother looking at the note. I know what it is – a note for his
girlfriend Ephigenia. I slip it into my pocket. The other men
work hard to secure things and lash them down. When the
alarm is over, Ezet and Usin offload crates filled with fish,
octopus, sea urchins, and a lobster. There is even a small shark,
hacked in two. They set the crates on the pier and wait for
housewives to come and buy fresh fish. The greater portion of
the catch has been sold to wholesalers on the mainland. 'Not
bad for this time of the year,' observes young Usin. He's so
emaciated that the clothes flap on his frame like rags. 'It's
nothing,' replies Ezet, tossing back his head. 'You wait till next
season.' Ezet's an old hand. He's lived through more storms
than Usin has hairs on his chin. 'The waters will be calmer and
the fish will be leaping out of the sea into the nets. You'll be
begging them to leave you alone!' He laughs, casting an eye
along the length of the pier. It doesn't look as if anyone's going
to brave the weather today. 'Next time we'll go as far as Sarköy,'
says my father, sauntering over with his hands in his pockets.
An unfiltered cigarette dangles from his mouth. My father is
long and slender as an eel. Aware of his height, he stoops to
avoid towering over people. 'That's where the real fish are. Too
many tankers in the Straits.' He goes quiet, as if he's spoken out
of place or for too long. Ezet laughs again. 'Go home, Stamo,'
he says. 'Your wife will make a nice fish soup and you can relax
with your family. And take this beautiful boy home with you
before I kidnap him.' He tousles my hair. Zotico comes down
the gangplank and lopes by with a plastic bag slimy with fish.
I'm tempted to go with him. School starts in under an hour,
and I don't want to be late. First, I have to take his note to
Ephigenia. 'Come see me before you go to school,' Zotico flings
over his shoulder. In battered leather jacket, he saunters like a
Turkish movie star. 'He's in a hurry,' says Ezet, eyeing him off.

'He's got fire in his loins,' my father adds. 'Let's hope he comes to his senses before it's too late.' They chuckle and sink into themselves. 'Don't be like that,' Ezet admonishes after a while. 'What else is there for a man to do? He works and he loves. There are no greater gifts.' My father tries to peg him. 'You can say that? After what you've been through . . . ' He plucks the cigarette from his mouth with two cracked claws. Under his breath, he starts humming a Turkish song. '*Ne bu sevgi ah?* Ah, what kind of love is this?' Two covered women arrive and bargain with Ezet for fish. Usin scampers off. My father pulls me close to his thigh. 'Aren't you cold?' he asks. 'You ought to go home. Don't you have school today?' Having made their purchases, the women scuttle off. 'Experience compels me to speak,' Ezet says, picking up from where they left off. 'There must be room for forgiveness. Otherwise what's the purpose of life?' My father takes a drag on his cigarette. 'You're a dervish, my friend,' he observes, breathing out smoke that is instantly shredded by a gust. 'Not a fisherman.'

Ezet is my father's drinking partner. When they're on dry land, they sit in the tavern, knocking back bottles of wine. They drink and stare into space, each man present in body yet elsewhere in his thoughts. Ezet studies the world through eyes filled with sadness and yearning. A devout Muslim – though not too exemplary because he's fond of 'a drop of lion's milk' – he puts a lid on his thoughts by wearing a skullcap as white as his hair. 'One day,' Ezet said to me, 'I'm going to Mecca for the ultimate pilgrimage. Then you'll address me as Ezet *haci*, not *dayı*. Though, of course, I'll remain your protector for the rest of my days, and happily so.' Before he cast his lot in with us, Ezet lived in Tekirdağ. He was married then. 'My wife's eyes were as beautiful as two suns at their zenith. Her face would have compelled sultans to abandon their thrones and palaces for her. She made those so-called movie stars look like the harlots that they are.' Life was paradise. The only thing lacking was a child, that indispensable product of their loins that would proclaim their love to the world. Then his virtuous wife shacked up with an itinerant truck driver from Bursa and, overnight, Ezet's world turned into a Türkan Şoray melodrama. One day, so the story goes, he came home to an empty house. The adulterers had packed up and fled. They'd sunk so low that they'd even taken the table and chairs, and the rugs hanging on the walls. Ezet was left with only the clothes on his back and a brass coffee pot. It turned out every woman in the neighbourhood had been in on the deception. Men said that Ezet was weak for letting a woman pull the wool over his eyes, and children crowned him a cuckold. To escape their scorn, Ezet settled on Bozcaada. 'Here I hope to leave behind the miseries of the world,' he told my father when they first met. 'And the shabby way people treat one another.'

Ezet and I clicked straight away. The first time we met, I was leaning over the side of the *Buğday*, vomiting. The caique was on its way to Çanakkale. Conditions in the Dardanelles were unusually rough for summer. Later, when I needed to piss over the side, Ezet held onto my belt to stop me from falling into the water. 'Hold on. Wait for the wind to change,' he advised. 'Or else it'll fly back at you.' It was too late. I'd already let go. Ezet laughed so much; he almost fell overboard. 'Don't worry,' he said. 'It'll dry off.' In the evening, when the other men trooped off to the tavern, Ezet stayed behind. My father tried to talk him into going with them. 'He'll be all right on his own,' Baba had said. Ezet wouldn't hear of it. 'I can drink any night of the week,' he replied. 'But how often do I get to be a father?' As another day fizzled out on the water, the Turkish man from Tekirdağ and the Greek boy from Tenedos walked hand-in-hand to an open-air cinema. They were going to watch a film under the stars. The boy sat on a wooden chair beside the man. The night was balmy and clouds of cigarette smoke intermittently obscured the screen. The patrons wore shirtsleeves and mosquitoes buzzed in the humid air. As the movie began, people fanned themselves with folded newspapers, and crunched peanuts and roasted sunflower seeds. In the half-light, the man from Tekirdağ kept turning his head. He'd beam at the boy as if Allah had given him a precious gift. 'Would you like another bottle of *gazoza, yavrum?*' he whispered, placing his mouth close to the boy's ear. 'How about more sunflower seeds? You must be cold. Here, drape my jacket over your shoulders.' When the film ended, the boy from Tenedos was asleep. The man from Tekirdağ lifted his charge and carried him back to the caique.

I have been thinking about the visit to my brother's grave. A solution must be found otherwise my mother will never rest and I'll be forever charged with preserving the memory of a dead boy. Before I deliver Zotico's note to Ephigenia, I have to tell my father about my plan. 'Baba,' I say, tugging his sleeve. The hairs on his wrist, clustered thickly around the fraying watchband, bend with the wind. 'Why is my brother's grave unmarked?' He looks at me as if we're about to topple off a cliff-top. His eyelids flutter uncertainly. 'What?' he asks, frowning. 'He ought to have a name on his cross, like everyone else. That way the world won't ever forget who he is.' My father turns away. When he faces me again, his eyes are marbles. For a second I think he's going to give me a backhander, but he's never hit me so I relax. 'Who's been putting this rubbish into your head?' he asks, crouching on his haunches. He takes hold of my shoulders and speaks directly into my face. I smell tobacco on his breath. 'There's no brother,' he says, emphatic. 'You are the first and Electra the second. There is no other child. God hasn't blessed us with more children; I wish that He would.' He speaks slowly, deliberately, the way people speak to Aristos's imbecile brother. 'What's got into you? Why are you saying these things?' He is upset and I am sorry I didn't think carefully before opening my big mouth again. He throws down his cigarette. 'There is so another child,' I persist. 'My mother took me to his grave. He has the same name as me, and he's buried under the almond tree.' Another squall drives the rain parallel to the ground. 'Listen,' my father says, 'I'm going to say this once and I'm not going to repeat it again. There is no child. I don't want to hear you say such things. What if someone hears? We'll be a laughing stock. You must have dreamed it,' he adds, wiping his hands and rising on two long legs. When Greeks talk among themselves they switch to their own tongue; Ezet's not in on the conversation. 'What's up?' he asks, sensing tension. He flicks his cigarette butt in the water. Orange sparks snag and die on the wind. 'Nothing,' Baba replies. He turns his back, cups his hands, and puts a match to another cigarette. 'He's talking shit. It's all the books he reads. They put ideas in his head and he can't tell truth from lies.' Ezet rests his hand on my shoulder. 'Take these fish to your mother,' my father orders. 'And tell her I'll be home later.'

I run off and give Zotico's note to Ephigenia. She is his not-so-secret girlfriend. By Pan's beard that woman's a sullen-faced cow. I can't figure out what Zotico sees in her. She's got a moustache thicker than the ones worn by Turkish men. If Zotico had Ephigenia's interests in mind, he'd give her a razor and tell her to shave. Kissing her must be like kissing a man. I give Ephigenia the note and dash across town. Going past Grandmother's guesthouse, I see the dentist coming out the front door. He's loaded with black bags. He pulls out teeth all summer long, and goes back to Ezine on the mainland for the winter. Like a shadow, he'll be back next year. When he first set foot on the island two or three summers ago, he announced that his aim was to have falsies in everybody's mouth before the decade was out. 'Real teeth,' he declared, pointing a finger at the sky, 'are a thing of the past. The future is false teeth.' The islanders were so impressed they lined up to get their chompers removed, whether they needed to or not. He hasn't had a slack day since. The only problem is that most of the new teeth don't fit properly. They are either too tight, or too loose. They cause too much pain or they fall out. I'll tell you one thing: that monster is not coming near me with pliers. When you walk past his rooms, you hear teeth dropping into the tin pan and people groaning with pain. I turn heel and run away from him. I might not be much of a fighter, but, with these matchstick legs, running is my game. As I rush past our house, I lob the bag of fish at Mama. 'He'll be home soon,' I yell. The soles of my shoes touch the schoolyard as the bell rings.

The class sits with its back to tall windows made of square panes of glass. The weak light streaming in from outside creates vertical and horizontal bars on Atatürk's portrait, and on the teacher's face. Pointing with a ruler at the writing on the board, she leads the way. The class chants by rote. We cover the nominative cases, the accusative, genitive, dative, locative and the ablative until our heads buzz with new words. The milk and soft sugary rolls we're fed at ten are well deserved. In the playground Refik and I repeat the lesson, singing the words and skipping up and down the schoolyard, arm in arm. We crack up laughing at our cleverness, thrashing on the ground. 'You're such children,' says Deniz, tossing her head. 'When are you going to grow up?' Refik lobs a stone at her head. She ducks and runs away, screaming and threatening to tell. It seems she hasn't mentioned me lurking in the Turkish Quarter.

It's just as well. If Refik asked about it, I wouldn't know how to respond. The air is a curtain of gold and bronze leaves. On the ground they rattle or float in scummy puddles left behind by the rains. Soon the trees will be naked as the dryads at Ayazma grove.

Baba comes home late. He is drunk. The house is locked and sleeping. Unable to find his key, he kicks in the front door and calls for my mother. 'I want something to eat.' His voice peaks sharp as a piece of shale. In the next room my mother isn't game to move. It's chilly and besides she's scared he'll smack her again. 'Come down and do your duty,' he persists. 'I'm your husband and I want something to eat. If you were any sort of a wife, you'd come down and do what I tell you.' His voice ebbs and flows. He trips and falls over something, swears. 'Keep it down,' she tells him from the landing. 'You'll wake the children.' She descends the stairs. The kitchen is directly beneath the bedroom; their voices rise as if the crossbeams and the floorboards did not exist. If I lean over the side of the bed and pretend the floor is made of glass, I'd see the tops of their heads moving in the light of the lamp. Mama busies herself at the pot. She heats the *tarhana* soup, and puts a bowl and spoon on the table. Not a word passes their lips. At least she's learned to leave him alone when he's in this state. But she can't let it be. While he eats, she begins to berate him: 'What do you call this? Drunk again. You've just come back from the sea. Your children haven't seen you yet. I haven't seen you yet. Coming home in the middle of the night. Drunk.' 'Let it go, wife,' he replies. 'In the name of God, let it go. May the devil take you! You're no better.' I pray that she will leave it at that. A woman ought to know when to stop. Instead, she keeps pecking at him. He continues eating his soup, the spoon chiming as it hits the side of the bowl. Peck, peck, peck; my mother goes on at my father's head. Next she'll peck on his manhood. 'I said,' he calls out, 'let it go.' When my father wants to he has a very loud voice. It booms like a cannon out of his thin chest. Electra is awake beside me. Her eyes gleam anxiously in the dark. She takes my hand. The bowl of soup smashes against the far wall. My mother lets out a surprised yelp. A chair clatters to the floor. He hits her. The sound rises through the floorboards as if it's got wings. Another slap. There's no sound of struggle. I picture her lying beneath him, taking it as it comes. 'You think you're better than us,' he says. 'You think you're a lily in the shit of the world, is that it? You think we're not good enough for you. Well, you're no better. You're like the rest of us. So cut the crap.' Silence. The wind whistles outside the window. A tile slips from the roof and smashes onto the cobbles, making a far-off and lonely sound. 'And what shit have you been feeding your son about having a brother? What's that about?' My heart stops beating. This time my mother makes a wounded-animal noise. He pummels her again. After that, things quieten down. She cleans up the mess. They talk in whispers. Later, they gently shut the door to their bedroom and sleep on the same rollout mattress. I fall asleep, still holding Electra's tiny paw.

In the morning, 'Come here,' she says. It's just the two of us. Electra's left for school with Evangelia. Now that the fishing season is over, Baba's gone to scratch for work at the Kostaraga winery. 'Come here.' Those two words freeze my blood. I'm at the table, finishing breakfast. She's standing over me, hands on flared hips. 'Why did you tell him? Didn't we say it's our secret?' I whisper, 'I don't know, Mama.' Her eyes shine, a savage crow. 'What do you mean you don't know? Did we say it's between us or didn't we?' I'm not like her; I can't be tough. I start sniffling. That's her cue. Her right hand flies back and away from her hip, high up into the air. 'I'll show you how to keep secrets,' she utters. The hand flies down again, a great swoop, like a scythe, and connects with the side of my face. My cheek stings and my ears ring. The hand completes a half circle across her body and flies back again. This time the back of her hand connects with my mouth. Her wedding band cuts my lip and strikes my teeth with a sickening crunch. 'Now go to school,' she says, turning her back. 'Stop sniffling, cry baby.'

On the street, Amya pulls me into her house. She sits me next to the woodstove in the front room. The heat penetrating my woollen pants feels heavenly. 'Athena, get some iodine and cotton wool,' Amya says, keeping her voice low. Sounds carry. 'Shush, *yavrum*, don't cry. I heard everything, last night and this morning. It's not your fault.' She encircles me with her loving arms and rests my head on her bosom. 'The blood,' I protest, pushing her away. 'It will wash off,' she says. Athena returns with a bag of cotton wool and a brown bottle of iodine. 'One day,' Amya says almost to herself, 'she's going to kill him and then what's she going to do?' Athena holds my hand. It is good to be the centre of her attention again. 'It must be second nature by now,' she mutters. 'Didn't I tell you not to say anything?' she says softly to me. It's odd but for the first time I see her for what she is: a woman, not a child like Lelia. Our eyes connect and a silent, unintended communication passes between us. The tears dry on my face. 'You shut your mouth,' Amya snaps at Athena, eyes blazing. 'Not another word.' A breeze flutters the curtain on the window and for a moment panic makes my heart scuttle. I don't want my mother to know I'm here. Reading my mind, Athena shuts the window. Amya cleans my lip. A clock ticks loudly on a side table. Athena is so calm. Her luminous hair creates a halo round her head. Maybe this means she's forgiven me for what I did to Costas, and we can go back to being friends again. Amya rises. She smoothes her dress and says, 'Better get going. You'll be late for school.' I stand up. 'Come back at lunchtime,' she adds in a softer tone. 'Zotico will be here and I'll cook you a potato omelette.'

Days before Christmas, Zotico folds another infernal piece of paper into my hand and tells me to take it to Ephigenia. She lives in a wooden house that faces the fortress, round the corner from Aunt Vasiliki's. 'Come back to tell me what she says,' he instructs, his eyes dilated with lust. I run off, eager to please. In my haste, I forget about the black ice that makes a treacherous path of the streets at this time of year. I race past the church, turn left into my grandmother's street and head for the Cauldron. Byron struggles to keep up with me. Everywhere is the sound of trickling water. I'm running past the priest's house when my feet go out from under me. I fly through the air and sprawl in the slush, biting my tongue in the process. When I arrive at Ephigenia's house, I'm nursing skinned hands and knees. Blood's smeared round my mouth. I've torn my pants and my gloves are caked with mud. I knock. Ephigenia's mother opens the door. She looks me up and down and calls to her daughter. 'There's a ragamuffin here to see you,' she says. 'It's your suitor.' The women inside cackle. 'What do you want?' says Ephigenia, stepping outside. She pouts and won't meet my eye. As if I'm the one that's stringing her along. I hand over the note and wait. Ephigenia takes her time reading. Hurry up cow; I'm freezing. She bends down to my level and whispers, 'Tell him I'll be there.' I look at her with wide eyes. 'Where?' I say, taunting. I know well enough where and how they indulge their shame. 'Idiot. Where do you think? The usual place.' She slams the door in my face. I'm black and blue from the cold. My teeth are rattling like castanets. The least she could have done was offer me tea. I walk to Aunt Vasiliki's. When I sidle into the living room, half a dozen young seamstresses throw down their

work and run around the room, chattering excitedly. 'Outside
with that dirty dog,' screams Aunt Vasiliki, pointing a witch's
finger. I tie Byron to the stoop and come back inside. In next
to no time, my every need is tended to. Cousin Zoe places a
glass of piping hot tea at my elbow, with a half-moon of short
bread covered in icing sugar. One of the girls rips off my pants
and settles down to mend them. Another cleans my gloves in
the kitchen. A brunette with coal-black eyes and lips so vivid
they could have been smeared with pomegranate juice kneels
beside me. I've never seen her before. Silently, in gentle strokes,
she applies cotton wool and iodine to swab the blood off my
face. 'Your mother would eat you alive if she saw you in this
state,' Aunt Vasiliki pronounces with queen-like majesty. She's
a sultana in a high-backed chair, and I am the little sultan in
his harem. Beside the sultana, the woodstove radiates enough
heat to bring our blood to the boil.

I tell Electra to go stand with Mama and Baba. 'You'll be warmer
over there.' She lets go of my hand and wanders off between a
forest of legs and flapping coats. It's the day of the epiphany in
January. A new year has begun. Greeks line the harbour front
from one end to the other, while curious Turks cling to the
fortress battlements, watching the show that's about to begin.
It's so cold I swear nothing will ever warm me again. The sea is
grey steel that moves in a piece. There are no seagulls, only a
hollow boom and shriek in the sky. People cluster together,
waiting for the priest to arrive. He will bless the waters and
expel the *kalikanzari*. I'm scared of *kalikanzari*. They're goblins.
From Christmas Eve to epiphany, they hide in dark corners,
snatching children and kidnapping the unfaithful. Only the
priest's magic can cast them out. My mother and father stand
side by side. Electra huddles in the gully between their legs.
Seeing my mother with her hand through the crook of my

father's arm, you'd never know they're constantly at war. In her fawn coat, she is a picture of elegance. She has no equal. Her hair is covered with a flowered scarf, and brown leather gloves sheath her hands. I'm standing with Timon. While the laggards vie for a better view, my eyes are glued on Zotico. He's standing in a rowboat, wearing nothing but sopping-wet navy bathers and a sleeveless black vest that is plastered to his torso. Under the wet skin, the muscles of his hairy legs tighten and gird his midsection like tree roots. His broad, flat feet spread, gripping the boat that pitches and bucks. It's a miracle he manages to keep his balance and not fall in the sea before he's supposed to. His eyes are like searchlights, scanning the crowd. He's probably trying to locate Ephigenia. I don't know why they don't declare their love and get it over and done with; I mean it's not like nobody knows that they use me as a go-between, carrying love notes back and forth. Some people would pay a hefty amount to read one of those letters. But I'll tell you one thing: they're boring as bat shit. Not an ounce of poetry in them, purely directive. 'Dear Ephigenia, please sit at your bedroom window at such and such time so that I can gaze on your dusky beauty from the fortress battlements.' That kind of thing. See what I mean? Unimaginative. All I can say is Zotico better marry her fast. Crouching on the battlements and playing with his hooded bird isn't going to endear him to his future in-laws, who aren't too keen on a big-lipped blackie like him anyway. He's too poor for their precious. More likely than not, they'll marry Ephigenia off to someone with a bit of money, and that will be the end of it.

The priest finally arrives, surrounded by acolytes and choirboys. The big man's crimson and golden sunset robes swirl round his body, making him look like a collection of rags eager to take off and fly to heaven. As he comes to a halt at the water's edge, a sudden gust snatches his stovepipe hat. For a second it floats inches above his cottony head. A boy lunges for it, but it's too late. It shoots off, twirling serenely over the waves and across the sea. People stifle sniggers. 'I wish he'd hurry up. It's bloody freezing,' says a smart alec in a loud whisper. 'Shush,' says the woman that's hanging off his arm. 'It's a sin.' She quickly crosses herself. 'You won't be saying that when my nuts freeze,' he tells her. 'That'll be the real sin.' He laughs coarsely. She whacks him on the arm and giggles. The priest is forced to finish the liturgy without his hat. It's probably in Africa by now. As he chants, another group of half naked youths are rowed out to join Zotico in the boat. He tries to intimidate them with his black eyes, but they're too cold to notice. Aristo is among them. They stand, bobbing in the rowboat, hands cupped over their genitals, as if they're scared frozen fingers will slink out of the water and pluck their balls from between their legs. Finally, the priest flings the last lines of the liturgy into the wind. When the words are dashed against the wall behind him, he throws the cross into the water. It sinks beneath the waves. Six young men throw their bodies into the air. They slice through the water, their white flesh rippling beneath the swirling froth. Then they too vanish. The water claims them for minutes on end. While we wait to see who will find the crucifix first, I stand there wishing Aristo drowns and never rises to the surface again. It is Zotico who bursts to the surface, gasping and holding the cross aloft. The crowd erupts into jubilant cries. He is clearly the favourite. Zotico locks eyes with Ephigenia and kisses Jesus' cold lips with all the passion he can muster. Then he raises the cross over his head again. Ephigenia can't contain her joy. She cheers and claps, hopping on the spot. Her sister elbows her in the ribs and Ephigenia goes quiet. I would have shoved her in the drink. Then we'd have seen whose side God is on.

From January to the end of February, rain and fierce winds have the run of the island. There is slush and mud everywhere. People venture out only if they must. The streets are deserted and smoke swirls crazily out of flue pipes. Even the stray cats and dogs have skulked off to shelter in disused basements and barns. In the long months, many will starve. Come spring their carcasses will be found, crawling with maggots. It's so cold even the warring politicians have pulled back their horns and retreated to snug rooms. Not long after my ninth birthday in February, in the night, silence thickens round the house. Then we know it: the snows have arrived. Without uttering a word, we throw back our bedclothes, slip our feet into shoes or slippers and step into the street. Only one or two lights, set far enough apart to create great pools of blackness in between, and the night above. Like cotton wool, thick snow falls, mysterious, adding to our wonder, absorbing all sound. Neighbours all, we stand looking up, wondering at such miracles. Then, without having uttered a word, we close our doors and return to our still-warm beds. The morning is a frozen world. A great hush presses down, covers everything. The village stops looking shabby and grimy and becomes beautiful, clean. As if it's newly born. Life crouches beneath the soil, waiting to breathe again. When the snow begins to melt weeks from now, crocuses will clamber out of the earth, pretty and innocent beside the matted carcasses of dogs and cats.

It has been snowing non-stop for almost a week. We haven't been to school in a fortnight. The coal to heat the classrooms ran out and the schoolyard was under several feet of snow. A couple of kids fell into snowdrifts and they had to be dug out by the janitor. After that, classes were dismissed; and, as the days passed, heaving white mounds slowly devoured the houses. Men dug busily from morning till night, clearing the streets, pavements and doorways. I wonder how Kokona is holding out by herself beside the ravine. Luckily the wind dropped some days back. The world went eerie, flat and still. You can't even hear the sea any more. I bet it's frozen over. You could probably walk from here to the mainland if you wanted to. Any more of this weather and the snowdrifts will be as high as the rooftops. Already an old barn has collapsed under the weight of snow, crushing a goat and some chickens. And there is more to come, says Mama's radio.

My mother finally snaps. 'Go to your grandmother's. Get out of my hair,' she yells. 'I'm sick of you.' She's been stuck in the house with Electra and me for weeks and she's going stir crazy. I slink out with my tail between my legs, leaving Electra at the mercy of the madwoman that claims to be our mother. Scrunched down in my coat, I take a right turn at the first corner and head for my grandmother's *pensione*. In minutes, my feet are soaked and numb. The hard-packed snow squeaking underfoot, timid as a mouse, is in complete contrast to the great crows that gather overhead, shattering the glassy air with their insane cries. On the way, I have to pass Hasan's house. He lives with his mother and policeman father in a house behind the Talay winery, where they are building the new Turkish bath. I usually avoid going this way but, in this weather, I figure no one's going to be outside. I'm wrong. As soon as I turn the corner, I spot Hasan. He is crouched in the snow, building a snowman. He looks up when he hears the snow squeaking. A flash of recognition lights up his oval face and he rises to his feet. He stands stock-still and stares. I'm tempted to turn tail and run, but I don't. I won't be intimidated. I put one foot in front of the other and keep walking. Hasan hasn't moved. He's still as a statue, bare hands hanging by his side, wet and bright red from digging in the snow. I swear I can see water dripping from his fingertips as if he's sprung a leak. His chin is tucked

into the collar of his jacket and only his eyes move, sizing me
up. He reminds me of a dangerous dog. This standing still is
really scaring me. I'd prefer it if he moved or said something. I
keep putting distance between us, one step at a time. Just as I
think I've made it and I'm going to get away, he opens his
mouth and says, 'Hey, *gavur*, infidel, where do you think you're
going?' It's like he's uttered a magic spell. I freeze to the spot. I
summon the strength Levent Efendi taught me to display, but
nothing comes of it. 'Do you think you can walk past my house
as if you own it?' Hasan says. The word 'infidel', it goes in one
ear, straight to my brain, and out the other. My temples begin
to throb. My vision clouds. Bile rises in my throat. 'Answer me
when I'm talking to you,' he calls. I turn to look at him but my
sight is obscured by big black dots. I feel faint and bilious.
Hasan crouches again, and digs with his left hand in the snow.
He rises to his feet, clutching something. 'This is a message for
that dog you call a cousin,' he says. 'Tell him he's next.' He
throws whatever he's picked up. It's a snowball with a rock
imbedded in its centre. It hits me on the forehead. I fall over
backwards. Oddly enough it doesn't hurt. I sit up in time to see
a shadow loom from the doorway behind Hasan. A hand reaches
out to grab him by the shoulder. And then I see that the hand is
attached to an arm, and the arm is attached to Hasan's policeman
father. The man is laughing so hard his face splits in two.

Acantha's mother Eleni finds me wandering the streets and
brings me home. She hands me over to my mother. 'He's been
beaten up – *again*,' she says, nibbling worrisomely at her lower
lip with buckteeth that would be at home on a rabbit. My mother
crosses the room. Eleni leaves. I tell Mama what happened. The
minute the words are out of my mouth, she is rigid with fury.
Her hands wipe themselves on her apron as if they don't belong
to her. Then they rip the cloth from round her waist, as if she is

shearing off her skin. 'That's it,' she screams. 'I've had it. I can't stand this any more.' The fingers clutch her hair as if she's going to rip it at the roots. 'Something's got to be done.' She dashes out. 'Galatea,' Amya calls from next door, 'be careful. His father's a policeman. You're digging yourself into a hole you won't be able to get out of.' Electra starts crying and runs to Amya. 'Policeman nothing,' my mother yells. She's halfway along the street. 'He can go to the devil. I'll show them. If the government isn't going to protect us, we have to look after ourselves. I'll be back in a minute.' She has left without putting on a coat, or changing out of her slippers. Because the front door is open, I can hear neighbouring women trying to talk sense into her. Galatea, don't do this, for heaven's sake. Galatea, stop in the name of God. Please think before you act. You'll get us all into trouble. You're making a bad thing worse, for all of us. Stop and think before it's too late. Let the men handle it. That's what they're there for after all. For all the attention my mother pays them, their voices might as well be the twittering of birds. When that woman's head is made up, nothing can shake her resolve. I dare not tell her that Hasan hit me in retaliation for what we did to Süleyman's house. Finally, silence returns to the street. Athena comes in with Electra in her arms. She puts down my sister and closes the door. 'Sit,' she says. 'I'll clean up the blood.' She is very businesslike. Electra is still blubbing. 'Shush, my gorgeous girl,' Athena says, caressing her. 'It'll be all right. There's no need to be scared.' She wipes Electra's face with a handkerchief and kisses her hair. 'Everything is fine. There is nothing to worry about. You'll see.' I touch Athena's hand. 'Don't,' she says, snatching it away. 'Why do I always have to nurse you? Am I your mother?'

I hear voices in the night. I open my eyes. The vigil light has gone out and it is pitch black. My father's voice rises through the floorboards. Careful not to wake Electra, I roll out of bed and tiptoe to the landing. I quietly descend the stairs, making sure to avoid the second one that creaks. I don't go down all the way. I stop before the mezzanine and sit at the spot where the staircase curves down to the living room. From here, I can listen without being seen. They're arguing again. My father is angry. It sounds like they're sitting at the kitchen table, Baba nearest the door. 'Who told you to go and take on the police?' he's saying. 'Are you crazy? Have you lost your mind? Because of you and your big mouth, the police dragged me out of the *kafenio* and interrogated me for an hour.' Blue cigarette smoke wafts out the kitchen door, carrying his words on its back. 'It's not right,' my mother responds feebly. Her voice sounds faint, as if she's been asleep. 'These things, they are wrong. A policeman has no right to behave in that manner, towards a child, or anyone for that matter. They're there to uphold the law. Not break it.' Because the kitchen door is open and the kerosene lamp is on the table between them, when my father moves, his shadow slides restlessly on the floor behind him. 'Wife, don't you understand? It's not a matter of right and wrong. It's simply that it is not up to you to behave like this. These things are beyond our power and control. Are you even aware of what you've started today? Do you care? Next time they're going to drag you down there. Is that what you want because it's not what I want. No wife of mine is going to end up in a police station.' My mother doesn't reply. 'So we just let them beat our children,' she says, finally. She sounds tired, defeated. 'We let them come in here and drink the blood in our veins. Is that it?' My father pushes back his chair and his long, spiky shadow leaps out of the doorway into the living room. The chair scrapes on the floor. But he doesn't stand up. He empties his lungs of air. The shadow's shoulders lift up and fall down. 'Ouf, you're going to be the end of me,' he tells her. 'I don't know what else to say and do. You will stay at home.' He emphasises each word. 'You will keep your mouth shut.' Mama tries to interrupt him, but he tells her to shut it. She goes on anyway. 'After what I lived through in Constantinople in nineteen fifty-five, I swore I would never again sit still and let them control my life.' She is speaking through gritted teeth, I can tell. Her voice is fixed and vicious. 'You don't know what we went through that night and in the days after. It was hell, sitting in that basement, waiting for who knows what. We thought they were going to slaughter all of us.' My father rubs the stubble on his face and I hear the sandpapery sound it makes. 'You don't need to tell me what you lived through,' he replies. 'I know. Don't forget that I was doing my military service in the city at the time. How do you think it was for us Greek guys, sitting there, knowing that they were burning Greek shops, smashing up houses, looting and doing God knows what to our women? We couldn't do a thing. We couldn't say a word. We couldn't object. You don't know what they did to the Greek soldiers after that . . . ' He trails off and they're silent for a long time. Baba strikes a match and lights another cigarette. The flaring light almost obliterates his double on the floor. 'What happened?' she asks. 'Never you mind,' he says. But she continues to push. 'Believe me, you don't want to know,' he says again. 'Tell me.' She's not going to give up. 'You really don't know when to let go, do you?' he retaliates, his voice rising again. An evening's ration of wine is gurgling in his throat. 'Well, someone's got to protect your family,' my mother says, changing tack. 'You won't do anything.' Her chair scrapes the floor. I hear her stand and walk to the washing trough. Plates and cups clatter. 'You're never here when I need you. I'm always alone.' Her voice is now coming from the kitchen window. She sounds weary and sorry for herself. 'I'm the mother and the father for these kids. I might as well be a widow.

I rely on Dimitro for everything. He takes it on without a word, but that much responsibility is not right for a child. He's only a kid. What does he know? It's wrong to place such a burden on him.' My father exhales and says, 'It'll make a man out of him.' They're both sounding tired. Sleep coats their tongues. 'Anyway,' Baba says, 'I don't want you going anywhere near the policeman again. It's not your job. And tomorrow you say you're sorry.' It's getting cold. My teeth are chattering and my toes are numb. 'Apologise nothing,' she whirls on him. 'They should apologise to us.' My father's voice goes up several decibels. It's the only way he can make her pay attention. 'You will obey me,' he shouts, rising to his feet. 'You are putting everyone in danger by behaving like this.' My mother makes a contemptuous noise. 'As if I care,' she says. 'Cowards.' As he launches his body onto her, knocking the glass ashtray to the ground, his shadow gathers wings, like a kestrel leaping into the void. The ashtray falls and begins to rotate on the floor. I shoot to my feet, hand over my mouth. I almost cry out. The ashtray is still spinning. Behind the sound of glass dancing on concrete is the sound of flesh pummelling flesh, grunts and cries, insults, protests. A body hits the ground. Then the ashtray sits, flat and noiseless. 'No!' she cries. 'Stop.' I scamper, silent as smoke, to bed. The hitting goes on for a while. Behind it is the sound of my mother making coughing, choking sounds and my father going, 'Aye, aye, are you going to listen or aren't you? Aye? I can't take this anymore. I can't . . . ' He too begins to weep. Then quiet. Not long after, the bedroom door opens and Mama comes in. In the dark, she crawls into bed with Electra and me, crying. 'I swear,' she mutters, 'in the name of God I swear, this is the last time.' My father comes upstairs and goes into the other room. As she sleeps, my mother grinds her teeth and Electra trembles as if she is lying on icy sheets.

In the morning they're both gone. The house is empty, from one end to the other. Not a peep. The woodstove is not ticking as it expands with the fire it usually contains in its belly, and the cold is causing our insides to flutter. Electra and I go next door to Amya. She combs our hair beside the heater and puts black tea and bread sprinkled with olive oil and salt in our mouths; she is poorer than us. Then she buttons up our black tunics and Athena walks with us as far as the school gates. 'Your mother will be back later,' she tells us. 'Don't worry.' In the evening, Mama is still not back. Neither is Baba. The house is frigid. They've really done it this time: they've abandoned us. More than anything I want to put my face in my hands and cry. Instead, I feed Byron and tie him in the backyard. Then I take Electra to Aunt Irene's. After that I walk to the village square. It's almost dark by the time I get there. On the way, I try not to sniffle but it's hard not to with the chill wind blowing in my face. Normally I enjoy the snowy streets. It's like walking on a piece of paper that no one's thought to write on yet, and the long trail left by my footsteps is the first mark. The first steps made by man. This evening there's no time for games. Teeth clacking, feet frozen, I walk from one tavern to the other until I find my father. He's drinking with Ezet. Two half-empty glasses of red wine sit between them on the grimy table. The ashtray is bristling with cigarette butts. Ezet and Baba, they're almost numb with drink and vacant as the dead. I tug my father's hand and tell him to come home. My fingers rub his wedding band as if it could summon a jinn. I'd make a wish, except I don't believe it would come true. 'Mama is gone,' I tell him. He looks at me as if his brain does not recognise the fruit of his loins. 'What?' he says, managing to sound irritated and puzzled at the same time. 'I said, I don't know where Mama is. Electra and I are scared to go to sleep on our own. Come home.' I tug his hand, hoping to make him stand up. A radio sitting high on a shelf is playing mournful Turkish songs. The words sound as if they are coming from a great distance. My father flicks my pesky hand away and his mouth releases a torrent of abuse, aimed at my mother and his luckless marriage. I stand still until he runs out of words. Then I take his hand again. His pupils burn in his small, red-rimmed eyes. They're scary. I cast imploring gazes at Ezet, but he's of no use tonight. He's off somewhere by himself. Stelios, the owner of the tavern, stands over my father. '*Haydi*, Stamo, it's time to go home,' he says to my father in Greek. Then he switches to Turkish. 'You've had enough. Both of you,' he says, looking at Ezet. 'Go home. I'm closing up; no one's out in this weather.' He nods encouragingly at me. I help my father to his feet. 'I'll take care of this one,' says Stelios, indicating Ezet. 'He lives in my direction.' My father and I, we walk home, in the dark and snow, and I don't know why it happens, but while he is leaning his weight on me, I start to cry. Really cry. 'Are you crying?' he asks. 'Why are you crying? You shouldn't cry. It's not right.' The tears come out of the cracks in my eyes and freeze halfway down my face. Even God doesn't want me to cry. So I stop. I take Baba home. Then I go out again to collect Electra from Aunt Irene's house. When I knock on the door, 'No,' Irene says. 'She's asleep. Let her stay here tonight. I'll bring her over in the morning. Timon,' she calls over her shoulder. Timon comes out. 'Take Dimitro home.' Timon throws on a coat and gloves. Hand in hand we walk through the empty lot with the Judas tree that scrapes the back of a derelict house. Beneath the streetlight on the corner, the wind rakes the cobbles with snow and ice. At the front door Timon says, 'Good night, I'll leave you here,' and quickly vanishes. I wait a minute before going inside. Baba is unconscious on the divan. The wick of the kerosene lamp is turned down low and the flame is sputtering. A string of black smoke rises from the glass funnel and coils beneath the ceiling. I remove my father's shoes and throw a blanket over him. For a second, I fantasise about dousing him with kerosene and setting him alight. That ought to put an end to everything. The clock ticking loudly on the kitchen shelf brings me back to the room. Wearily, I climb the stairs and get into bed. My feet, my fingertips, the roots of my hair, everything, is so cold, it feels like I'm burning up. For some reason, the room seems to have shrunk. I am a giant squashed between four walls, sandwiched by the ceiling and floor. And then I am floating outside the room, seeing through the wall, as my body tosses and turns in bed, desperately trying to keep warm. I keep going in and out of the room. One minute inside my body, the next minute out of it and floating away. My head begins to throb. My eyeballs hurt. I'm so tired I don't even say a prayer to the saints. Grandfather Dimitro sits beside me. 'Look where we have arrived,' he says, spreading his hands, palms up like a beggar. 'When I was a young man I had an Arab neighbour. He was a good soul. When there was trouble brewing and he was at a loss what to make of the turn of events, he'd say, "*Yegallek Allah!*" See where we have arrived.' When I don't reply, Grandfather puts his hand to my forehead. 'You have a fever,' he says. 'Shall I tell you a story to make you sleep?' I nod, not caring so long as someone is beside me. 'Tell me again how Tenedos got its name,' I manage to say. 'All right then, close your eyes. Here it is . . . '

'A long time ago,' he begins, stretching out beside me, 'before the Christian and Muslim God knew who He was, many gods ruled the world and they each had a name. During their time, there lived a mighty king called Cycnus, who lived in Colonae, where Lapseki is today in the Dardanelles. This king had a son called Tenes. He and his sister Hymethea were the grandchildren of Poseidon, the Girdler of the Earth. For what Cycnus did not know, though he might well have suspected it, was that Tenes was the product of a union between his first wife Proclia and the god Apollo. Those were the days when such things happened. The gods delighted in dalliances with mortals. It's said that Cycnus himself was the product of just such a union, between Poseidon and his mortal consort Calyce. After the death of his first wife Proclia, Cycnus married again, this time to Philonome, daughter of feared Tragasus. But, as the Fates would have it, Philonome preferred her stepson Tenes. When the good-hearted boy rejected his stepmother's unwanted advances, furious Philonome falsely accused him of having raped her, adding that his virtuous sister Hymethea had helped her brother in the deed. She even managed to convince Eumolphos, a flute player who had been rejected by Hymethea, to support her story. Cycnus was heartbroken to hear of such treachery and determined to have nothing more to do with his children. Suspecting Tenes' divine origins, he dared not kill him outright and risk the fury of the god of light and music. As the next best thing, he locked Tenes and Hymethea inside a chest and cast them into the Hellespont. As the pitiless currents carried the children out to the Aegean, Poseidon, whose stables are beneath the waves between here and Imvros, heard their cries. He took pity on his grandchildren and guided them safely into the harbour of a nearby island, pushing the chest with its precious cargo toward the hut of a fisherman whose frequent sacrifices to the god had not gone unheeded. The man did not hesitate to bring up the children as his own when he saw his favourite god's hand at work. As for the island on which the children found themselves, all that can be said about it with certainty is that a seafaring people known as the Pelagians had settled its shores before the dawn of history. Content to live simply off the bounty of the land and sea, they were neither empire builders nor craftsmen of renown. Theirs was a basic existence. Whatever charms the island boasted were of nature's making. Song and legend has it that from Troy on the opposite shore, the white cliffs of the island, towering over the turquoise sea, shone like gems and earned the island the epithet Leuphcophrys, "white brow". In time, Tenes became king of Leuphcophrys. In his honour, the people changed the name of the island to Tenedos, which means "the place of Tenes". As for Hymethea, she became the goddess of caves and of openings in the earth. While all this was happening on the island, in Colonae King Cycnus discovered his wife's deception in a vision given to him by his divine father Poseidon. He had Philonome buried alive as an example to liars, and decreed that Eumolphos be stoned to death. They didn't do things by halves in those days ... Having heard that his children now lived on nearby Tenedos, King Cycnus set out with a small crew to bring them home. But he was in for further heartache. While attempting to land at Tenedos, he was repelled by Tenes and a group of fearsome islanders. Obstinate Tenes still held a grudge against his father. He cut the mooring of Cycnus's ship, and his men hurled rocks and verbal abuse at the sailors. Cycnus left, hoping that his son would eventually calm down. It was not to be. Some time after this show of impetuosity there came another hothead to the island, thus proving that Tenedos really is too small for two rams hell bent on clashing horns. The new arrival was Achilles, near-invincible hero and son of the nereid Thetis. (She's the one that lives in the big well on your summer property, by the way.) Little did Achilles know that by setting foot on the island he was sealing his own fate; an oracle had told Thetis that if Achilles killed Tenes, he too would die. Achilles arrived on Tenedos with the Achaean armada on the way to fight at Troy. While his men were replenishing their provisions, he wandered about the island. During the course of his explorations, he came across a cave sheltered by a copse of fragrant pines. Mint and dogbane grew in profusion in the waters of the spring by the entrance, and from inside the cave emanated an enchanting song. Achilles was bewitched. Poking his head in, he found a young woman seated in a chair, busy at her loom. The instant their eyes met, Cupid's work was done. The young woman, isolated all these years with only her brother and the most uncouth of men to look at, had never seen such a dashing specimen of manhood. As for Achilles, he was immediately won over by this wild girl who, all the same, showed signs of refinement beyond her circumstance. So Hymethea met Achilles. She must have invited him inside, for the two were entwined as two vines in summer when Tenes returned. Outraged, yelling at the top of his voice, Tenes dragged Achilles off his sister and began to beat him with his fists. Surprised, brutal Achilles struck at his assailant's head. There was a mighty crack and Tenes crumbled to the ground, blood spilling from a wound. Hymethea screamed her brother's name, bringing Achilles to his senses. When he heard that he had killed Tenes, son of Cycnus, he knew that he had also sealed his own doom. He fled to his ship and immediately set sail for Troy. Many months later, Achilles vanquished King Cycnus on the battlefield. As the mighty king fell to the ground, he turned into a swan and flew to Mount Olympus. For her part, Hymethea buried Tenes' body inside a mound and, in time, joined him there. Today the mound is known as the hill of Saint Elias. The Turks call it *Göz Tepe.*'

I wake up. Beyond the curtain, the morning draws a frosty veil across the glass. The winery rooftops are covered in thick bristling snow that reflects the sun in dazzling shards of light. The sky is baby blue. There is not a cloud in sight. I dress and set to doing what I like best: drawing pictures on the frosted glass with my finger. I am sketching a cottage with a smoking chimney nestled beneath a palm tree when I hear the front door open. It's Grandmother Evangelia and Aunt Vasiliki bringing my mother back. They're talking in hushed tones. One of them sets to lighting the woodstove, while another lights the hearth in the kitchen. 'You must forgive him,' I hear Aunt Vasiliki say. 'Leaving is not an option.' In a short while, Grandmother calls them into the kitchen. 'I've made tea,' she says. 'It'll warm us up.' Mama hasn't uttered a word. Now she opens her mouth. 'I don't want tea. I want to go upstairs and pack my things. I'm not staying in this house another hour.' I open the bedroom door and stand on the landing, the better to hear. She wants to leave us. 'You'll do nothing of the sort,' Grandmother replies. She sounds hard and uncompromising. Aunt Vasiliki is more beseeching. 'Think about the children,' she adds. 'You can't leave them. Besides, we'll be a laughing stock. You know how people talk.' I'm ready to run downstairs and beg Mama not to abandon us when Grandmother's voice says, 'Listen, Galatea, this is how things are. It hasn't been easy for any of us. Just about every woman on the island puts up with this sort of treatment. The men drink and they take it out on their wives. It's time you accepted the way things are.' Vasiliki butts in with, 'Thanks be to God my Yanni doesn't drink.' I can almost see her crossing her breast, eternally grateful to the Lord for sparing her. Grandmother goes on as if Vasiliki had not interrupted. 'This is our lot to bear and you will have to make the most of it . . . ' My mother interrupts. 'No, it's not right. Look at my face. Look at my throat. What have I done to deserve this? Next, he will kill me and kill the children, too. I'm telling you that I'm scared.' She's stubborn as a mule; I'll grant that. 'Galatea, I sympathise, I really do,' implores her sister-in-law. She's not as stony as Grandmother; her voice is almost frightened. 'It's not right that he should treat you like this, the mother of his children. Though you must admit that you are a bit of a handful. You do ask for it.' Then quiet. They must be drinking their mountain tea. My nose twitches. The sweet aroma of the slopes

is inside our home months before it has any right to be. I'm
hungry. 'Listen,' Vasiliki goes on, 'leave it with me. He's my
brother. I'll talk sense into him. I will stop at the winery and
ask him to come see me after work. If he hears you want to
leave him, he'll get scared and stop. He's not a bad man. It's
the drink. You know as well as I do that the bottle talks louder
than his conscience, that's all. I'm begging you, for my sake,
don't leave him. He'll be lost without you.' Mama sniffs. 'I
can't stand to have him near me,' she says softly, her voice
shuddering. 'That's something else again,' responds Vasiliki.
'These are private matters, between you and him. All I'll say is
that he is your husband and what you are saying is wrong.'
The early morning sun is coming in through the sitting room
window, brushing the table with the creamy lace cloth. The
woodstove is crackling and roaring behind the metal door.
'You cannot leave him,' Grandmother says, sounding like she's
winding things down. 'I won't have you in my house if you
do.' My mother begins to whimper. It's as if something is
broken inside of her. 'You have your children to care for. Put
your thoughts and energy into that. I've got work to do at the
pensione. Vasiliki is going to stay with you for a while. I'll
collect Electra from Irene's and then you will get on with your
day as if nothing had happened. Is that understood?' Mama
doesn't respond. 'Dimitro,' Grandmother calls. Her voice is
usually filled with kisses. Now it's sharp as a thorn. 'I know
you're upstairs. Come down at once. You've got work to do.'
In the kitchen, I'm too scared to look at my mother. I'm afraid
of two things: I don't want to see the bruises and I don't want
to see that she's hardened her heart against us. Luckily, her
face is buried in a tiny wet handkerchief. Vasiliki has her
wrapped up in her wings. 'Your mother is not feeling well,'
Grandmother says, turning to me. 'She fell down. It's your job
to look after her. I must go to work, but your aunt will get you

ready for school.' Vasiliki nods, looking sad. A tiny voice in my head tells me to listen to Grandmother and obey. Otherwise Electra and I will be out on the street, frozen kittens before nightfall. I stand by my mother. If my father goes near her with a raised hand, I swear I'll kill him. I gingerly touch one of Mama's fingers. She lifts her head and then lowers it again, sobbing harder. The fire in her gut seems to have gone out and I'm wondering how to stoke it back to life again. As Grandmother walks out the front door, she says, 'It might be best if you didn't go out for a few days. You don't want people talking any more than they are already.'

In the night's endless river of cold and darkness, barely anyone ventures out once the streetlights flicker on. The wind shrieks at the door, trying to find a way in. The radio predicts more snow. Baba and Timon's father Uncle Petro sit at the living room table, smoking. It's as if all the words in the world have been spoken, and there is nothing left to say. Uncle Petro's rheumy eyes are red from drink. Broken capillaries run wild beneath the thin skin on his nose. Mama and her sister Irene are speaking quietly in the kitchen. Mama is stirring the Turkish coffee she's brewing on the hot coals of the brazier. When it comes to the boil with a furious hiss, she emerges bearing two steaming cups and places them on the table before the men. Uncle Petro says, 'Thank you, Galatea.' From the sheepish way he offers his gratitude, anyone would think he's the one that beats her. My mother walks back to the kitchen without acknowledging him. Despite a face that bears a resemblance to orange pulp, she is regal as a queen. She won't even glance at my father, who sits shame-faced and gloomy by the heater. Evangelia and Electra are perched at the end of the divan, trying to make sense of a Turkish primary reader. Cousin Evangelia is better at reading than my sister. 'What's this say?' Electra asks, showing me the book. '*Evvel zaman içinde*,' I tell her. 'It means "Once upon a time".' Timon and I are playing games on the mezzanine. We've built a mountain pass and winding valley with cushions and rugs. Timon's toy Chevrolet is rushing toward a head-on collision with my red Mini. When the cars round the bend, there's going to be an almighty crash. If there was a donkey with a rider caught between the vehicles, the destruction would be truly bloody. The cars collide. Timon and I make crashing noises, the screams of survivors and the dying. 'Will you shut up,' yells Timon's father. 'Devils! Get out of here.' He makes to hit us. The girls frown their disapproval. Chastened, we remember the gravity of the situation and quieten down.

I'm desperate for a pee. But it's too cold to go stand over the cesspit in the yard. If I wait for our guests to leave so that I can use the potty upstairs, my bladder will burst. When I can't hold on any longer, I tell Timon where I'm going and leave the room. As I walk through the kitchen, my mother says, 'Where are you going?' For some reason I'm angry with her. 'To the toilet,' I snap. I close the door behind me and fumble in the dark. The cesspit is several paces from the back door. Two planks of wood are thrown over the hole. To do your business, you stand on them and aim. I shuffle forward. Snow stings my face and hands. It quickly turns to slush underfoot. When my shoes touch the planks, I unbutton my trousers and take it out. It is freezing. In seconds, my teeth are chattering. The urine feels like solid ice forcing its way out of my body. I'm almost done, when I hear a cracking sound. One of the planks breaks. I tip over and drop into the hole without a sound. I'm up to my chin in frozen human waste. I try to keep my mouth closed, but each time I call out, stuff goes in. It's pitch black. I can't see a thing. I go under. I come up again, coughing and spluttering. Snow falls on me. I'm floundering and calling my mother. No one comes to rescue me. I can't climb out on my own. It's too steep and deep. When I leap up, I see safe golden light spilling into the night from the kitchen window. It seems so distant. I yell until my lungs hurt. Finally, the back door opens and a rectangle of light cuts into the night. 'What are you doing out there all this time?' my mother says, sounding irate. 'Mama, I'm in the hole. Help me,' I yell, gargling shit. She screams. 'Stamo, the boy is in the hole. Hurry. Quickly before he drowns.' In seconds, the men are standing over the cesspit. Together they reach down and grab an arm each. They yank me out as if I am a feather. 'Phew,' says Uncle Petro, pinching his nostrils. 'What a stench!' He waves a hand in the air, pulling a face that gives him sardine lips. My father lifts me in his arms and rushes inside, kicking the door shut behind him. 'Quick, get the clothes off him before he freezes,' he says, tugging at my jumper. Mama strips the soiled clothes off me while reliable Aunt Irene pulls the tin tub from under the stairs and fills it with boiling water. By this time, I can't feel a thing. I'm numb from the shock and cold. My mother lowers me into the steaming water and attacks my skin with a soapy washcloth. My blood begins to circulate again. My skin tingles and prickles. Electra, Evangelia and Timon stand by the door, barely managing to contain their laughter. 'Throw out the clothes,' my mother orders over her shoulder. 'Get the smell out of here. Electra, go upstairs and bring me the *eau de cologne.*' When I'm wearing clean, warm clothes again, Timon grins. I know what he's thinking. 'Hey, shit boy,' he chirps, 'you stank out the place.' Everybody bursts out laughing. 'I think we could all do with a cup of tea,' Irene says. 'Thank God he's safe,' my mother mumbles, slapping her cheek.

The next morning, we discover that Kokona's house burned down overnight. They say she fell asleep without putting a fireguard across the grate. A log rolled out and, before you knew

it, her life's work was reduced to ashes. Even though her neighbours raised the alarm, it was the blacksmith from the foot of
the hill who clambered up the ravine from his workshop, half-
naked and bleeding from the dangerous climb, and pulled the
old woman from the flames. Had it not been for him, Kokona
would be in paradise now, and her sons in America would be
whipping themselves with grief. Timon told me all of this on
the way to Kokona's place. 'Where is she now?' I ask. We're
standing a safe distance from the charred remains of the house.
The still-smoking ruin is surrounded by slush. Blackened beams
point at the overcast sky like spiky hair. 'The priest is letting her
stay in that little room inside the church gates,' Timon replies.
'You know, just before you descend the stairs to the courtyard.'
A crow is wheeling overhead. I shudder when I think of the
calamity that's befallen the old woman. I don't know what's
worse. Losing the roof over your head or living inside a church-
yard filled with ghosts and saints. 'Let's get a better view,' says
Timon, pulling me through the mud. We are both wearing
boots, gloves and beanies against the cold. There's a sickly
stench in the air and I don't really want to get closer. 'That
must be the mule,' he says, pointing at the charred remains. I
can see a sooty snout and one perfectly formed ear, stiff legs,
hoofs. The animal's gut is grotesquely bloated. As we watch, a
crow lands on the roof and shatters the air with a harsh cry. It
flaps its wings, dislodging a loose beam, which falls to the
ground, spearing the mule's gut with an ugly crackling sound.
Powdery ash puffs out of the hole, and something that's neither
snow nor muddy rain falls into it. Disgusted, I think of our
donkey Train, who lodges just a few metres away. A neighbour
comes out of his house. He pretends to grab a stick he keeps by
the door. 'Get away from there, you ghouls,' he yells. 'Get away
before it collapses and takes you to hell with it. Will you have a
look at this, they've come to pick poor Kokona's bones and

she's not even dead yet.' His wife joins him, tut-tutting and shaking her fat head. 'Wait till I tell your mothers,' she yells, her chins wobbling. We pelt off, slipping and sliding in the snow.

'Children.' The teacher calls the class to attention. 'I want you to open your history books. I have a special surprise for you today.' She names a page number and smiles, keeping one finger on the open book before her. There's a rustle of paper as the class obeys. 'I reckon she's stacked on the weight,' Refik whispers, burying his nose in the book. 'It's the island air,' I put in. 'Either that or she's pregnant.' Refik splutters. To cover up he pretends to have a coughing fit. The teacher continues to smile as if she's had too much to drink. Lelia glares at Refik from the other side of the aisle. 'Well,' the teacher says, 'what do you see, children?' When no one responds, she exhales impatiently and says, 'It's our beautiful island, Bozcaada. Do you recognise it?' In a French illustration of the eighteenth century, the island is serene as a Muslim graveyard. Beside the illustration is a map from the seventeenth century. It shows a lighthouse in exactly the same spot where an almost identical one still brings fishermen home of an evening. In the French illustration, the fortress dominates the foreshore; while behind it, in the gentle folds of valleys, poplars and cypress trees sprout, piercing the pregnant bellies of clouds. Inside the fortress walls is an elaborately tiered palace, and a mosque with no fewer than three minarets. 'Well, that's gone now,' I mutter. 'It's beautiful,' breathes Refik. The smile returns to the teacher's face. 'That's right,' she says, moving to stand in front of the woodstove. 'It is beautiful. I thought this might interest you. It is our island as it used to be in times past. It's a paradise.' I can't tear my eyes away from the book. Everything seems so clean and new. The houses huddled beside trees, the people at work or on the promenade along the still and placid shore. It's like seeing your grandmother as a young girl starting out in life. Behind the healthy expanse of the township, the hill looks distant and indomitable as a mountain, rather than the mere hillock it is; maybe time has eaten it away. Apart from that, nothing seems to have changed over the centuries. 'Turn the page,' the teacher instructs. 'This illustration was drawn by an Italian artist, one Koronel.' She seems genuinely surprised and pleased by our response to the pictures and can't stop smiling. I've rarely seen her this animated. Maybe she is not so bad after all. The class is hushed. 'He sailed these waters in the late sixteen hundreds. What can you tell me about this picture? Anyone? Remember to put up your hand first.' I raise my hand. The teacher points to me and I stand up. 'My teacher,' I say, 'this drawing bears no resemblance to Tenedos whatsoever. Everyone knows that Tenedos is a triangle, like a cheese *börek*.' Kids snigger and smack their lips. Someone says, 'Yum!' The teacher smiles indulgently. 'This picture is more like a wrinkled apple with a large chunk bitten off for the harbour,' I go on. 'But the fortress and the lighthouse are the same, as is the hill behind the village.' The teacher puts up her hand to stop me. 'That's excellent, Dimitri. Good boy. Now, can someone correct him on one small point?' she asks, glancing round the room. Her straight wheat hair pivots. No one answers. 'All right, then, I'll tell you,' she says, touching her cheek. 'The name of our island is Bozcaada, not Tenedos. Now on the next page, children, you will find an illustration showing the illustrious Ottoman navy liberating Bozcaada from the Venetians in fourteen fifty-six.' With a rustle of paper, everyone turns the page. I sit, puzzled and confused. I wanted to tell the teacher something else that I had spotted. In the bottom right-hand corner of the drawing is a banner announcing, '*Isola del Tenedo*'.

That night I'm eager to tell Mama and Baba about the history lesson. Baba glides against the divan. He reaches across to turn on the radio. He sees the disappointed expression on my face and withdraws his hand. 'Go on then. Tell us,' he says. He looks like a grasshopper with bushy eyebrows. 'Can't he do it after the news?' Mama says, picking up her knitting. She's taken to wearing seeing glasses with thick, black frames. They make her look older. My father rests his eyes on her. 'No, now,' he says, lighting a cigarette. 'I want to hear.' He lifts Electra onto his knee. 'You make tea if you're not interested,' he tells Mama. She doesn't reply. Even though her bruises have almost disappeared, she still sits away from the light. 'So,' my father says, plucking the cigarette from his mouth and exhaling a plume of smoke. 'What did you learn?' I take a deep breath and start. 'This is from the teacher's mouth,' I say, excited. 'It's in the history books, too. She said that Fatih the Conqueror wrested Tenedos from the Venetians three years after the Ottoman conquest of Constantinople in fourteen fifty-three. But she didn't call the island Tenedos. She said back then it was called Boğaz Adası, Straits Island.' My mother snorts and rolls her eyes. I ignore her and go on with the story. 'Until the Ottoman take-over, the island had been constantly changing hands between the Byzantines and the cities of Venice and Genoa.' My father is gently stroking Electra's hair. 'Never heard of them,' he interrupts. 'Where are they from?' My mother looks up from her work. 'In Italy,' she snaps, radiating scorn. 'Go on.' Now she's interested. I start up again; glad to have her attention. 'Hoping to regain control of the island,' I continue, 'Venice clashed with the Ottomans for almost a decade in the late fifteenth century. In the end, Gedik Paşa took charge of Tenedos, and in fourteen seventy-nine he rebuilt the partially destroyed fortress left behind by the Venetians. They had built it on the foundations of an older Phoenecian castle. That's the fortress on the harbour today. The one Timon and I play in!' I finish off triumphantly. My father's eyes brim with pride. He turns to Mama and says, 'He takes to learning pretty well, doesn't he?' When my mother doesn't respond, he adds, 'Just one question though. Who were the Byzantines? Were they Muslims too?' My mother can't believe her ears. She throws the yarn and knitting needles in her lap and turns to face him. 'Stamo,' she says, exasperated, 'don't you know anything? The Byzantines were Greek Orthodox Christians. Anatolia was theirs until the Ottomans took over. We're their descendants. They built the Hagia Sophia.' Goodness, how she heats up. Baba is silenced by the rebuke. His face says this is too much for him to absorb in one go. Behind his thinking, the wind moans and batters the door. Electra climbs out of his lap and parts the curtain over the window. 'What are you saying?' Baba says finally. 'I thought the Hagia Sophia was a mosque.' Someone runs by in the street. The metal caps on the front of his shoes strike the stone, making a pleasant ringing sound. 'It was a basilica first,' Mama tells him. 'Then they turned it into a mosque and now it's a museum. Who else do you think built those churches? The Muslims?' I wish she would cut it out. Baba is asking because he wants to know and she's making him feel smaller than an ant. Electra lets the curtain drop and settles in Baba's lap again. 'Tell me,' Mama says, turning to me, 'did your clever teacher also tell you that Alexander the Great fought the Persians for possession of the island? And that from there on Tenedos followed a more or less Greek course until the Otto-mans came along?' I shake my head, shamed by my ignorance. 'I didn't think so,' she says, picking up her knitting again. 'The Venetians, the Genoese, the Arabs, they've all been here,' she says. 'All the same, the island remained culturally Greek. The rest came and went, but we've remained. And we're still here. Find that in your precious books.' Mama has a way of weeding out know-it-alls and telling them exactly where they stand. She sits back content in the knowledge that she's put us in our place. Baba floods the room with radio noise. 'See,' he says in a low voice, 'that's why it's important to go to school. You're not to go to sea, do you hear?' From the other end of the divan Mama pipes up, 'You can say that again. When he's old enough he's going to university in Constantinople.'

Zotico shouts through the wall. 'Dimitro, come. I need you.' Without asking Mama's permission, I scoot out the door and zip into Amya's house. The cold is quick to nip at my ears and fingertips. 'Ah, the light of my life.' Amya beams from her usual spot: the kitchen sink. She seems to be held there by invisible chains, never moving more than five or ten feet away from it. Athena sits at the table, morosely sipping tea. Her face is sad, brooding and distant. There are dark circles round her eyes and her cheeks are hollow. 'Come sit here,' says Zotico, patting his knee. I clamber up. He wraps an arm round my waist and pulls me closer. 'This morning, before school,' he whispers. 'Can you?' He slips a sheet of paper into my pocket. His eyes are restless and wet, making him resemble a tomcat in May. 'As if we can't hear you,' mutters Athena, glaring at him. 'What is it, another message for your whore? Mixing up a child in your sordid business. Aren't you ashamed?' I squirm in Zotico's lap, not wanting to get caught up in anything that is going on between them. 'You shut up,' he yells at his sister. 'Who are you to talk?' Amya turns from the sink. 'Don't shout,' she protests in a practical voice. 'Your sister is right, Zotico. You should be going down there yourself and doing the right thing, or asking your father to speak for you.' Athena snorts. She tips the remaining tea into a silver pail by the door, bangs her cup on the sink and walks out. 'Zotico.' Amya lowers her voice. 'You're the oldest now. I want you to marry so that we can marry her off too,' she tips her chin at Athena's back. 'She's well past the age when she should be married. It's not right that she is still single. She's already too old and I'm afraid we'll be stuck with her.' Zotico nods, pursing his full lips so that his movie star moustache undulates. 'Go now,' he says to me. 'You haven't got long to go before school starts. Don't forget to come back and tell me what she says.' His moustache tickles my cheek with a kiss. I slide off his knee and walk off. Athena is in the front room, gazing out of the window. A paper bag floats by outside as if it's a new breed of bird. Cold light bathes Athena's blotchy face, making her seem paler than usual. She senses my presence and turns to face me. 'Get lost,' she snaps, allowing the embroidered curtain to fall across the window. 'Go do your dirty job. I'm sick of the sight of you. All of you are pimps.' Her voice sounds watery. I'm out the front door, wondering what the devil is wrong with her.

Refik grabs my arm. He's bundled up in heavy clothing so that only his red nose and cheeks are visible. 'Have you heard?' he asks, keeping an eye out for teachers. 'Heard what?' He rolls his eyes. We're walking the concrete lip that skirts the school building. Since the snows started to melt and the rains came, the students restrict their movements during recess to the narrow path. The rest of the schoolyard is a muddy field, best avoided, unless you have to dash to the toilet block or the drinking taps. 'She's gone,' he says, threading his arm through mine. I have no idea what he's talking about. 'Who's gone?' Soft scurrying steps approach from behind. Refik waits till a solitary kid passes. 'Idiot,' he says, when the kid has passed, 'who do you think I'm talking about? The teacher. She's gone back to the mainland to have her baby. There's no hospital or doctor on the island and she wanted to be close to her parents and her in-laws. So she left this morning on Captain Yakar's boat.' He sounds glad, relieved. 'Aren't you happy?' he asks, when I don't say anything. 'We're getting a new teacher.' I shrug. I'm neither happy nor sad. Since I turned nine in February, I've been trying to master my emotions, the way a man is supposed to. The teacher's departure simply means we have to break in a new taskmaster, and who knows what he or she is going to be like. 'I don't understand why we can't have Levent Efendi,' I say, preferring the known to the unknown. Lelia and Acantha stroll by, arm in arm. They too are bundled up in thick gear, except Acantha's shoe has a hole in it and you can see her black leggings. When they see us, they lift their noses in the air and stalk by on thin legs. 'For all we know, the new teacher could be worse than the last one,' I point out. Refik shakes his head, smiling. 'You worry too much,' he says. 'I thought you'd be happy. My father was telling my mother about it over breakfast. He's friendly with the teacher's husband, you know.' We stroll arm in arm, passing other kids. 'What about the husband?' I ask. I'd seen him arrive at the school earlier. 'He stays, but he's not so bad,' Refik says, and that's true enough. A sharp-faced student squelches through the mud from the direction of the toilet block. He stands before us, grinning and trying to scrape off the thick mud caked to his shoes and the cuffs of his dark trousers. 'Don't try it, boys,' he advises. 'Better to do it in your pants than risk crossing that swamp.' He laughs. Overhead, buds are bursting through the trees' tough skin. The bell rings over the first bird song of the season, and the sound of goats bleating washes from the hill. Green is returning to the world. Soon the sound of tortoises mating will be all over the island.

The new teacher is very handsome. Tall and slender, with coal-black hair and green eyes, his beauty has no comparison; even the sun's rays pale before him. He glides along the edges of the room, speaking in a deep reverberating voice, a black and white, sharply angular angel. My eyes follow him of their own accord.

I am hypnotised. I haven't heard a thing he has uttered all morning. My ears are blocked. My eyes have tunnel vision. The classroom contains only him and me. He smiles and the creased skin either side of his mouth forms brackets that protect his lips. I am dazzled. I hear the rose-coloured starling indulge in an outburst as a ray of sunlight breaks through a chink in the thick cloud. Over the heads of the students, the teacher's eyes lock with mine. He lengthens his stride and continues to measure the room's perimeter, hands behind his back. When he is almost on the edge of vision, my head pivots to keep him in its sights. By some miracle, he is suddenly standing behind me. His body is a towering column of smoke. I freeze, my heart thumping out of sheer embarrassment rather than fright. 'What are you playing at?' he demands. Beside me, Refik squeals and almost leaps out of his skin. On the other side of the aisle, Lelia covers her mouth to stifle a giggle. 'What are you staring at?' the teacher says. I am speechless. I can only gape in horror. 'I've had my eye on you all morning. You two are troublemakers, intent on disrupting the class.' He smartly knocks our heads together and walks away. Refik begins to weep. 'From here on,' the teacher says, turning, 'you two may not sit together.' Refik lets out a stifled sob and rubs his head. I am furious. I grit my teeth and tremble with rage. I am fed up with being a punch bag for whoever comes along. I swear that I am going to get that bastard; I am going to make him pay . . .

After school, I hide behind the fountain outside the school gates and wait. It's cold and damp but I am determined. An eternity passes. When someone comes to collect water, I pretend I am playing a game. Finally, the teacher emerges carrying a black bag. Levent Efendi is with him. 'Please don't let them share a house,' I pray, 'because I will have to burn it down, and I don't want to make Levent Efendi homeless.' I wait till they reach the

Dadaoğlu house before I follow. From the Dadaoğlu doorway, I poke out my head and spy them go down to Republic Street. When they are a safe distance, I pad after them silent as a cat. They stop at the corner bakery. The teacher buys a loaf of bread and Levent Efendi buys two *simit*, sesame rings. Then they cross the road and walk in the shadow of the winery, deep into the Turkish Quarter, chatting quietly. They both have long legs and I have to trot to keep up. Occasionally, they laugh, these two gentlemen in suits and ties. I want to throw a rock at the pimp's head. Instead, I skulk from door to door, nursing my desire for revenge. At the start of the street that leads up to the high school, they stop before a grey wooden house with a faded green door. Still chatting, the teacher takes out a key and unlocks the door. The handsome one shakes hands with Levent Efendi and enters the house. Levent Efendi leaves. Whether he meant to or not, I don't know, but the teacher left the front door ajar. I flatten myself behind a streetlight until Levent Efendi takes a corner and disappears. A dog barks and children laugh from behind a high wall. My mother will be wondering where I am. Just as I've resolved to tiptoe over and peek into the house, the teacher comes out again. He's taken off his jacket and tie, and slipped a black woollen vest over the white shirt. Almost entirely in black, he is so eye-catching he could easily be the devil. It is a pity I have to make him suffer. He is holding a white enamel bowl. In the silence, I hear the metal scrape stone as he carefully places it on the cobbles. A black cat dashes out from between his legs, mewing. It has a white nose and brown speckles on its hind-quarters. A small bell tinkles at its throat. The cat gazes adoringly up at him before burying its snout in the milk. He crosses his arms and stands there, admiring his pet. He scans the sky and, after a while, goes back inside. The door shuts with a clatter. The breeze ruffling its fur, the cat continues to drink contently. I kneel and extend my hand. 'Puss, puss, puss,' I say. The cat looks up and goes back to drinking milk. I persevere. 'Puss, puss, puss.'

Refik has been away for almost a week. This morning his sister Deniz arrives at school furious. I ask after her brother. Instead of replying, she says she is angry with me because Refik got into trouble with the new teacher. To top it all off, Refik has been ill and they had to call the doctor. Deniz tells me all this before she comes to the crunch. 'Stay away from my brother,' she warns, pointing a finger in my face. 'You're a bad influence. Refik is a good student and you're just average.' I want to interrupt and tell her that it's not true. Levent Efendi told my mother I am very good at my books and only need maths tuition. But haughty Deniz goes on and on, like women do, never knowing when to stop. I almost punch her in the mouth. Then she delivers her final thrust. 'What can anyone expect from you,' she says, 'apart from herding goats? Nothing. That's what. From now on, stick to your own kind.' As she walks away, I fight the urge to scoop up some mud and rub it into her shiny hair. Instead, I grit my teeth and clench my fists. Tears spring to my eyes, but I push them back into the well that lives inside of me. Ever since I started harnessing my emotions and biting the bit, I don't cry. I must be strong. I swallow countless times until my throat is dry and my temples ache. During morning recess, I seek Lelia and Acantha's company. But they mock me. 'Lost your Turk have you?' says Acantha, tossing her ponytail. 'And now you expect us to take you back as if nothing's happened. Well, think again. That's not how it works, my boy. My mother says we don't mix with Turks and they don't mix with us. That's what you are, Dimitro, a Turk. Go play with them.' Lelia's lily-pond eyes never leave my face. Her fringe is too long. It touches her eyelashes and causes her to constantly flick it back with pudgy fingers. Right there and then, I would have kissed those dear little digits if she'd only smile at me. Instead she turns her back. That evening, I'm standing in the shadows opposite the handsome teacher's house, waiting . . .

The green door opens. Out he steps, wearing a flash navy coat. In profile, his angular face cuts the cold night air like a knife. In his hand is the white ceramic bowl. He puts it on the cobbles. Milk wobbles, but doesn't spill. It's the only patch of white in the crowding darkness. The cat with the white nose dashes out. It sniffs the milk and drinks. Its master locks the door, pulls the collar of his coat against the cutting breeze, and walks toward the lights of the town square. From here the sea is audible, washing the hard, smooth pebbles. The sky is clear and already sparkling with stars. Tonight, I am prepared. Earlier, I'd managed to steal a sardine from my mother's kitchen. I'd wrapped it in newspaper and put it in my pocket. I take out the sardine and step out of the shadows. The cat looks up and then goes back to lapping milk. He's used to me now; I've been visiting almost every night since the bastard hit us. I hold out the fish and say, 'Puss, puss, puss. Come on. Come and eat some real food.' The cat raises its head again and studies me with eyes that are as green as its master's. I wave the sardine. It sniffs. 'Come here, puss.' Cautiously, the animal creeps over. I hold the sardine away from it. When the animal is close enough, I reach out and gently stroke the side of its head. It turns quickly and sinks its fangs into my hand. I am just as fast. I grab its throat and step on its body to prevent its claws from doing harm. The cat manages a last strangled cry before I break its neck. I pull out some string from my pocket and use it to hang the carcass from a nearby Judas tree. When the teacher opens his front door in the morning, it'll be the first thing he sees. I want to set fire to the house, too, but I'll save that for another time. I run home. The cat's bulging eyes follow me through the deserted alleyways.

No fur. No body, only large, green eyes. And one horrible, life-depriving yowl. When I open the front door to our house, my limbs are trembling with the enormity of what I've done. Byron dashes in from the backyard and leaps into my arms, yapping madly. 'Out,' my mother screams, 'I want him out of the house. Now.'

The first thing Refik says to me when he returns to school is, 'I'm not supposed to talk to you.' The second thing he says is, 'Have you heard what some crazy did to the teacher's cat?' I feign ignorance, preferring to forget about it. 'News travels slowly from your side of town to mine,' I point out and we nod as if it's a law of nature. Truth be told, killing that cat has done something strange to me. All I can think about is how good it made me feel, how powerful and strong. I dream about squashing the life out of another defenceless creature so that I can feel that energy surge through my limbs again. We're sitting outside the unfinished school building, facing the paddock. Green fingers are pushing out of the mud; yellow and pink flowers nod in the sun. Half a dozen men are gathered out there, carrying picks and axes and shovels. There's a white van parked by the roadside. Muddy footsteps lead from the van to where the men stand in the middle of the field. They're not villagers. 'Some nut killed it and hung it from a tree,' Refik goes on, awed. 'How creepy is that? It serves him right, though, aye? Bastard for hitting us.' He laughs maliciously and nudges me in the ribs. I nod and manage to scrape together a smile. It's good to have him back; I get lonely when he's away. I want to tell him that I did it, that I killed the cat for him, but I keep my mouth shut. Here's another learning I made recently: it doesn't pay to reveal everything. Some things are meant to be secret. The day after I'd killed his cat, the teacher came to school pale and shaken. All that day and into the next, he was distracted and uncertain. Gone was the confident air, the self-assured smile, the strut. It made him less attractive and I stopped spying on him on the sly. At first, I was certain everyone could see my guilt. But nothing happened. No one said a thing. Nonetheless, I'd rather forget about the incident. Then why does my blood sing when I think of hurting and killing something else? I feel untouchable. Just thinking about it fills me with shame and yet my heart beats faster, my skin comes alive. 'We're not allowed to sit together,' Refik is saying, scuffing his heel into the wall. 'But no one said we can't play together at break.' The poplars by the road shake out their leaves and spangle the air. The sweet aroma of roses and citrus is billowing out of the Dadaoğlu garden with something that feels like steam rising out of the earth. The world is brimming with bird song and goats' bleating. Mists are rising from hollows. Two turkeys scratch in the rubbish heap against the top fence. One tries to mount the other. He is rejected and the two birds fight noisily. Exhausted yellow wagtails flying up from Africa alight in cypress trees to rest. 'What about Deniz?' I say. 'She'll tell your parents.' Refik shrugs. He seems to have grown larger and more daring since his illness. 'She'll keep her mouth shut, if she knows what's good for her.' It's time for the first class of the day. As we walk back to the school building, Levent Efendi strolls by, hands clasped behind his back. 'There's no keeping you two apart, is there?' he says, smiling. 'Remember to behave.' He taps my nose with the tip of his finger.

Lately, Athena has been going out alone. When she thinks no one is watching, she dolls up, grabs her basket and heads for the hill. Today, I am determined to find out what she is up to. With Byron in tow, I follow her through the streets. Earlier, when I asked if I could accompany her, she told me she was going to collect docks and nettles, but she did not want me to come

along. Looking comely in a butter-coloured cardigan and dusty
pink skirt, she walks between the last two houses and steps into
the mass of earthy aromas that rise from the new grass on the
hillside. She stops to greet the sky, breathes in, as if she is
drinking freedom. The wind has dropped and birds swoop,
doing the great dance. Bees dive into flowers. Waters burrow
and trickle and gurgle everywhere. Nature is making so much
noise you can barely hear yourself think. During the rains, the
force of the water ripped up velvety cushions of moss to expose
brown earth. Worms coil and arch their backs, digging their
heads into the underworld. Their wiggling tails are an invitation
to the birds. Fleecy, woolly, furry creatures run everywhere. I
stop in front of a barn to catch my breath. A noise is coming
from inside. Byron sniffs at the door and growls. Athena is
almost out of sight. The noise comes again from inside the
barn. I push open the door. Byron charges in. I grab his collar
and hold him back. It sounds like someone is crying. Inside it's
dark and smells of donkey piss. Cobwebs flutter in high corners.
Eight kittens are huddled in the straw. Byron starts yapping. I
tell him to shut up in case Athena hears. He goes quiet and I
turn my attention back to the kittens. Their eyes are closed and
their pink mouths are wide open, begging for food. They crawl
over each other with stiff, jerky movements. The light streaming
in the door bathes their red fur like a ray of hope, and they
crawl toward it. I don't think. I just act. I pick them up one by
one and dash their tiny bodies against the wall. Again and again,
until they stop moving and are dead. When they are masses of
fur and shattered bone, and the barn stinks of death and shame
and humiliation, I hear a bluebottle fly buzz thickly in the air. I
quickly cover the still-warm bodies with straw and cap the
whole thing with a rusty pail. I'm hoping the worms will devour
them before their mother notices and starts to cry. I am sweating
and breathing hard. While I was taking my anger out on the

poor kittens, Byron has been cowering in a corner. I call him over and run out of that horrible place, through the streets to the sea. I forget about Athena. My heart is beating fast. I know that what I've done is wrong, but I can't help myself. I couldn't stop it even if I wanted to. I'm so used to being on the receiving end, people hitting me, picking on me, that it feels good to take it out on something that's smaller and weaker than me. For once, I'm the strong one. I'm in charge, the one in control. I feel like a hawk. At the far end of the fortress, where the rocky causeway juts out to the sea, I scrub my hands with salty water until they're clean and the nails sparkle in the sunlight. Then I gather Byron in my arms and hope that he won't judge me harshly. I pray that he, at least, will not be scared.

A crow chases a greenfinch across the cloudless sky. The green-finch dips and twirls, dives and flips, climbing higher and higher before dropping faster and faster to earth again. The crow stays behind it, a trail of black smoke. Lelia moves the basket hanging off her arm to a more comfortable position and watches them. We're walking home after collecting water parsnip for our mothers from behind the smithy's. Byron sniffs her heel and she gently kicks him away. 'Flea bag,' she says, shuddering. Aside from that blemish she is pristine as the egg-yolk coloured irises that are growing in ditches and fields. Lelia points at the birds. 'Will you look at that,' she says, shaking her head. 'Every-thing is out to kill everything else. Why can't God's creatures just live in peace?' And there was me thinking the crow was chasing the greenfinch for love. 'Have you heard about Zotico's Ephigenia?' I ask. I am eager to share the gossip, even though I've been sworn to secrecy. She tips back her head and makes a clicking noise with her tongue: No. I tell her that the love affair is over. Fed up with his daughter's disobedience, Ephigenia's father Praxitelis packed her off to relatives in another country.

She's probably halfway across the world by now. Needless to say, Zotico is heartbroken. He sits at home, cursing 'this wretched isle', as if Tenedos is to blame for his sorry state. His mother's tears won't bring him to his senses and his father's threats have next to no effect on him; any day now, he keeps saying, any day now, he's off to France. Lelia is not that interested. She's got more gruesome things on her mind. 'I heard that your grand-mother found three dead kittens in the hotel basement,' she says. 'Someone had crushed them with a rock.' She shudders. 'That's the second lot in as many weeks.' I remain silent and hope she drops the subject. 'Mind you, whoever is responsible is only killing cats in the Greek Quarter,' she goes on. 'They're saying it's one of the crazies that have been shipped here from a loony bin, trying to scare people.' I hang my head in shame. I don't like it when people are blamed for things they didn't do. It's not fair. 'If he wants to scare us then why doesn't he kill people? What's a poor animal ever done to him?' I throw in, for the sake of contributing to the conversation. 'Thank God he doesn't kill people! What a thing to say,' Lelia says, crossing herself. 'Still, better an animal than us,' she finishes off, crossing herself again. I relieve her of the basket. There are enough parsnips and camomile in there to feed an army. Byron is sniffing a carcass in the ditch. I whistle twice before he comes.

On the way, we pass the men that are digging in the paddock behind the school. They are sitting beside their van, eating lunch. Everyone's curiosity has peaked. Who are these men? What are they doing here? But no one is game to ask. They're foreigners and we don't talk to them. Nevertheless, rumours abound. Some say that the men are laying foundations for a new building, while the more pessimistic reckon that they are digging a pit, a mass grave. They reckon that with the Cypriot business going from bad to worse, the Turks are going to slaughter all the

Greeks on the island and toss them in the hole. Two Greek men have been killed on nearby Imvros. Coming on the heels of that, it's not hard to believe we're next. Then they will burn our corpses and no one will know what happened to us. All in all there are half a dozen workmen. The two that are doing the hard labour are obviously Turks, or maybe Kurds – I can't really tell. The soft ones with the new clothes are obviously foreigners. The men see Lelia and me approach. They stop eating and stare as if they've never seen children before. One of the blond foreigners is whistling. When he sees us, he says something in another language. Then he licks his lips, slow and lascivious. When they are moist and shiny, he rubs between his legs, flicking his tongue as if he's spotted a delicious ice cream and wants to give it a good lick. 'All right then, kids,' he says in bad Turkish. 'If it's romance you want, come over here and I'll teach you a thing or two.' His blue eyes gleam in the noonday sun, and beneath his unshaven beard, his skin is fair. The other men guffaw. Without missing a beat, I step between Lelia and the pervert. Byron trots over to them. The blond guy gives him a savage kick. Byron yelps and runs back to me. When we're a safe distance, I pick up a big rock and throw it at the van. It hits a side panel, making a satisfying bang. The men yell 'Hey!' Lelia and I run off, giggling.

I crouch above the new toilet. Mama is sitting at the back door with a textbook in her lap. With her short hair pulled back and glasses perched on her nose, she's testing my knowledge of multiplication tables. But, I ask you, how can a man concentrate on two things at the same time? It's impossible. When I point this out to her, she snorts contemptuously. 'If I can do five things at once, so can you.' There's a rustle of pages on the other side of the curtain that separates me from her scrutiny. 'What's four fours?' she asks. I ransack my brain. There is no answer in there. I wish she'd leave me in peace. Right now all I want is to enjoy using the toilet. As soon as the weather warmed up, Baba hired a man to build a proper one in the backyard. 'I don't want the neighbours saying that my family drowned in shit,' he had said. True to his word, he hired a man to empty the cesspit and fill it in with dirt. Then another guy built a concrete box, like a closet, a few feet away from the house. The concrete box doesn't have a window; just an entrance covered with a frayed old curtain. Inside is a hole with a sloping base and two raised blocks for the feet. After you've done what you need to do, you dump a bucket of water in the hole to wash it away. Now that it's there, I make sure to use it as often as possible. Over dinner one evening, Mama says that Old Pagona across the street breathed a sigh of relief and, no doubt, some fresh air, when our toilet was built. It means that I will stop using the lane that runs beside her house as a latrine. I've noticed lately that Mama is losing her city ways and becoming more like the women in the village; in the past, she would not have talked about such things at the table. 'I asked you,' my mother barks on the other side of the curtain, 'what's four fours?' Now she's gone and broken my concentration. In the long silence that follows, I pray that an answer will fall from the sky into my head. But the only sound comes from the earthquake in my belly. I've eaten too many green plums with salt again, and now I am paying for it. The plums are called *erik*. It's a Turkish word. I like eating *erik* more than anything in the world, except for *simit*. When *erik* are in season, as they are in May, I fill my pockets and chew on them all day. Be careful, though. If you eat too many, your gut blocks up and then you have a job and a half unblocking it. 'Nineteen?' I hazard a guess, hoping she's given up and gone back to doing whatever she does. Her voice rises on the other side of the curtain. 'Wait till you get out of there. I'm going to break your thick head.' I get such a fright that my guts open and everything inside of me rushes out.

Mama announces that it is time for a wash – a real one this time, not that bit of splashing that we do once a week in the tub. She packs a wicker basket with a loofah, face-washers, towels and a huge bar of olive oil soap. Then she takes Electra and me by the hand and we set off. At the bathhouse beneath the Christothoulo house, I'm the only boy there. Once in a while, when the spirit of generosity possesses her, Chrysanthe Christothoulo invites the neighbourhood women to bathe in her *hamam*. Men are strictly not welcome. Timon was kicked out last year, so I think it's my turn next. The Turkish bath is a bewildering place. Steam obscures everything. The air is wet and unreal, as if you are breathing something that doesn't exist. A narrow window in the thick wooden door lets in light from the naked bulb that hangs in the changing room. When the steam parts, it reveals women with big breasts, lolling on the shadowy benches. They resemble gleaming seals, water streaming off them in rivulets. It's odd to see familiar women without a stitch on. Away from home, they turn into different creatures. They behave as if they've left their husbands and children at the door and will pick them up again when they step outside. The pale brilliance of their thighs is hypnotic. They remind me of the season's first figs, when the purple skin is carefully peeled to reveal the juicy white flesh beneath. Like a thunderclap, it dawns on me why the boys in the gang spend so much time thinking about girls, why they pant like dogs when a good sort walks by. Two women are speaking quietly. Others remain silent, contemplative. Their wet eyelashes are captivating. The dark-haired beauty that works as a seamstress for Aunt Vasiliki tosses aside her towel, displaying a dark patch between her legs. The night coalesces into a triangle between her milky thighs. 'For heaven's sake, Larissa,' says Yanoula from up the street. 'Cover up. No one wants to see your pudenda.' Larissa turns up her nose, but doesn't bother to draw a veil over her privates. She's Pontian from the Black Sea. Maybe they do things differently there. 'Sow,' mutters Yanoula, turning her back. 'Prostitute,' shoots Larissa, smiling at me. I ask Mama to explain the black patch. 'It's what women piss through,' she whispers. 'Don't look.' I scrutinise the woman's cleft, baffled. Her birdy must be nesting within the hair. Amya catches me at it. '*Haydi*, Galatea,' she says. 'He's almost a man. Can't you see? When they start asking questions, it's time to cage their little bird. Don't bring him here again.' Beside her, Athena covers her pink buds with wet hair and primly turns away.

My father knocks on the door of his sister's house. While waiting to be let in, we're serenaded by Cousin Zoe's mandolin. Delicate notes float through the walls and merge with the gentle sounds of the sea. She is very good at it, and manages to make the instrument sob sadder than a Zeki Müren dirge. 'Knock again,' my mother says, impatient. 'Maybe they didn't hear over that racket.' My father is about to knock again when Uncle Yanni opens the door. 'Ah,' he cries out, delighted, 'we have visitors.' He adjusts his vest and pats down his hair. Inside, Zoe's mandolin falls silent. Uncle Yanni ushers us into the living room. Even before we've been offered seats, or exchanged the customary greetings, Aunt Vasiliki, looking frazzled, launches into the talk she's been impatiently sitting on all day. If she doesn't get it off her chest immediately, she will burst. 'The archaeologists digging in the paddock behind the school,' she says, 'uncovered a necropolis. Infidels that they are, they didn't stop at that. They went on to desecrate the graves by breaking the seals and lifting the stone slabs. Ah, Mary, Mother of God. Have you ever heard of such a thing? They exposed the skulls and skeletons of ancient Greek warriors to the light of day for the first time in centuries.' Her beady eyes are virtually popping out of her horn-rimmed glasses with excitement. It's old news but we pretend it's new to us. For the last month or so, during recess, the kids at school have been gathering to watch the archaeologists, for that's what they have turned out to be; not assassins. Nothing much happened from one day to the next. All there was to see was men digging and shifting dirt from one spot to the next. It seemed a useless task, work for fools. Then, about two weeks ago, the men threw down their picks and shovels, and raised cries of jubilation to the sky. As if in answer, it began to rain and the sweet smell of earth and water overwhelmed our senses. Teachers and students rushed under the portico. From there we watched through streaming rain as one of the men drove off in the van. In minutes everyone in town knew where he'd gone in such a rush: the post office. He was calling the museum at Çanakkale. In next to no time, news of the great find was in the newspapers and magazines that gather at Grandfather Elias's feet. After that the heathens went about their grisly business more seriously and with more care than before, while day after day villagers gathered to watch, aghast. Under their breath women prayed that whatever curse erupted from the ground, for it was sure to happen, would rain its pestilence on the grave robbers and bypass us altogether. Even at school the teachers talked of nothing else. During morning assembly one day, Levent Efendi said that the graves dated from the seventh to the second century before the birth of Christ. This meant nothing to the kids standing before him. When he saw the blank uncomprehending faces, Levent Efendi added, 'That's very old.' We nodded in unison, appreciating the weight of his words if nothing else. 'All together, two dozen graves have been uncovered,' he went on, barely containing his growing excitement. 'This great find is sure to put our island on the map and tourists will come.' The four teachers that stood in a row beside him nodded and clapped. The men drinking in the taverns have a different take on events. They reckon that the graves are the final resting place of Odysseus and his men. My father has his own theories. He tells his sister that the graves belong to Jason and the Argonauts. 'Now that they've found the bodies,' he declares, hand on chest, 'their spirits can rest in peace. They sailed right by here,' he adds, 'and went all the way to the Black Sea for the golden ram. They even stopped off at the Hagia Sophia in Constantinople to make a sacrifice. What a journey that must have been . . . ' He nods, impressed by what his mind's eye conjures. My mother, who'd been daydreaming, reels herself back into the room and says, 'How do you know all this?' Baba laughs as if she's made a great joke. 'My father, may he rest in peace, used to read these histories to us when we were children gathered round the fire, in this very room. Isn't that so, Vasiliki?' His sister nods. Her face softens as she recalls her adored parent. 'It's true,' she acknowledges, 'our father, bless his soul, was wise indeed.' She sighs and her eyes fill up. The room goes quiet. Zoe strums her mandolin. Her eyes close as each delicate note falls like a dewdrop from her fingers.

They come for my father at daybreak. The house is still asleep when a fist pounds on the door with such force that the windows rattle in their frames. It's the kind of knock that demands an answer, even though everything about it spells trouble. Baba descends the stairs. I hear him pull back the bolt on the front door. Daylight is seeping into the bedroom and I can see the dim outline of various objects in the room. Electra sits up beside me, sleepy and alarmed. She asks what is going on. I tell her to be quiet so that I can hear. Downstairs, Baba is speaking to someone in a low respectful voice. A man responds in Turkish. His deep voice is familiar. My father replies. From the tone of his speech, I can tell that he is afraid. He denies something. A second voice joins in. Instead of talking like a normal man, this one has a soldier's bark. My father tries to keep his voice steady, but the other man shouts over his head. When he answers, my father's voice is unsteady. Again, he emphatically denies an allegation. One of the men calls him a lying dog and there is a brief scuffle, followed by a long silence. I hear the door on the other side of the landing open. Mama enters our room. She is wide-eyed with fear and still in her nightgown. 'Quickly,' she whispers. 'Get into your school uniforms and go next door.' She's ashen and can barely contain herself. 'What's going on?' I ask. 'Not a word, just do as I ask,' she says, her lips white. When we don't move, she screams, 'Now!' Electra and I scramble out of bed and get dressed in a hurry. 'Next door,' my mother says, already dressed. 'Get going.' Downstairs, the door is wide open onto the street. It's as if whoever left it in that state believes that the lives inside are so inconsequential it does not matter if the front door is open or closed. The street is deserted. There is not a sign of the two men or my father. They have spirited him away in his long white underwear. In the cool blue light, I sense that the neighbourhood is watching, holding its breath. A light seeps from Aphrodite's house diagonally across the street. At the end of the laneway someone is peeking out of Lelia's window. A curtain moves and then falls into place again. I take Electra by the hand and knock on Amya's door. It flies open and Amya drags us in by the arms. She quickly shuts the door and stands with her back to it, breathing heavily. She is still in her flannelette nightdress. They have obviously heard everything. After a while, we hear Mama calmly closing the front door. She leaves the house. While Electra and I eat bread soaked in hot salty milk, Mama's footsteps recede into the distance. Electra looks up from her meal. 'What's happening, Aunty?' she asks. I put my arm round her. 'I don't know, *yavrum*,' Amya replies, stroking Electra's hair. 'I don't know . . . May God protect us.' She seems terribly afraid. Athena and Zotico sit quietly in the shadows, still in their pyjamas. Uncle Haralambos stirs upstairs.

The whites of Zotico's eyes blaze in the semi-darkness. I place my empty bowl on the table and climb into his lap. He wraps his arm around me. 'I'm so fed up,' he sighs in my ear. 'I'm so fed up with being treated like an animal all the time.' Beside him, Athena twists her handkerchief into ever tightening knots. I gently nudge her with my toe. She doesn't look up. Her knuckles are red. If she doesn't breathe soon, she'll turn blue and collapse on the floor. Zotico continues talking to himself: 'Sometimes I wonder what would have been our fate if, like the Palestinians, we had fought, actually fought, for the right to exist on our native soil, rather than scamper away with our tails between our legs.' Amya stands up. 'Shut up,' she says harshly and slaps him hard across the face. Zotico leaps to his feet. I fall to the floor and sit there, stunned. He stands above me, fists clenched, and the two of them challenge each other with enraged eyes. Finally, Zotico backs down. 'Thank your lucky stars you're my mother,' he says. The hair on his head bristles, making him look like the bastard child of a gipsy. Athena takes Electra by the hand. Together they leave the room and go upstairs.

My father comes home the next day. He is badly bruised from the beating he received at the police station. One of his eyes is swollen and his ribs are mottled purple and an ugly yellow. He hasn't moved from his bed since my mother brought him home. A doctor from Ezine has been to see him. My father says it hurts wherever you touch him. Sometimes he cries out and my mother spends a great deal of time upstairs with him. From what I can gather, this is what happened: two nights ago, some-one stole one of Elif's chickens. Elif is a young Turkish woman who lives with her husband Sefer on the corner. Aphrodite from across the street told Elif that she saw my father climb into Elif's chicken coop and take a chicken. When she saw that one of her birds was indeed missing, Elif reported the matter to the police. And that's how my father ended up in prison. He told us that they beat him with a rubber hose to make him talk. He couldn't confess to something that he didn't do, could he? So he denied everything. Between blows, he tried to tell them that he was innocent, that he didn't know what they were talking about. His family hadn't eaten meat in months. He didn't get further. One of the policemen punched him in the gut and then kicked him in the groin. After that my father couldn't say much, except scream for mercy. 'We have witnesses,' the policeman shouted, 'who saw you steal the chicken. Confess or we'll break the bones in your feet.' When my mother arrived at the jail, they wouldn't let her see him. She then rushed round town, begging my father's Turkish friends for assistance. She called on the lowest – Ezet – to the highest – Talay. She even went to Levent Efendi. The band of friends intervened and the police finally released him. The worst of it was this: a day later, they caught the real thief. He was a gipsy who'd come to the island in search of work. Aphrodite admitted to lying when she said she saw my father stealing Elif's chicken. She said she only did it to pay back my mother for insulting her. She didn't mean to cause harm. When my mother heard this, she rushed across the street and attacked Aphrodite. There was a fierce scuffle and it took the neighbours ages to separate the two women. Athena pushed my mother into the house and stood guard at the front door, holding the doorknob so that my mother would not be able to go out again. Mama was livid. 'What's that in your hand?' I asked when she calmed down a little. In her fist was a nest of Aphrodite's red hair. She cursed and flung it into the fire where it sizzled before bursting into flame. 'May she burn in hell,' my mother spat, gritting her teeth. Now that the days are warm, women sit outside to gossip in the sun. If Aphrodite spies my mother with them, she won't step out of her house for all the money in the world. My mother calls her *patzavura*, old rag, which is about as low as you can get. My father told Mama to forgive and forget, but Mama is not the sort. She is the reason why they say a Tenedian is as obstinate as a mule. In his condition, my father won't be going anywhere for a while. 'And where's the food going to come from?' my mother snaps when I gladly point this out. 'No work means no money. No money, no food. Have you thought of that, idiot son of mine?' She viciously raps her knuckles on my forehead. I pull away, angry at her for treating me like this.

The next day I grab Byron and go to the country property. It's a half hour trip on the donkey's back. I cast my eyes over our garden. Everything is the same as we left it last autumn. The house squats silent and still. The chapel is safely locked. Nothing is out of place. There is no noise other than the sound of tortoises clicking as they mate, and someone's rake among the sharp rocks over the next rise. I lead the animals to the spring. While they drink, I walk to the ruin between the house and kitchen, curious to see how the tomatoes planted last season fared during the cold months. The wind has blown the plastic sheets off the vines, exposing juicy red balloons clustered beneath fragrant leaves. I collect them and head back. In the village, I set aside four tomatoes and sell the rest. At home, 'Where have you been?' my mother says. 'I've made myself hoarse calling for you.' She's beating eggs to make potato omelette. Electra is stirring butter in the frying pan. 'How's my father?' I ask, ignoring her remark. 'Fine. He's at the dentist, getting false teeth.' Electra drops the chopped sage into the butter and glances over her shoulder. 'What's that in your hand?' she asks. The kitchen is full of cooking smells. Without uttering a word, I place the money and the four tomatoes on the kitchen table. My heart throbs with pride. Now my mother will see that I am not useless. Her hand freezes in the bowl. She frowns. 'Where did this come from?' I tell her and her face breaks into a smile, bright as the fruit on the table. She pockets the money and tells Electra to chop two tomatoes for the omelette. 'Go and wash your hands,' she tells me. 'Lunch is almost ready. But first, come here.' I approach reluctantly, afraid that she is going to hit me. She bends and puts her lips to my cheek. 'My little boy,' she whispers, stroking my face. 'You are our only hope and salvation.' Electra drops the chopped tomatoes in the pan. They hiss and spit in the butter.

Days before we're due to move into the country house, Baba strides into the kitchen. He sits at the table and sticks a cigarette between his lips, using the kerosene lamp to light it. He is almost back to normal, though a little jumpy and given to thoughtful silences. My mother chops cucumber and tomato for the salad. She sprinkles the pieces with oil from the can and a flat, earthy aroma fills the room. Electra squeezes lemon for the dressing. Although it is summer, the weather's turned. It's cold out. The four of us huddle at the table, eager for some food to warm our bellies. Mama loads the plates with rice and lamb *pilav*. Electra carefully brings each dish to the table. Baba is served first. Then me. Finally, Electra and Mama sit down with steaming plates before them. The meal has been baked at the Dadaoğlu ovens on Republic Street. I carried the tray back with two towels wrapped round it to stop my hands from getting burnt. 'Got any yoghurt?' Baba asks, his lips working hard to keep the false teeth in his head. They're loose and keep slipping out. My mother scrapes back her chair to stand up. 'I'll get it,' I say, leaping to my feet. I retrieve the yoghurt pot from the pantry under the stairs. 'Turn on the radio,' my mother says to Baba. 'The Americans are going to land on the moon tonight.' My father's hand automatically reaches for the radio. Then it freezes in mid-air. 'What did you say?' he asks. My mother picks up a piece of meat with her fingers and nibbles. If her Istanbul friends saw her now, they would be horrified. 'Just what I said,' she counters, sucking the marrow out of a bone. 'An American is landing on the moon.' Electra and I exchange glances. Our mother has finally lost her mind. 'Mary, Mother of God,' my father says, crossing himself. 'What next?' My mother licks her fingers. I can't help smiling. She is behaving like the peasants she claims to despise. 'Turn it on. What are you waiting for? This is a once in a lifetime event. You don't want to miss it.' My father switches on the radio. Mama tells him which station to tune it to. His long thick fingers fiddle with the knob. Static scrapes out of the speakers. From behind a pregnant bleep a man's voice waddles forward. He's talking rapidly, his voice excited, awed, as if he can't believe that his throat is actually reporting the miraculous events that are unfolding. His voice drops before picking up again. Behind each word is an impenetrable night sky with miles of emptiness. Inside the house, all is heavy with expectation. Outside, rain drums on the roof. Forks down, eyes at half-mast, we are all ears as we try to picture this amazing thing that is happening above our heads. I'm thinking that any minute now the American is going to lose his balance and fall off the moon, out of the sky, and onto our house. We will be crushed to death. Careful not to make any noise, my mother stands up to get a second helping of food. Terrified, I follow her to the fireplace and press against her as she serves herself. When she walks back to the table, I'm her shadow. She stops and I bump into her. 'Hey, you, sit down,' she shouts, pushing me away. My father tells her to keep her voice down. His ears are glued to the radio. 'He's such a scaredy cat,' she complains. 'Wife, will you be quiet?' My father's cigarette is a forgotten grey cylinder in the ashtray. 'Eat,' my mother orders, pointing at my plate. I'm so alarmed I've barely

touched my food. I shut my eyes and feel the pulse quicken in
my neck. 'The rocket ship,' I say. 'It's going to fall on our house
and destroy everything.' Everyone at the table bursts out
laughing. 'That's so stupid,' my mother snorts. 'Haven't I taught
you anything? Rocket ships don't fall out of the sky. They go to
the moon and then they come back and land safely on earth so
that the Americans can walk out, knowing that they are the
masters of the earth. Tell him,' she says to my father. 'What can
I say, wife?' he says, shrugging. He seems as bewildered as me.
Electra is still sniggering. I give her a mean look. She quickly
goes back to eating. I have no idea what a rocket ship is or what
it might resemble. Nonetheless, I see a vague shape in space,
heading toward the earth, motionless as death.

Now that it's summer and the school holidays have started,
most of the Greeks lock up their town houses and move to the
country. Train and Byron thrive out here, where they can forage
and fossick all day. From May to October, the Greek Quarter is
almost empty, fit only for ghosts and strays. People come to
town for the night if there's something good screening at the
open-air cinema, and then go back in the morning. Others make
the trip to sit with friends beneath the pine trees in the park and
enjoy a cool Pepsi or *gazoza* – alcohol is not served because the
mosque and upper primary school are across the square. In the
morning they mount their donkeys and head back to the cool
and fragrant airs that wash the valleys and rises. Like the village,
the countryside is split into districts. From the peak of Saint
Elias's hill you can see across all of them. Grandfather Dimitro's
finger moves from one end of the island to the other. 'Over
there,' he says, 'is Kambo. There it's flat and open. An old man
like me won't have a hard time getting about.' I shudder. 'It's
full of snakes,' I remind him, pulling Byron to me for protection.
'I saw one last summer. I was going with my father to the vine-

yard that's out there and a big snake was hanging from a tree. Someone killed it and hung it there as a warning to travellers.' Grandfather laughs. 'You said it right,' he says, 'it's teeming with snakes, big as me and capable of swallowing two whole goats without a hiccough.' He takes a deep breath. His grey eyes cast loving glances over our island. He sighs. 'That district over there,' he says, pointing, 'is called Çayirya. Over there is Sulu Bahçe where there's plenty of water and the fertile soil yields most of what we eat. Then there's Orta Koliba, Çardak and Saint Theodoros.' Our property is at the foot of Saint Elias's hill in the latter district. Amya, Uncle Haralambos, Zotico and Athena live across the meadow. To get there cross-country, you make your way over bare, stony fields and a treeless road. All the same, we rarely see them in the hot months. We mainly keep company with our good neighbours, Chrostalenia and her two daughters, dark-haired Evdokia and golden Despina. They live on the rise beyond the creek that runs at the bottom of our property.

'What's going on over there?' Grandfather says, bringing me back to the present. He shades his eyes and squints into the distance. A warring cloud of crows has dropped to earth. It shrouds Amya's house and the straggly trees beside it. As we watch, a tall, lean man runs out, swinging a broom overhead. That would be Uncle Haralambos. The birds billow into the air and settle down again a few feet away. 'What is it?' I ask, alarmed. 'Death,' Grandfather mutters, nodding. 'Crows are harbingers of death.' I increase my grip on Byron and bury my face in his fur. He wriggles in my arms, trying to escape. I can't help it, tears come to my eyes. 'Hey, why are you crying?' Grandfather says, putting his arm on my shoulder. 'I'm not,' I reply. 'It's only that everyone's talking about death and the horrible things that are about to happen.' Grandfather wraps me in his arms. He takes out a big blue hanky and dries my tears. Byron grabs his chance and takes off. 'Shhh,' Grandfather says. 'Nothing bad is going to happen. More than half of what people say is rubbish. I'm no different. I am an old fool for saying such things. An old fool . . . You must remember that your mother and father love you. And I will always be there to look after you.' I dry my tears and give back the handkerchief. 'Sometimes I hate this place,' I tell him. I don't know where that came from. Usually I can't distinguish Tenedos from my body and the air that I breathe. I never want to leave, despite the fact that we live with the threat of expulsion hanging over our heads. Strange, inexplicable things have been happening. Nothing makes sense any more. 'Where will you go?' Grandfather asks, studying me carefully. I don't understand what he means. 'If you hate it here so much,' he clarifies. 'Where will you go?' I think before answering. 'I don't know.' I shrug. 'Maybe we can pack our bags and go to the other side of the world. We could go as far as Istanbul and see all the places Mama talks about and then we can hop on a ship and go to Greece where life is easy.' Grandfather sighs. His eyes soften with pity, as if he's seen more than I have. 'When I was a young man, I saw a thousand shooting stars. They came like flames from the sky and disappeared into the sea. One day, I followed those shooting stars to the other side of the world, only to find that they had moved. They were now where I had started.' I don't know what he means. Sometimes you need an encyclopaedia to make sense of what he says. I snap a twig of sage and crush the leaves between my fingers. It has a pleasing, heady aroma that hits you in the back of the nose and in the temples. This time of year the hills are full of wild herbs. I must remember to take some back to the house.

My mother is holding a terracotta pot. She's wrapped it with a red and white tea towel to stop her hands from getting burned.

She sees me sprawled on the cushions like a *paşa* and her face collapses. If there's one thing she can't abide, it's laziness. I deliberately don't move. Dutiful Electra scrambles to help set the table for dinner. 'Did you lock the chapel?' Mama asks. I tell her that I have. In the summer, it's my duty to lock it for the night. I blow out the candles, close the shutters on the windows and bolt the entrance. 'It's my job, isn't it?' I throw a challenge with my eyes. 'Don't play games with me,' Mama says. She sets down the pot and casts her eyes over the landscape. 'Here we are again, stuck out here by ourselves,' she adds. 'When is Baba coming back from the sea?' I ask. Not that I am interested in my father's whereabouts. I ask because she expects me to keep the conversation going. Her eyes sweep the darkening meadow as if she is reading the minor chorus of sounds hidden behind the night's familiar murmurs. Then she turns to me. 'Go to the vegetable garden and bring me a cucumber and tomato for the salad.' I rise reluctantly to my feet. To reach the vegetable garden, I have to walk past the well beneath the fig tree. That's where the nereid Thetis lives. If I get too close, she'll leap out and drag me under the water. 'Can't Electra go?' I ask. '*Haydi*, scaredy cat, go,' my mother raises her voice. I whistle for Byron and run off, hoping for the best. 'Bring a small watermelon, too,' my mother calls behind me.

When I reach the mulberry tree, I look back at the house. It is a low stone building with a flat roof. In Turkish, this style of building is called a *dâm*. It means stable. Built of stone and clay, it might as well be a troglodyte's home. As soon as the weather warms up, Baba kicks out the goats and other animals that shelter there in winter. Then he sets Byron on the rats and mice. After the massacre, he smokes out the scorpions and giant millipedes that hide between the cracks in the walls. When the vermin and the rodents are vanquished, Mama moves in with a broom and dust cloth. She cleans out the straw, the animal droppings, and paints the walls a fresh, clean white. As a final touch, she blesses the house by burning incense. The living room is on the ground floor and the communal bedroom on the mezzanine. The kitchen with the built-in oven is at the far end of the property, next to one of the wells. In between is the ruin where Baba grows tomatoes in the winter. Because the external walls of the building are daubed in the red soil of the valley, the compound looks like it sprang out of the earth in the night. In the right light, it resembles a golden loaf of bread. Outcrops of rock hem the house on two sides. Rain, wind and human use have rounded them into smooth, flowing forms until they resemble gentle waves bursting from earth. On balmy evenings, like tonight, Mama spreads a tablecloth, blankets and a scatter of cushions to create an outdoor dining room.

I return safe and sound with the cucumber, tomatoes and melon. Mama slices the first two and flings them in a bowl with oil, a little vinegar, salt, and basil. While we eat, there is nothing but loneliness and quiet as night falls. The olive grove and the vineyard rustle softly. A dog barks in the distance and Byron answers him. The creek cackles over the flat, grey pebbles. The bamboo sighs. The hills turn pale mauve. They become indistinct and merge with the sky. The only light comes from Aunt Chrostalenia's lamp in the distance. Electra goes to bed after dinner. Mama carries the dishes to the kitchen and I light the way with the kerosene lamp. When we return to our spot, Mama sits with her back to the wall and turns on the radio. A Greek song spills into the night to compete with the cicadas. I lay my head in her lap. 'The stars are close tonight,' I whisper. 'Maybe they will come closer when we are ready to join them,' she says, running her fingers through my hair.

Not long after the Americans land on the moon, it's Saint Paraskevy Festival. It's the biggest religious celebration on the island, and a sure sign that summer has arrived. People come for the three-day celebrations from far-off Istanbul and even northern Greece, where many Tenedians went to live after the 1923 population exchanges. From dawn, an unbroken stream of donkeys, mules, horses and carts trundle through the country-side. They are going to the blessed chapel at Ayazma. In honour of the day, houses along the way are beautifully decorated. They are painted with flowers, fruit and vegetables, a cornucopia. People try to outdo each other and there's a festive feeling in the air. The valley resounds with laughter and jubilation. Families stand outside their houses, waving paper windmills, blowing whistles, banging tins and singing songs. The place rings with noise and it's making Train skittish. I rest my hand on his neck to steady him. Electra is sitting on his back between two panniers that brim with food, picnic blankets and utensils. I tell you, half the house is in there. We had to leave Byron at home because Mama said a festival is no place for a dog. She has been cooking for the last two days and is feeling crankier than usual. She walks arm in arm with Baba several paces behind us. Whatever Aunt Vasiliki said to Baba seems to have done the trick. He and Mama haven't argued much lately. Mama is wearing a wide-brimmed straw hat with a red ribbon and holding aloft an umbrella to protect them from the scorching sun. Baba is wearing a clean white shirt and nice trousers with a sharp crease. To reach Saint Paraskevy's chapel, the road twists and turns through fields, vegetable gardens, orchards and vine-yards. This side of the island is fertile and the soil is a coffee-coloured loam, fragrant with wild flowers. Lush grasses sprout in ditches, and the fields are a riot of colour – crimson and yellow and purple. As the road begins its final descent to the chapel, it skirts the pine forest. Cooling shadows splash on our

heads and shoulders. Mama sighs as the thick canopy blots
out the sky. The dark fir-clad hills moan gently in the breeze.
Cicadas fall silent when we approach and start up again as we
pass. I wipe my brow and dry my wet hand on Train's dusty
coat. 'When we get there, wash your hands at the spring,' my
mother says, 'both of you. I don't want you touching food with
dirty hands.' The chapel is located high above the beach, in a
shady grove. It's not as grand as ours, but it is better situated
and blessed with abundant fresh water. There is the holy spring
beneath the chapel, and the two fountains on the lower terrace.
All year there is the restful gurgling music of water, and the
rustle of the plane trees. No wonder nymphs live here. Electra
leaps off the donkey and runs ahead. When we arrive, the terraces
teem with people milling round picnics. They wander from
group to group, talking, laughing and eating. Everyone is dressed
to impress. 'Stamo, over here,' calls Uncle Yanni. He's with Aunt
Vasiliki, Zoe, Timon, his sister Evangelia, and their mother and
father, Irene and Petro. Zotico, Amya and Uncle Haralambos
are there, too. Athena is not. I sit beside Zotico and ask her
whereabouts. 'She's gone to stay with her sister Penelope in
Istanbul,' he says, taking a drag on his cigarette. Well, that's a
new one. It seems strange that she left the island without saying
anything. I ask Zotico what's going on. 'It's nothing serious,' he
says, shrugging. I can tell from his manner that something is
not right. I persevere with the questions. 'She's a bit sick and
she's gone to see a doctor. That's all,' he insists, even though he
can see it'll take more than that to convince me. 'They've got
good ones in the big city. It's nothing to worry about. She'll be
back soon. Go off and play now. Come on, off you go.' He
draws heavily on his cigarette and turns to talk to my father.
Amya leans across and says, 'It's true, *yavrum*. Athena will be
back soon, good as new.' I last saw Athena in spring. That's
when Mama fought with our nosy neighbour Aphrodite, and

Athena stepped in to separate them. After that she rarely left the house.

The sea shines invitingly between the thick white tree trunks. The Turkish musicians are setting up in front of the Malamatina house. There is an Armenian clarinet player with them, too. Manolis Malamatina and his wife Diamanda are the custodians of the chapel and the official hosts for the next three days. When the priest arrives, he will sit at the table that is set up in front of their house. Right now husband and wife sit quietly, gazing at the gathering before them in a royal fashion. Their mongrel Boreas is under the table, forepaws folded, patiently waiting for scraps. 'Let's go to the beach,' says Timon, leaping to his feet. Like me, he's dressed in shorts and sandals. I turn enquiring eyes to my mother. 'Go,' she says. 'The water will do you good. I might come down myself later.' Our friends Apostoli and Yerasimo join us and we run through the brambles and thistles, down the escarpment to the sand. Music blares from the chapel, the clarion and the tambour making a forest sound. 'It's starting,' yells Timon, excited. 'The festival's beginning.' The four of us clasp each other's shoulders and spin round, dancing footprints in the sand.

When we rejoin the party, Ezet is sitting between my father and Uncle Yanni. I'm surprised to see him. Except for the musicians, it's not normal for Turks to come to Greek religious celebrations. When I ask him what he's doing there, Ezet says, 'The sad thing is that we have two people, two cultures, living side by side and we know so little about each other.' He sips red wine and sways to the music. I notice that he is not wearing his white skullcap. When I point this out, he smiles. 'It wouldn't be right, given the circumstances.' He makes a sweeping gesture that encompasses the gathering. 'Does that mean you're no longer a Muslim?' I ask. He laughs. 'Hardly,' he replies. 'I'm still saving to go on the pilgrimage to Mecca.' Erimos Leonidas is sitting with his family beneath the next tree. He's been eyeing us off for a while. Hands in pockets, he saunters over. Erimos is a stocky man with dark sunglasses and slicked-back hair. He hitches up his trousers and crouches beside my father. 'Stamo,' he says in Greek, 'what's he doing here?' He jerks his head in Ezet's direction. My father tenses up. He's not good in situations like this. 'What does it look like? He's eating and drinking like the rest of us.' Erimos is floored. 'Is he Greek? Is he Christian? If he is, he is welcome. If not, then he has no place here,' he counters, raising his voice. 'He can't help not being Greek,' my father replies, trying to make him see reason. Ezet looks from one man to the other. Even though he does not understand what they are saying, he senses that something's wrong. 'Perhaps I ought to leave,' he offers, touching my father's wrist. 'Don't be in such a hurry,' my father says. He is slightly tipsy and he slurs his words. He wraps an arm around Ezet's shoulders and clings to him. Uncle Yanni has been quietly watching from the side. Even though he does not really know Ezet, he steps into the fracas. 'If you object to him being here,' he tells Erimos in a firm voice, 'you had better go and tell the band to leave as well. They're Turks, too, every single one of them.' When Uncle speaks usually no one dares contradict him. But not Erimos. He turns on Uncle fast as a scorpion. 'That's different,' he snaps. 'They're playing music. Not eating and drinking with us.' Uncle feigns puzzlement. 'Well, they're human,' he counters. 'Sooner or later they're going to want to take a piss, eat and drink something. Are you going to deny them that privilege?' He's thrown down the gauntlet. My uncle is a diplomat, but things are hotting up between them. Aware that people are starting to notice, my father tries to defuse the situation in the only way he knows. 'Here, have another wine, you too Erimos,' he offers.

'Let's drink to the saint's name.' He pours a round. 'A blessing on Saint Paraskevy.' The four men raise their glasses and drink. Erimos reluctantly drains his glass. He thumps it down and stalks off. 'Trouble maker,' Uncle Yanni mutters. One of the musicians is playing a ballad on a mandolin. The music weaves through the branches overhead. A bird, dazzled by the splendid notes, breaks into spontaneous song. People clap their hands and raise their voices in response. Others jiggle on the spot and click their fingers like castanets. The next number is a fast one. Captain Starenios leaps to his feet. Adjusting his fisherman's cap, he comes over, waving a white handkerchief and wiggling his hips like a houri. He grabs my mother and father by the hand and pulls them to their feet. They dance. More and more people link hands with them. Soon a wide circle is whirling, faster and faster, round and round the clearing. 'Dancing is a way of living in the moment,' Ezet whispers. 'When the dance takes over, people forget the pains of the past and look more kindly on the future.' I feel sorry for him. He seems lonely even in company.

The hours pass. When it's time to leave, Mama packs the remains of our picnic, while Baba loads the panniers on the donkey's back. The priest was late. As soon as he arrived, he set to singing the praises of Saint Paraskevy, the Holy Virgin, and the Son she produced through her celibate union with God. The priest will preach till dawn, and who can take that much saintliness? Forgetting for the time being that nymphs haunt the grove, some of the celebrants will spread blankets beneath the trees and sleep outside. A small group of the truly devout will stay awake to keep the holy man company, as he preaches in the waning candlelight. Others will cat nap, grabbing some shut-eye between prayer and gossip. Most people, though, will leave this evening. Unlike us, they will probably come back tomorrow to continue the revelry. Truth be known, my parents aren't all that religious. Nor are they keen revellers. You pray and you sing and dance in moderation. That's my mother's dictum, because too much of a good thing is unhealthy for the soul. And sooner or later, God will exact a high price for all the good times He's given you. I say good night and happy celebration to my friends and favourite relatives. As soon as we leave the clearing, the night is black as tar. Baba lights a lantern. We journey with only a golden circle of light to protect us. The sky is teeming with stars, some intensely bright and others faint and barely shimmering. Shooting stars come out of nowhere and vanish above the jagged treetops. An owl flies by, hooting. The pine trees release resin onto the forest floor in a slow rain. I sit on the donkey's back holding Electra. She falls asleep as soon as the saddle starts to sway. I'm having trouble staying awake myself. Train lurches from side to side. It's like being at sea. I'm scared that if I fall asleep, I'll tumble out of the saddle and be left behind. We travel without uttering a word. My father walks ahead, holding the lantern high and giving hushed instructions on where to step and what to avoid. It is surprisingly light now, the world aglow. You can make out trees, the occasional slumbering house, and shadow-rich orchards. My mother presses close to Train's head, holding the reins. It's hard to believe that somewhere behind us life still goes on. Lights blaze, people pray and the priest raises his arms to the heavens. Out here, miles from anywhere, surrounded by an endless void, it feels as if the world has ended. I breathe a sigh of relief when Train finally turns off the road and heads up toward Ali Berber's ruin. Our property is on the other side of the rise. The olive trees close overhead. The darkness thickens and the smell of poppies and olives ripening envelops our senses. Train stops to graze in the long grass but Mama urges him on. 'Almost there.' She whispers because the ghosts that haunt the ruin have big ears and don't like disturbances. A fox leaps out, eyes gleaming, and bares its fangs. My father is taken aback. 'What about that?' he says, outraged. He throws a stone and the animal vanishes in a flash. Train stops outside the *dâm*. I pass Electra to my mother and dismount. My father goes off to tie Train under the fig tree. Byron is letting off short sharp yelps from inside the house. I open the door and he bounds into the night.

Time passes slowly in the country. Each day lasts a year. Out here, I don't need to drink water. All summer, the hills and the daisy-strewn valley floor are the only sustenance a boy needs. Especially at night, it's a circus of crickets, cicadas, bats, snakes, owls, foxes, scorpions, and wild dogs come from the hills to feed. And we, the occupants of the *dâm*, bolt our shutters and cower behind closed doors, hoping that a call of nature will not force us, kerosene lamp in hand, to brave the dark at three in the morning. This year, Timon's family is renting a *kula* across the road. That's a house with a pitched tiled roof, not flat like ours. When Timon can't play with me, I spend most days in the trees. One day I nest in the mulberry and climb down in the evening covered in red juice, looking like I've been skinned alive. The next day, I shift to the broad branches of the fig tree that throws its arms over the biggest and deepest well on the property. Byron sits at the base of the tree, watching my every move. From the topmost branches, I survey my kingdom. My father's vegetable garden is spread out in neat rows beneath me. The olive grove borders it on one side and the bamboo on the other. To pick vegetables, we walk through the avenue of sour cherries. At the bottom of the property runs the creek in a green belt of spiky poplar and frowsy willows. That's where the fauns live; I've often seen them play in the shade of the noonday heat. Beyond that begins a ring of hills interspersed with summer-houses and chapels tucked beneath pomegranate, fig, mulberry, almond and pink oleander trees. Looking into the well from the top of the fig tree is like gazing into hell's maw. I must be alert. At any minute Thetis the nymph could throw up thick tendrils to drag me down to unimaginable depths. All the same, I go back every day. I scramble out on a thick bough suspended over the wide-open mouth of the well and sit there talking to the bumble bees and birds that come to visit. Up here I am king, commanding the lower and upper realms; even nature obeys my call. With one word from me, the poplars will lance a passing cloud so that I might have a ball to play with. When Electra tries to climb up, I tell her to leave me alone. She's growing fast and becoming a pest. Half my energy goes into avoiding her. Sitting in the trees is better than scrambling up to perch on a rooftop because a tree is a living being. After you sit in the arms of a tree for a long time, something else takes over, something magical; suddenly, you come to and it's late. A whole day has passed with you sitting there, speaking nature's secret tongue. After a while the spiders, worms, caterpillars, birds, shed their suspicions and resentments and come to sit with you. Trees hold a great attraction for people. The nomad workers camp under them in autumn. Locals gather in grottoes to kiss, to cry, to laugh, to sleep, and, at the end of the day, to shit. There are turds everywhere. Every now and then you hear of some unlucky sod who'd gone to sleep beneath a tree and woken up to discover that he'd been using someone's leaf-covered turd as a pillow. Alekos, the neighbour's son, is in the habit of carving a round hole in a tree trunk and unloading his passion into its depths. He is older than me. Older even than Timon. 'Aren't you scared of splinters?' I asked him one day. 'I put moss around the edges,' he replied, showing me how it's done. 'See?' His parents sell eggs. When I go to their farm to buy some for my mother, he calls me over to watch. 'Hey, look at this,' he says, pumping away. I put down the basket and step back to enjoy the show. 'This one's for the dryads,' he says, humping the tree ever more vigorously. I've no idea what he's talking about, nonetheless I am aware that he derives enormous satisfaction from his regular deposits.

Weeks later I wake up in the night. It's because of the noise. The weather has warmed up but it's nowhere near as hot as it's going to be in August. The sheet I'd thrown over myself when I came to bed is bunched at my feet. I strain my ears and listen. The grown-ups are talking outside. I can hear my mother's voice, my father, my mother's sister Irene and her husband Petro. Our neighbour, Chrostalenia from across the creek, and Zotico are there as well. They are sitting in the starlight, yacking away without a thought for those of us that have to sleep. Judging by the tone of their voices, though, it's serious. Something is up. A male voice rises and a female voice battens it down. 'Hush. The children. They're asleep inside.' I strain hard to listen but I can't make out what they are saying. I need to get closer to the window. Hopefully, Electra is asleep in the bunk above me. I slip out of bed and crawl to the window. The shutters are partly closed and there is a kerosene lamp on the other side, feeding thin, broken streaks of light into the room through the cracks in the wood. 'What are you doing?' Electra whispers, sitting up in bed. I tell her to be quiet and go back to sleep. 'You'll get into trouble,' she whispers. 'Get back to bed.' I ignore her. I put my eye to the opening in the shutter. It's a still night – a night when sounds carry far. Beyond the lamp, I see the tops of five or so heads. Amya is there too, but she's not saying anything. She seems preoccupied, in another world. Beside her, Zotico is saying, 'I'm telling you; they've already packed. They're leaving tonight, as we speak.' He drops his voice and goes on. 'As soon as the moon sets, a fishing boat will pick them up. It's going to take them across the border into Greece.' The women gasp. 'If they're caught, there'll be hell to pay,' puts in Petro in his peevish voice. My mother cries out, 'No,' and slaps her cheek. Her sister Irene takes out a handkerchief and begins to weep. 'Be quiet wife,' her husband says. 'As if we haven't got enough troubles we've got to listen to you.' Chrostalenia butts in. 'Leave her alone,' she says, rubbing Irene's broad back. 'Mind your own business,' Petro growls, scowling. His balding head tips back as he takes a drink of wine. 'They're leaving like ghosts in the night. Is this what we've been reduced to?' Irene says between sniffles. She must be very upset; she's not easily reduced to tears. 'Well, what do you want them to do,' her husband retorts, 'make a general announcement? It's meant to be a secret. If the authorities found out . . . ' There's a long silence that is filled with the creaking of cicadas. 'Anyway, what happened?' enquires my mother. 'What brought this about?' She casts her eyes round the circle of anxious faces lit eerily by the lamp. 'Yes, tell us what happened, Zotico,' mutters Chrostalenia. 'You're the closest to their son.' Zotico's glossy head leans into the light. 'As far as I can make out, this is the story,' he begins. He puffs a cigarette as he speaks. Occasionally he stops talking to sip red wine, or cast worried glances at his deathly silent mother. It appears that something happened two nights after the Saint Paraskevy Festival at Ayazma. Manolis Malamatina, the custodian of the chapel, woke up to a disturbance in the night. His dog Boreas was barking, making a dreadful racket outside. Manolis calmed his wife Diamanda and went to investigate. He found the poor dog nailed to a tree. Panicked, he fled back to the house and spent a night of terror behind closed doors with his wife and two sons, rifle in hand. In the morning the eldest son Laos discovered a message scrawled on the chapel wall. It had been written in the dog's blood: red on white. 'What did it say?' my father asks, stunned. He creases

his brow and leans forward to hear properly. 'Yes, tell us,' pleads
Irene. 'Leave,' Zotico said, sounding grave. 'It said, leave if you
don't want to end up like the dog.' Chrostalenia gasps and
crosses herself. She calls on God and his Son in heaven to protect
us. 'The cowards,' Uncle Petro erupts. 'They're all brave under
cover of darkness. Get them one by one in the light of day and
it's a different story.' Now it's Aunt Irene's turn to placate her
husband. 'Hush,' she tells him, placing a hand on his shoulder.
From behind the shutters, I see him shake her off. 'You never
know who is listening,' Irene adds, casting doubtful glances
into the dark. Zotico swipes a mosquito and says that it's true
enough. 'Did Malamatina go to the police?' Chrostalenia asks.
I see a volley of heads turn as everyone looks at her dumb-
founded. 'Why bother?' my mother cries, 'if it's the nationalists,
and you can bet they're behind this, the police won't do a thing.
They're in on it themselves. I mean to say, what did they do
when the Greek cemetery was desecrated? They smashed the
crosses and covered the ossuary in shit.' Zotico raises his glass
to his lips. 'It's the animals they're shipping in.' Everyone silently
agrees. 'Poor Diamanda,' my mother says, shaking her head.
She sounds exhausted. 'Where will they go? What will they do?'
My father turns his head and whistles sharply into the darkness.
Byron's white body trots out of the black and settles by his side.
Baba feeds him white cheese. 'If they make it across the border,
they'll be fine,' Zotico tells Mama. His back is so hunched he
looks as if he's about to roll into a tight ball. 'They have relatives
in Chalkidiki, close to Thessaloniki. They'll be all right there.
Hopefully we can sell their property and send on the money
later.' Petro snorts. 'The government will probably expropriate
it.' He removes the cigarette from his mouth and when he speaks
again, there is such bitterness in his voice it would outclass a
lemon. 'Anyway, I hope you're not expecting a high price. We're
being kicked out and they're buying what is rightfully ours for a

song. Most of the time they just move in without a by your leave. We're all going to end up homeless and destitute, that's how we're going to end up, take my word for it.' He picks up his glass and tosses back the wine. My father fills it up again. Zotico gives Petro a poisonous glance. The two don't see eye to eye on much. Zotico asks the time. My father tells him. 'We'd better get going,' Zotico says, turning to his mother. He cups his knees with his hands and pushes himself up to a standing position. He helps his mother up. Then he turns to Chrostalenia. 'We'll walk you home,' he offers. Chrostalenia takes his hand to help her get up from the cushions. 'We better get going, too,' says Irene, looking at her husband. 'The children are alone.' They say goodnight and disperse. My mother cleans up. I crawl back to bed. I'm busting for a pee but the toilet is at the edge of the vineyard and there's no way I'm going out there in the dark.

My mother has a toothache. Baba is at sea again and there is no one to care for her. So she locks Byron in the house and we leave for town. While she's at the dentist, I go to the fountain to fetch water. The streets are deserted. It's as if no one lives here except air and birds. Most houses are closed, the curtains drawn. As I approach the fountain, the sound of bubbling water eases my anxiety about my mother. The basin is full and a muddy stream wends its way in the middle of the street. Beyond the fence, the schoolyard is empty, patiently waiting to be filled with students. I step with relief into the shade of the big old plane tree that grows behind the fountain. I place the bucket under the stream of water and wait for it to fill. The cloudless sky is visible through the trembling broad leaves. I am standing there, waiting, when I hear an unusual sound. A deep, menacing rumble comes from the sky. It's unlike anything I've heard before and it's coming closer. There aren't any clouds, so it can't be thunder. The nearer it gets the more it sounds like a roar, steady and throbbing in my gut and in the soles of my feet. My heart begins to pound. Could it be an earthquake? We haven't had one of those in a while. The noise grows to a crescendo above my head. The earth trembles and with it my limbs. It's right above the tree now. I look up. Through the leaves I see a demon streaking across the sky. Its body is long and silver. Two great wings hook the air on either side. I scream. My knees buckle and I keel over in the mud. I cover my head with my arms and whimper. Keep still, I tell myself; be quiet. If the demon hears you, it will swoop down and eat you. I don't know how long I remain in this position. It seems like forever. A hand grabs my shoulder. I scream again and spin around. 'What are you doing?' It's Costas Hrisostom. 'The devil,' I say, pointing at the sky. Costas frowns before studying the clouds. When he looks back at me again, his eyes soften with pity. 'It's all right,' he says, taking my hand. 'Dimitro, it's only an aeroplane. Calm down.' When he sees that I am still agitated, he adds, 'Haven't you seen one of those before?' 'What's an aeroplane?' 'It flies in the sky. It carries people from one place to another. Like a bus only it flies.' This barely makes sense to me, but I figure that if there are people inside that thing, its belly must be full. It can't want me. 'Well, if you're sure it's not going to eat me,' I say, relaxing a little. He throws back his head and roars with laughter. 'It won't eat you,' he reassures me, trying not to fluff the words. When he stops laughing, his fingers flutter over the pink cleft on his lip. 'I promise. But God willing something like it will soon carry all of us away from this place.' I want to ask him how he is going. It's the first time I've had a chance to speak to him in a while. He's as good a student as we have on the island. Even so, I know that he's worried. He hasn't been offered a place in an Istanbul university because they give preference to Turkish students. Before I utter a word, Costas stands up and, hands in pockets, walks away. When my mother returns from the dentist, her face is twice its normal size. She can barely speak. She tells me to bring Train. 'We're going back to the country before it gets dark,' she says, through a mouthful of bloodied cotton wool. We lock the house, put Electra on the donkey and leave.

And so the summer days pass. The Malamatina family has been gone a long time. I've barely heard a whisper about them since the night they left. Presumably they made it to safety. Only weeks after he rescued me from the aeroplane, Costas Hrisostom passed from our lives, too. One moonless night, his parents entrusted him to the care of yet another fisherman bound for Greece. You would think they would be happy now that their son can attend university and continue his studies. But their hungry and haunted eyes tell another story. One day I asked his mother where Costas was now, how he was doing at university, and she looked at me as if she didn't have a clue what I was talking about, as if she didn't have a son. I can't get over Costas's disappearance. It's a puzzle. One day he was there and the next he was gone. Never to be seen again. Like Athena, he didn't even say farewell. 'That must be what it's like when you die,' I tell Timon. He and I, we're sitting in the fig tree. The sun is blazing on top of the thick, flat leaves that act as umbrellas over our heads. Timon shrugs and the light dances on his striped t-shirt. His cheeks are hollow and his eyes sad. 'That's how things are,' he says, harshly. 'Get used to it.' I think about the people that have left our island. The place is emptying. Every day there is another deserted house or shop where, once, people lived, voices rang, children laughed. Friends, neighbours and relatives, they are vanishing, leaving, going someplace else. They mustn't love Tenedos any more is all I can say. Timon snorts. 'What's there to love?' he says, leaping off the tree. Spider-like, he clambers over the fence and jumps onto the road. Hands in pockets, he crosses to a thicket of poplars that hide the house his parents are renting for the summer and vanishes among the trees. Around him the red buds on the pomegranate trees are turning into tiny green fruits. When they ripen they'll go back to being crimson again. 'Don't go there,' I yell after him. 'There are snakes in the water.' He doesn't pay attention to me. An uncle went to Russia to join the communists and hasn't been heard of since. Athena went to see a doctor and never came back. I wonder who will be next.

It is very hot. Mama is cleaning okra, while Byron pants at her feet, tongue lolling out. Sitting beside her outside the kitchen, I am twitchy with shame. Minutes earlier, I'd used a sharp rock to crack open a tortoise's shell, and left the glistening creature exposed and flailing on its back, food for the crows that gather in the trees. 'What's wrong with you? Stop coiling like a snake,' my mother snaps, elbowing me out of the way. I dare not tell her what I did; she would kill me. She flings the knife in the bucket of water between her knees and says, 'Go, go. Both of you; get out of my hair; leave me alone. Go see Amya. Just give me some peace for a minute.' Electra begins to whimper. She is such a sombre, withdrawn little girl. My heart sometimes goes out to her. I dry her tears and take her hand. I give my mother a sidelong glance. I want her to know that this is her fault, but her head is down and she doesn't see my accusing eyes. 'Come on,' I say to my sister, 'let's go see what Amya is doing.' She calms down. 'I'll get my hat,' she says, running off. Hand in hand, we trudge across the paddocks to Amya's house. Except for the occasional almond sapling there is no shade. Amya's house is set well back from the road, in the middle of a dun-coloured field. It's a barn like ours, with broad steps that lead to the flat roof. This time of year, the fields that surround it stretch bronze and golden to the horizon, occasionally broken by a red poppy, struggling out of the hard-baked earth. In my shorts and sandals, I am a scratching post for the burs that line the path. By the time we get there we are parched and boiling. A couple of bony goats give us the evil eye from beneath an apricot tree. A featherless chicken scratches listlessly in a yard full of junk. Unlike our place, it is a pretty shabby house. Amya is sitting on a chair under the bamboo veranda, her arms folded across her round belly. The ground is streaked with slivers of light and shade. Amya could be hibernating or maybe waiting for something, anything, to happen. When she sees us emerge from out of the blazing light, she makes a shelter over her eyes with her hand and squints. 'Ah, it's you two,' she chimes, breaking into a smile. 'Look who it is,' she says to no one in particular. 'It's the children . . . come to see us.' She hoists herself up and rushes into the house. She emerges a short time later, bearing a tray. Two glasses of water and fruit sit on a white embroidered cloth. Amya sets down the offerings and asks after my mother. Electra reaches for the water and tells her that our mother is doing as well as can be expected. Now that the baby fat is melting from her face and her limbs are shooting out, she's beginning to speak like a grown-up. I ask Amya how Athena is doing. 'When is she coming back?' I ask, eager for news. 'She's been gone a long time. Is she still sick?' Amya doesn't answer. She studies her pale hands instead. They twitch in her lap. She opens her mouth to speak. Before she can utter a word, Uncle Haralambos charges out of the house and cracks her one across the mouth. Amya gasps and stumbles back, almost falling. 'Not a word,' he yells, drawing himself up until he resembles the god Cronos about to devour his young. 'How many times do I have to tell you? You will not mention that slut's name in this house.' Amya covers her mouth, her eyes misty. Terrible accusations come out of Haralambos's mouth. 'It's your fault,' he shouts, crying too now that his body has almost regained its human dimensions. 'It's your fault. No one in my family has ever done such a thing. It runs in your family. You're all sluts.' His eyes are red slits in a narrow, heavily lined face. I've always been terrified of him and with good reason. The man's got a mean streak in him. Even at this time of day he reeks of alcohol. He turns on us, trembling with rage. 'You,' he bellows, pointing at Electra and me, 'get lost!' It doesn't take long for us to figure out that we'd be having more fun if we had visited Aunt Chrostalenia and her serene daughters, Despina and Evdokia. We leave, feeling puzzled and alarmed. 'What's eating him?' asks Electra, clinging to my hand. 'Who knows?' I respond. 'Come on, I'll give you a piggyback.'

Baba is back. 'I want to treat you to a night on the town,' he declares solemnly, and we're glad of the distraction. It can get boring out here after a while. 'First,' he says, 'we will go to the movies.' For some reason, he is very excited. 'After that, we can have a drink in the park.' It sounds like a good plan and we speedily prepare to leave. But when we get there, he realises that he does not have enough money to pay for four cinema tickets, and he's too proud to borrow from friends. He tells Mama that most of what he'd had in his pocket went into buying a train ticket to Ankara. She shrugs. 'That's how things are. What's there to do?' There is a new tone of resignation in her voice that I have not heard before. What's more, that is the second trip Baba's taken to Ankara this summer. I can't imagine what he could be doing there. Far as I know, it's not close to the water and you can't sell fish there. The disappointment unexpectedly lifts from his face. 'I've a good idea. You'll like this.' He borrows the rowboat from the *Buğday*. 'Get in,' he orders, 'come on, don't be scared.' After Electra and I clamber in and settle down either side of my mother, he grabs the oars and with powerful strokes cuts through the dark water, streaked with the broken multi-coloured fairy lights strung along the shore, and rows the boat to where they set up the open-air cinema at the base of the fortress. 'Won't we get into trouble if someone catches us?' Mama whispers. 'Who's going to see us out here?' he replies. The movie begins. The actors' voices are muffled by distance, and glassy with having to cross the still water. The black-and-white picture is clear and sharp. From our location, we can see the back of the projection booth and we have a side-on view of the sizeable audience, hypnotised by the moving image. The screen sheds flickering pale blue and white light on everyone. From this floating distance, they look as if they too are in a movie, or on an eerily lit stage. For most of the movie, I am happy to watch them instead of the zombies that are eating a group of people in an isolated farmhouse. The night is calm. The boat bobs in the slight swell that reflects the moon and stars. Water laps the hull. After a while, I doze off. When I come to, Baba is handing me over to Mama who is standing on the shore. Electra is beside her, crunching roast chickpeas out of a paper cone. The movie has ended. Crowds are spilling out of the cinema. 'We'll get a *gazoza* at the park now,' Baba says to me. 'That'll wake you up, won't it?' He rests his hand on my shoulder and gently steers me away from the water. He seems inordinately happy about something, and I am wondering what has gotten into him.

Recep Efendi, the Turk that runs the café in the park, has placed tables and chairs under the pine trees. He's even strung fairy lights through the branches to create a festive atmosphere. The sharp, green pine needles seem artificial with the different coloured lights shining on them. Music is coming out of speakers hanging in the trees at both ends of the establishment. As is the law, the songs alternate between Greek and Turkish. Most of the people that had been at the cinema are lining up here for a table. Some join friends while others, mainly young couples, sit by themselves where the shadows are deepest. Two waiters with bronze trays bearing tea, Turkish coffee and chilled drinks zigzag expertly between shrieking kids. Uncle Petro and Aunt Irene are already seated. When he sees us, Petro stands up. He whistles sharply to draw our attention, and waves us over. Aunt Irene tells Evangelia and Timon to move up so that my father can squeeze in four more chairs round the small table. We sit down. A waiter takes our order and leaves. Timon waits till my *gazoza* arrives to say, 'Let's go play.' The two of us wander off between the trees. It's a balmy night and the town is reluctant to sleep. Some kids are playing hide-and-seek on the border of the park, where it's dark. On the way to the water, we pass Levent Efendi. He is with a group of teachers. Even on a night like this, he wears a dark suit and tie. He looks very smart. The handsome teacher is beside him, talking to a blonde woman with a yellow, short-sleeved blouse. She is wearing too much perfume. I can smell it from ten feet away, and it makes me dizzy. When he sees me, Levent Efendi nods in my direction without interrupting his conversation. I nod and smile back. Refik leaps up from a nearby table and falls into step on my left side. I hook my hand through his elbow and then I do the same to Timon on the other side. The walk to the water takes us down a short flight of steps and across a narrow street lined with linden trees. No one speaks. We come to a standstill on a small wooden pier. Rowboats are tied to it and they bob in the gentle swell. It's so dark over the sea you'd think an inkwell had been emptied from heaven. Timon breathes in deep and lets it out slowly, like an adult with too much on his mind. Refik tells us that a new Flying Man versus Skeletor movie is screening at the fleapit. 'We should try to sneak in,' he says, looking eagerly at Timon. It's a well-known fact that they don't sell tickets to kids who aren't accompanied by an adult, and there's no way our parents would take us to see that stuff. 'Maybe,' Timon murmurs, distracted. 'We'll see . . . ' A shooting star appears in the sky and falls into the water, leaving a streak on the surface. 'Did you make a wish?' Refik asks me. 'Did you?' I ask. He nods. 'What's going on?' Timon says, turning. Something is happening in the park. Raised voices. Someone is shouting. The three of us run back to watch.

A Turkish woman is hurling herself from table to table, thrashing and yelling. Aside from her voice and the music coming out of the speakers, it's dead quiet. Everyone has turned to stone, unable to believe what they are seeing. 'Turn that heathen music off. Why are you playing Greek music here? Is this Greece? Is this Greek soil that you should play their music here?' I recognise her instantly. Her name is Iraz. She's a new arrival, a Turkish-Albanian. She was born and raised in Thrace and she speaks Greek as well as any of the Greek islanders. She's wearing a white headscarf with tiny pink roses sewn around the edges. As she screams, waving her arms, the flowers seem to turn blood red, staining her forehead. Everyone is holding their breath and staring at her, aghast. A woman seated in front of us gasps and takes her husband's hand. Another woman begins to weep. Somewhere a spoon clatters into a dish, making a clear ringing sound. A man swears. Then, for what seems like an eternity, the only thing to hear is the Greek song coming out of the speakers. It reminds me of a bird singing in the wake of an earthquake. 'Do you know what these pigs did? Do you know?' Iraz is screaming herself hoarse, pointing at the seated people. Even Turks shrink from her accusing finger. 'I'll tell you what they did. They locked everyone in my village inside the mosque and set it alight, these accursed Greeks. My sister, my mother and my father were burned to death because of these monsters. And you're sitting here listening to their foul music, drinking with

them. I spit on you. Turn that music off, I say. Are you Turks?'
No one is game to reply. 'No, I can see that you are not. You're
dirty pigs,' she spits again and bursts into tears. The screaming
woman's husband is an electrician. He's a good-natured man
called Ali. He is on friendly terms with everyone and often
drinks with the Greek men in the tavern. He's sitting red-faced
and stunned at a nearby table. He stands up, trembling, and
tries to placate his wife. She pushes him aside. 'Get away from
me,' she screams. 'Get away, traitor. You're worse than all of
them put together.' With renewed energy, Iraz leaps up and
tries to tear down the speaker hanging from a low branch. Still,
the Greek music plays on and on. Ali is as powerless as the rest
of us. People are tied to their chairs, petrified as wood. No one
dares speak or breathe. 'This is how it always starts,' Timon says
under his breath. 'It takes only one person to speak up and then
there's no stopping it. It always begins like this: the riots, the
killing.' Refik turns his eyes on him. 'No,' he says, shaking his
head. 'No.' His mouth remains open in a pale face. Just when
everything seems lost, Levent Efendi stands up. He resembles a
column rising out of the ground. 'What this woman is doing is
illegal,' he shouts, cloaking himself in the security and authority
that comes with being a teacher. 'Call the police immediately.
Have her arrested.' But the police from across the way do not
come. It takes Recep Efendi, the owner of the café, to calm
things down. He bustles over, flustered and wiping his hands
on a stained white apron, and grabs hold of the woman's
elbow. 'Get out of my establishment and don't come back.' He
says it loudly so that everyone is sure to hear. 'The music stays
as is. If you don't like it, leave! You are not welcome here. You
too,' he says, gesturing to the mortified husband, 'take your
ill-mannered wife and get out. Teach her some manners. You
shame us. Get out. There is no place for you here. Shame!' His
voice echoes through the trees. It stays in my head for a long

time. Even as we walk home in silence, I can still hear it: 'Get out. There is no place for you here.' That evening we do not go back to the *dâm*. We stay in town, making do on makeshift bedding. I spend a sleepless night, worrying about Byron alone in the country.

We are climbing to the roof of the world. Soon we will be able to touch the sky's belly. Timon and I, we are high up, very near the peak of Saint Elias's hill. In the mid-morning silence, the only sound comes from the rhythmic squeak of Train's saddle and the occasional call of a crow that hangs low above our heads. Butterflies, the colour of dried rose petals, flit among the rocks and settle briefly on thistles and milkwort before being chased away by a hyper-charged Byron. The scent of oregano and thyme permeates everything. Timon is leading Train by the reins, while I sit on the donkey's back. An empty milk can is fastened to either side of the worn saddle as, with sure-footed confidence, Train navigates the narrow path that winds up the hip of the escarpment. The sheer hillside rises on our left and falls tumbling on our right down a ravine that ends in a cleft far below, clattering with stones and a cackle of water among a thicket of trees. Aside from us, there is no sign that beast or man exists this far up, where the winds lord it over the crags. The day is already wilting under the intense sun. Every now and then, much to my alarm, Train steps too close to the edge and a cascade of pebbles falls to its doom. 'Easy, easy, Train,' Timon warns, tightening his hold on the reins. 'You should have brought a hat,' he adds for my benefit. 'It's going to get hotter by the time we turn back.' An enormous silence closes in once more, broken now and again by a snort from Train, a yip from Byron. Mysterious gusts come out of nowhere, whiz round, and vanish. The air is filled with the buzz of bees and the fresh, heady fragrances of clover and crocus and the ever-present saltiness of the sea. The thing that everything and everyone smells of: sea-salt. 'We should give Train some water,' I say, barely above a whisper. I don't want to speak too loudly in case the great god Bacchus hears. I remember a story Grandfather Dimitro told. To secure the favour of Bacchus, the ancient islanders used to tear a baby to pieces with their hands during their rites. In return their bountiful land burst into the bright pomp of summer, its ultimate accolade the grapes as fat, firm and juicy as the cheeks of a babe at the breast. According to Grandfather, Plutarch announced that Pan died at the exact moment Christ was being crucified in Palestine. 'The passengers of a ship anchored off Paxos,' he said, 'reported a great wailing that erupted from the sea to announce the passing of the pagan world and the arrival of the Christian era. But we on the island know better. The old gods are still with us. Many shepherds see the half-goat, half-man god traipsing across a field, or playing his pipes beneath a pomegranate tree.' Timon mumbles something. 'What did you say?' I ask, coming out of a dream. 'I said he can have a drink when we get to the sheep sheds. It's not far now.' I squint back the way we have come. The hazy wreath of the fertile plain is visible far below, dotted with lines of spindly poplars and thick stands of mulberry that surround the summer-houses. Oleanders burn a soft pale pink and blazing crimson into the air. Nature's ungoverned abundance and fertility threaten to burst the stone barriers. Everywhere vineyards, crawling with men and women at the harvest, erupt with a froth of emerald frills. The runnels of red soil and bleeding poppies give the impression that bursting arteries connect the fields, and that the famous clarets of Tenedos require not water but blood to gain their unique taste and colour. 'I can see the sheepfolds,' Timon cries out. He points to the left, into the hillside. I squint and spot a mound, a squat pile of black rock that looks like a volcanic island in a sea of dun and jade folds. It seems that whoever built the place had gone to great pains to disguise the building's true purpose and identity. It's so weathered it resembles an artefact from another age. Out of nowhere, a dog barks, sheep bleat and cause the bells round their necks to clang. A squat, burly man appears at a wooden gate and waves, breaking the spell. What stands before us now is a low stone building, welded together with a thickness of earth and moss. The entire complex seems to have been carved out of the hill. Into view come doors and windows covered with the roughest wood. There are long sheds and pens for the sheep to the left, living quarters for the shepherds on the right. Inside a large enclosure trudge the luckless sheep amid their own droppings. They're looking for a blade of grass on soil that has been trodden into the firmness of cement. After the clean-smelling hills, the stench of animal waste and unwashed human skin hits hard. The complex is built in the lea of a plateau, ringed by gentle undulations and outcrops of lichen-infested rock. 'What are you doing here, boys?' The shepherd shouts in Greek as he opens the gate. 'Our mothers sent us to get milk for the *kapiratha*,' Timon answers. To make *kapiratha* you need fresh milk, dried thyme, salt and cracked wheat. I slide off the saddle and stretch my legs. Then I help unload the milk cans. 'Well, you've come to the right place,' says another shepherd in Turkish. He is barefoot and leaning against the shed door. 'Just keep the dog away from the animals,' he adds, nodding at Byron. He is a lean, craggy fellow with hollow, unshaven cheeks. I tie a rope round Byron's neck, and fasten the other end to a fence post. Then I turn my attention back to the shepherd. He is obviously a Kurd who understands Greek. He notes my curious eyes on him; he smiles crookedly, scratches the thick, jet hair beneath his flat cloth cap, rubs the pad of his thumb along his hooked nose, then sits on a nearby rock. With one heavily veined hand he takes out a cigarette from his pants cuff and lights up. I tend to Train while the milk cans are being filled. When they are ready, the men load them on the donkey. Timon frees Byron and hands the Greek guy some money. I mount and we are on our way again. 'Be a good boy and bring us some *kapiratha*,' the Kurd shouts as we pass through the gate. In minutes we belong to the wilderness again.

When we return to the house, our mothers want to know how the trip went. We answer in reluctant monosyllables until they give up and go back to cooking. Timon and I sit in the shade, waiting for the scrapings from the bottom of the cauldron. They're the best, crispy and burnt. It's after midday. Electra and Evangelia are sleeping inside a makeshift tent. Nearby, salted goatskins bake in the sun, flies buzzing round them. Our mothers continue to work. Mama pours the milk into the cauldron, while her sister Irene stirs with a large wooden paddle. She has arms thick as a grown man's thighs and is strong as an ox. If she ever got into a fight with her husband, she could probably throttle him. 'Have you heard?' she says to my mother. 'What?' Mama asks. Irene stops stirring and pulls up the sleeves of her dress. 'Ali the electrician was electrocuted yesterday. He's dead,' she whispers. 'Pity it wasn't his wife,' my mother mutters. 'He was a good soul. He deserved better.' She flings salt into the cauldron and pours in more milk. Irene continues to stir. 'Well, we won't have to put up with Iraz much longer either,' Irene answers. 'I hear she's leaving the island.' My mother doesn't miss a beat. 'May she go to the devil,' she says loud enough to be heard by all and sundry. 'I hope the boat sinks . . . ' Her sister is shocked. 'Hush, Galatea,' she says in a conciliatory voice. 'You mustn't say such things. You ought to be more forgiving.' My mother snorts and wipes sweat off her brow with the back of her hand.

A few days later, Electra and I are sitting with our mother in the shade of the mulberry tree. Heat pours from the sky, scorching the land. The chittering of sparrows and the occasional tortoise plopping into the spring are the only sounds. That and the voices of men working the vineyard behind us. It's noon. Where we sit, the heat is almost bearable. Earlier Mama had baked bread and *börek* filled with white cheese and pumpkin. As we eat, our gestures are slow, laden with sleep. Baba came back from the sea several days ago. Uncle Yanni and Uncle Petro are helping him harvest the grapes. They won't break for lunch until the job is done. Tomorrow they're supposed to be working the vineyard in Orta Koliba district. Their voices are audible from behind the gnarled tree trunk. I'm looking forward to the day when I will be old enough to help. In front of us is a yellow tea towel on which sit cheese, bread, a tomato, a bottle of water and the *börek*. Inside the bottle a sprig of mint gathers tiny bubbles to its leaves. A while ago, Mama had plunged her hand into the spring and plucked it by the root. Byron comes to sniff the food. Mama shoos him away and takes a pomegranate – the season's first – from the basket, holds a small knife to the fruit and, as she splits it open, mouths an old Turkish riddle. 'A rose unsmelled or a pomegranate unpeeled . . . ' Being an old Sufi, Ezet told me once that the answer is the Beloved. Mama gives a piece of the fruit to Electra and one to me. I crunch on the ruby seeds and suck the blood that fills the cusp of the tough skin. My chin and fingers grow sticky red. 'I have something to tell you,' Mama says. 'Your father and I are going to Ankara.' She notes the delighted expression on my face and quickly adds, 'You can't come. We have urgent business to attend to. As soon as that's over we will come back. Two or three days at most.' Electra places the fruit on the tea towel and wipes her hands on its edge. Ever the practical one, she asks who is going to look after us. 'You will stay with your cousin Evangelia and Dimitro can stay at Aunt Vasiliki's,' Mama answers. 'You must promise to behave.' And that's that. A few days later, Captain Yakar's boat takes both our parents to the mainland. From there they'll catch a bus to Istanbul and a train to Ankara. For some reason, Uncle Yanni went with them. He wore his best suit and carried a small valise.

Next day, I drop in on Grandmother Evangelia. I figure she will know why my parents went to Ankara. I have to find out because I have no stomach for mysteries. Instead of answering my questions like an adult, Grandmother gives way to tears, sniffling and wiping her eyes with a handkerchief that's too small for the job. I hate seeing women cry. Something bigger than me, more powerful, seizes my heart. If I could banish Grandmother's problems to the ocean floor, I would do it. Truth is I can't, and that knowledge only increases my helplessness. When I am old enough, I will marry a woman that looks like Athena. I will treat her with respect and I will never raise my hand to mar her face. That, Grandfather Dimitro told me, is the civilised way to treat a human being. Grandfather Elias, on the other hand, is as cold as a lizard. He sits there, combing his Hitler moustache with a stiff black brush. Rather than comfort his wife, he curls a lip and curses. 'Get out of here,' he bellows, 'and leave me in peace. You've been crying for weeks. What the hell is the matter with you?' Grandma takes my hand. 'I've been crying all of my life,' she mutters. 'Not that you'd notice.' Of course he doesn't hear a word. 'Soon you'll have all the peace you want, you cantankerous old man,' she flings over her shoulder. 'When all your children are gone and you're left here by yourself.' Grandmother must be thinking of the daughter and son she's lost to emigration. They flew away to a country called Australia. I don't know where that is exactly. Levent Efendi pointed it out on a map once, but I couldn't get a fix on it in my head. Last year, we received a postcard from Australia. On the back it said: 'Australia is a big red country. There's a fence down the middle. The whites live on one side and the blacks on the other.' Ever since then, I carry a vision in my head of hostile natives wearing elaborately feathered headgear. Their dark bodies are streaked with paint. They are wielding spears, bows and arrows, and dancing on one side of the rusty fence that stretches across this orange nation, from one end to the other. One day they are going to break through and eat everyone.

It's official. We're leaving Tenedos. Come February, we're migrating to the country called Australia. Mama and Baba broke the news to us over dinner when they returned from Ankara. They talked in hurried, excited voices, but for me everything had slowed down and stopped. Something inside me fell asleep and is yet to wake up. They made it sound as if the family is going on a wonderful picnic. I don't believe it. I don't think it's going to be a happy trip at all. Their strained, anxious faces showed as much. They told us that Uncle Yanni, Aunt Vasiliki and Zoe are coming with us, and that Grandmother will accompany us as far as Istanbul. Yanni and Vasiliki will sell Grandfather Dimitro's house and leave. Now I know why they've made repeat trips to Ankara and Istanbul – to apply for passports and visas, to book aeroplane tickets, to take us away from here. I don't want to go anywhere; I want to remain where I am.

Autumn is turning into winter when Timon takes me aside to tell me things I would much rather not hear. He grins as if this is going to be really amusing. 'Guess what?' he whispers, leaning close. Up until then, we had been sitting on the floor in his room, reading comics. The door is closed. Electra and Evangelia are in the next room. For the first time in ages, Timon's brown eyes are sparkling and there is life to him. He seems almost like his old self again. I shrug, uncaring. 'Don't you want to hear it?' Timon asks. If he has something to say, he better speak up. 'You haven't heard then?' he taunts. I tilt back my head: No. Mama hates gossips. She brought us up believing that to take part in idle talk is the worst thing you can do in life. 'Most of the world's ills come about because people don't know when to shut up,' she said once. When someone starts whispering, I block my ears and walk away. Timon glances over his shoulder as if the world is teeming with spies and we're going to be overheard no matter what precautions he takes. 'Athena has eloped with a Turk,' he says. This is too much. I can't believe my ears. My jaw drops. Words fail me altogether. And, for some reason, the person that fell asleep inside me when Mama and Baba told us we were leaving Tenedos wakes up and leaps on Timon like a savage dog. I grab him by the throat and try to throttle him. He thinks I'm joking and falls back, laughing. 'I'm telling you the truth, I swear,' Timon says, cackling. He pushes me off and sits up. 'Turns out she went to Istanbul not because she was sick but because she was pregnant. How about that? Athena doing it with a Turk . . . Now that's something!' He shakes his head, considers the possibilities. Then he slaps his thigh and laughs. I'm too shocked to speak. I can only stare at him, horrified. My head starts to buzz as if a hive of bees has taken residence in my brain. And then everything begins to make sense. No wonder Uncle Haralambos has been drinking more than usual and beating his wife. I hear them through the walls, bickering and sniping at one another. The light has gone out of Amya's eyes. When she looks at you now, it's with tiny black pinpoints, her lips hard and drawn. Not even Grand-mother Evangelia, her sister, can distract her. Not that Uncle Haralambos allows anyone to come to the house. He's banned visitors. That's why my mother and Grandmother only speak

with Amya when he's at work. 'Anyway,' Timon goes on, 'they
sent her to Istanbul to hide the pregnancy or to get rid of the
baby, I'm not sure which, and she ran away. She's gone off to
join her Turk in some village. Everyone is talking about it.
Who'd have thought she had it in her, that mouse? They're the
ones you've got to watch.' I try to stand; my legs have no
strength. I am convinced he is lying. 'Who told you?' I manage
to ask, feeling sad and betrayed. Why didn't she tell me? 'Your
mother was telling my mother yesterday. They were in the
kitchen and I was up here, doing homework.' It's impossible,
beyond belief. 'It doesn't make sense,' I say. Not her going off
with a Turk – I don't care about that – but her running away,
like a criminal, and not coming back to say goodbye. 'I'm only
telling you what I heard,' Timon replies. He's already losing
interest in the story and picks up his *Tom Mix* comic book. 'She
can't run away,' I holler. 'She's got to come back and say goodbye because we're leaving Tenedos and she'll never see us again.
She can't . . . ' I'm shouting at the top of my lungs. Timon tries
to calm me down. 'Hey,' he warns. 'Be quiet or you'll bring my
mother up here.' He cups his hand over my mouth. I stare at
him over the top of his hand and I feel my love for Athena
wither and die. It falls in a heap at my feet. All those silent and
withdrawn months she had been saying farewell, she was pulling
away from us, and I did not know. Electra and Evangelia are at
the door, holding hands and staring at us. In white dresses, with
cream coloured bows in their hair, they resemble startled, life-
size dolls. Timon tries to calm me down. 'I learned English at
high school. I'll teach you some words, all right? How about
that? You'd like that, wouldn't you? I bet you would. When
you get to Australia, you'll be able to speak English and make
new friends.' I nod. 'Now,' he begins, 'the word for "Hello" in
Australian is "Get fucked". Say it after me.' He says 'Hello' in
Greek and 'Get fucked' in English. I repeat after him, easily

coiling my tongue round the unfamiliar words. Electra mouths them with me. 'Good,' says Timon, smiling, 'you're doing well. Now, "Please" is "Get lost". Repeat after me,' he instructs. I repeat the words and Electra is my echo. 'Great,' says Timon, rubbing his hands. 'Speak to the Australians like that and you'll have no problems.'

'I have something to tell you,' says Levent Efendi. We have moved back to town again. It's early evening, after dinner. The front door and window were open when he arrived, but now they're closed because the minute he walked in, he politely asked if we could close everything. Hence the stuffiness in the room. The teacher seems agitated, and it's making my parents nervous. 'Well, what is it?' my father wants to know, indicating that we should all sit at the table in the living room. My mother leans forward. 'Yes, tell us.' Levent Efendi's eyes light on mine. 'Please excuse me,' he apologises. 'Now that I am here, I am lost for words. May I have some water?' He is so polite, such good manners. My mother fetches a glass of water. He drinks and goes on. 'I don't know how to tell you this – ' My father interrupts. 'Is it Dimitri?' he asks, looking at me. 'Has he done something wrong?' Levent Efendi assures them that it's not me he's come to talk about. 'Then what is it?' my mother asks. Levent Efendi rolls up his shirt sleeves and pulls them down again. 'I don't suppose it really matters any more,' he utters, almost to himself. 'I mean now that you are leaving . . . ' Mama and Baba wait for him to continue, perplexed by his strange behaviour. 'I don't want you to leave this country embittered,' he says. My father begins to protest. Levent Efendi holds up a hand to silence him and goes on. 'That's why I will tell you something I have never told anyone.' My father looks at my mother. She is intent on the teacher, leaning forward to catch his every utterance. 'You see, the situation is this,' the teacher

says. 'I am not really a Turk. I am Greek, raised as a Turk.' My
parents gasp and draw back. Levent Efendi won't meet their
eyes, he is buried deep inside his thoughts. 'My real parents
were Greek,' he continues. 'I was born in Smyrna. In nineteen
twenty-two when the Turkish army pushed the Greek army
into the sea and Smyrna was burning, I was two years old. My
father was a baker. We were well off, you might say. Or so I'm
told.' He pauses. The poor man is almost hyperventilating.
'We lived in an apartment above the bakery, not far from the
harbour. Oddly enough, the house still stands.' He smiles wryly
and wipes his brow with a handkerchief. 'What I am telling you
now was told to me by my foster parents after the event. I was
too small to remember.' He smiles almost shyly. My father nods
and pushes back his dentures with his lips. 'On the day of the
Disaster, our usually placid neighbourhood, where Greeks lived
side by side with Turks, was in turmoil. Soldiers went from
door to door, shooting Greeks, looting, setting fire to houses.
The screams of women and the dying were in the air we
breathed. Many people fled to the harbour. Some jumped into
the bay and tried to swim to the French and English ships
anchored out there. Many drowned. Wives were separated
from husbands, children from their parents . . . ' He pauses
again. 'That's what happened to you, isn't it?' my mother asks,
reaching for his hand. The teacher nods and tears fill his eyes. 'I
lost my mother and father that day,' he answers. 'In all that
chaos, I had nowhere to go, no one to turn to. Somehow, I
made my way back to our house. The streets were deserted.
There was only smoke from the burning buildings and blood
on the pavement. The door was kicked in. I went inside. I spent
that night in a niche on the staircase, alone in the house. In the
morning, someone heard my cries. He came to investigate and
found me. He was a Turkish neighbour and a good friend of my
father. He and his wife were childless. When my parents did

not return, they decided to raise me as their own.' My father interrupts to ask if at any stage Levent Efendi tried to find his real parents. 'For many years we tried to track them down. But we did not know where to look, or even if they had survived. No one came to claim me. So I remained with my new family. I was raised as a Turk and a Muslim. That said, my new parents were adamant I remember my Greek heritage. Even though I could not speak Greek, I remembered who I was.' My mother nods, patting his hand. 'That explains some of the strange things you said to Dimitri when you came here last winter. I was wondering where you were going with all of that.' My father asks, 'Why are you telling us this?' After some consideration, Levent Efendi raises his head. 'Because I don't want you to leave this country thinking we're all animals. There are good people here. Many do not agree with what is happening. A lot of people are trying to change things.' My mother leans back and folds her arms. 'And yet,' she says, 'here we are leaving, going who knows where.' Levent Efendi lowers his head. His hands are trembling from the effort it has taken to speak. Damp stains have spread under his armpits. 'But you are choosing to leave. You can choose to remain.' My father too lowers his head in shame. My mother instantly flares up. 'We did not choose to leave,' she retorts, slamming her hand on the table and causing everyone to jump. 'How dare you? We were coerced into leaving.' She pulls herself together and adds, 'Besides, what's there to stay for? More fear, more poverty, more discrimination. There is no future for our children. You know that.' She puts an arm round Electra. 'At least in Australia we will have some money and they can have a good education. Otherwise, they'll be no better than us.' Levent Efendi doesn't give up. 'He who fears birds doesn't plant corn,' he persists, quoting a Turkish proverb. 'If you are afraid, you should go. But answer me this: how will you be able to look yourselves in the mirror in the coming years, knowing you have abandoned your homeland? By leaving you allow the nationalists to triumph. What will you tell your children when they ask why you left and why they are growing up on foreign soil?' My mother is almost in tears. I can see she is wavering. 'We're afraid,' she whispers.

Winter is here again. Last year we had to coax it out of the woodwork. This year it arrived unbidden. But with only a week to go before Christmas, snow is still a way off. Timon says it doesn't snow in Australia, and I'm hoping we get to see the first flurries one last time before we leave. Every night the rains fall, thick and heavy and straight, pounding the streets and rooftops. I cuddle beside Electra under the duvet, thankful for the roof over our heads. Shrieking gales rattle the glass in the window. Rubbish twists and coils like ropes over the rooftops and sweeps out to sea. Everything is desolate, icy. The sun scarcely rises above the horizon; the streets run with horizontal bars of metallic light and shadow that appear to chase one another. I sit inside with Mama and Baba and Electra. I am glad the light is on and the woodstove is burning. Little by little, Baba is selling what little we own. The country property has been sold to a Turkish man. The vineyards went to one of the wineries, Talay or Kostaraga. I'm not sure which. And now Baba is trying to close a deal on the two town houses. 'We'll get peanuts for them,' he complains, 'but what can I do?' He shrugs, resigned, and takes a long drag on his cigarette. When the house is gone, that'll be it. There'll be nothing left to keep us here. 'Have you found a buyer for the donkey?' my mother asks. Her voice is constricted. She and Train have a special bond. It will be hard for them to part. 'Not yet,' my father replies. 'It's not going to be easy. He's old and troublesome . . . ' My mother nods and goes back to spooning food into her mouth. It is as if she were eating straw. She catches me looking at her. 'Eat,' she says, softly, 'stop staring.' She sighs and surveys the meagre kitchen. It feels colder than ever before. 'Byron?' I dare ask. 'What's going to happen to him?' My father puffs smoke over the table and flicks his bushy eyebrows. 'Someone will want him,' he says, finally. 'He's a good rat catcher. Don't worry, he will be cared for.' I reach under the table and stroke Byron's head. His soft, smooth fur. His wet nose. 'Don't do that,' my mother admonishes. 'Not at the table.' I swallow hard and hold back my tears. I wish I could be more like Electra. She sits at the table and stares at the world with big glassy eyes. She utters not a word, yet I am sure she does not miss a thing, making up her own mind as she goes along. I've had to learn very quickly what to say and what to leave unsaid. For a while, it seemed that every time I opened my mouth, with every word, every question, I caused my parents to break out in acid lacerations. Until one day my mother cuffed me hard across the mouth. 'Stop it,' she screamed. 'Stop it with the questions. Fuck your mouth. Don't talk any more. Just hold your tongue.' She cried until I thought she would break into pieces. Australia is an island. We swim round it, but we never go near. 'We're going,' she said with finality, 'and that's that. There is no need to keep talking about it. It's not as if we have any choice. So shut up and learn to live with it.'

It's Christmas morning. Mama kneels beside my brother's grave and touches the soil. It is overgrown with weeds. The iron crucifix is once again on a wild angle in the frozen earth. Only this time she does not bother to fix it. The almond tree has grown, its branches bare and rattling in the strong gusts that sweep in from Point Aeolus. 'Well, well . . . ' she intones. Then she is quiet for so long that I think she's fallen asleep beneath the tree with its skeleton fingers. A slick crow tears the air with its sharp beak. As if in response, the poplars whip their heads from side to side. My mother lifts her chin. She breathes in deep and stands up, placing her hands on her knees to push up her body. Her lips are set. 'Well, well . . . ' she repeats, and this time the tears come, a slow trickle down her face. The wind is so strong and persistent that it pushes them sidewise across her full cheeks. She doesn't bother to wipe them. 'So, it has finally come to this. No one will visit your grave when we're gone.' She drops to her knees and digs her fingers in the slush. For a moment I think she is going to dig up my brother's body and bring him home – set him up in a chair so that he can dine with us. She pulls her blackened fingers out of the ground and slips them into her coat pocket. 'Let's go,' she says. 'There is nothing here for us now.' On the flat open road to town, she is silent as the forest. Our shoes crunch too loudly on the hard-packed dirt. The air is bespattered with snow. Mama stops between the school and the Dadaoğlu property. 'It was all a dream. Do you understand?' she says, turning to face me. 'None of it was real.' I nod without understanding what she means. I take her hand. 'I should never have told you. It wasn't fair, but you came after him. I truly thought you were him, come back to give me a second chance . . . ' She shakes her head as if her folly is too great to contemplate. 'To make up for the sin, God help me.' She pivots on the spot, desperate and agonised. 'I see now that I was wrong.' Even though it's not yet noon it's almost dark. Snow slips from the sky, sharp as blades. There is darkness between the tree trunks. 'Let's sit here,' she says, indicating the steps that lead up to the schoolyard. 'No, Mama, the storm is coming. Besides, we have to go to Aunt Vasiliki's for lunch, remember? Everyone's going to be there.' She nods. 'Yes,' she says, as if she is anaesthetised. 'After what I've put this family through, after all that I've done, it's the least I can do for them.' She slips her hand out of mine and turns her back on the village. Her eyes coast over the frigid landscape as if she is looking at it for the final time. A black-clad man makes his way toward us through the swirling snow. 'How can God ever forgive me?' she asks the water trickling in the ditches. I don't know what she's talking about. My heart is set on getting us back home. That's all. 'Come on,' I say in my loudest, firmest voice. 'Let's get going.' The man trudges past on heavy feet, leaving a trail of footsteps in the sludge. The collar of his coat is pulled up and his face is buried in it. At the last minute he casts a quick, wary glance in our direction, as if he's only just become aware of our presence. He passes without uttering a word. His failure to acknowledge us makes me feel as if Mama and I have died and become ghosts, flapping in our white sheets by the roadside. I take her hand again and turn her gently round. 'Come,' I say. 'Let's go home.'

Levent Efendi says, 'Dimitri, write. Write to us from Australia. Don't forget us. Whatever you do, do not forget us. Don't disappear, like so many others that have gone before you.' His voice almost breaks. He clears his throat, swallows, and the sharp ridge of his Adam's apple rises and falls above the starched white collar. 'One day,' he adds, swallowing again, 'when you're a man, you must come back. You must tell us what this new country is like.' He is holding me before him. His hands rest lightly on my shoulders. Our eyes are locked. When he finishes, he turns me round to face the class. 'Isn't that true, boys and girls?' he asks, brightening. 'We all want Dimitri to write us a letter from Australia. Don't we?' Together, the class says, 'Yes, sir.' As soon as he lets me go, I snap back to my desk. It's as if I am tied to it with an elastic band that pulls me across the room against my will. I sit down and lower my head. I don't like it when attention is drawn to me like that. And now I am scared to lift my head and look my friends in the eye. I sit at my desk, trembling. When I look up, they regard me with a mixture of puzzlement, terror and suspicion. My family is not yet gone.

Even so people stare right through us, as if we don't exist. They think we are traitors, abandoning a sinking ship. I want to grab Refik and Lelia and tell them to cut it out. I am still here. I am still the same. 'Nothing has changed,' I want to say. 'Nothing. See, I am still the same Dimitri you have been playing with for years.' I want to say it even though I know it is not true.

After school, I visit Usin the grocer. I tie Byron to the front door with some string and go inside. The fire is blazing in the wood-stove. Usin is glad to see me. He places a chair beside the stove and I sit. Without uttering a word, he gives me roast chestnuts to eat. He walks behind the counter and lowers his body onto a stool. He too sits, staring at me as if he can't quite make out what his eyes register. Finally, his son Kemal comes in and says, 'It's closing time.' I leap to my feet. The front door opens and Electra walks in. 'Mama says to come home now.' Her plump cheeks are red with cold. 'Come on then, we better go,' I say. At the door, Kemal, in his quiet voice, says, 'Dimitri, remind your father to pay his account, please. He still owes us money.' I nod and step into the cold. The church belfry looms across the street, a stony spine wreathed in mist and snow and behind that, way back, a darkness so thick, so eternal, that I become frightened and run – I was going to say 'run home', but it is no longer home. I stop running and let Electra and Byron catch up. 'Don't,' she says, panting. 'Why are you running?' She looks at me with pleading eyes. 'Give me your hand then,' I tell her. And hand in hand, we walk in the direction that is so familiar to us we can accomplish the deed with our eyes closed. It's incomprehensible that soon we will have to get used to walking different paths.

It began early in the morning with a short, sharp cry whose anguish was prolonged by the sound of something breaking.

The whole set-up could have come from a stage play or a cheap movie. The noise came through the walls, from Amya's side of the house. I shoot up in bed. Almost immediately there is an urgent knock on our front door; and for some reason I think of Timon's words when Iraz went mad last summer: 'It always begins this way.' In a flash, my mother opens the door and Amya flies into the house, sobbing hysterically. That's unusual in itself. Mama is hardly ever up this early. It's as if she had been expecting this, waiting for the curtain to rise so that she can speak her lines. I leap out of bed and race downstairs. I watch the drama unfold from the safety of the landing. Amya's hair is in disarray, her face wet with tears, her mouth a red hole. 'Athena is dead,' she wails, collapsing into my mother's arms. Between sobs she manages to say, 'My little girl . . . They killed her, my little girl. They tricked her into going out there and they killed her.' The two women cling to each other and then part. I sit on a stair, shaking. I can't feel my toes. And there is a monstrous, throbbing pain behind my eyes. My mother collects herself. 'Calm down,' she says gently. 'What are you saying? What happened? Speak to me.' Amya is beyond reach. She cannot speak. My mother shakes her. 'Say it,' she urges with a ferocity that is unwarranted. Uncle Haralambos comes in and closes the front door. Neighbours are gathered outside, roused by the fracas. Haralambos doesn't go near his wife. It's as if she carries a pestilence. My father, still in his long johns, comes down and stands behind me, a bleary-eyed Electra in his arms. Haralambos takes a seat and tells us what happened. It seems that Athena ran away from her sister's house in Istanbul to join her lover in an Anatolian village, but then she went missing. When the police finally found the man, he denied knowing Athena. No one knew anything. Nor had they seen her, a Greek girl in a village full of Turks. She would have stood out, with her honey hair and fair skin. After an intensive search, says

Haralambos, the police found Athena in a shallow grave. 'They raped her,' Amya screams, 'and slit her throat.' And as if we'd been watching a play, Baba turns and walks away, muttering, 'I won't have any part in this.'

After Athena was buried on the mainland, Zotico left for France. During the day, I go to school and I come back. I don't think too much about anything any more. It's best to keep your head down and go from here to there, and back again. I don't see anyone, not even Timon. The only people I have contact with are Mama and Baba and Electra. I don't talk like I used to either. Most of the time, I feel like I am made of wood. Nothing sinks in. My lessons go to waste. When I think of Athena, I cry, but it's as if the tears are forcing themselves out of something that is dry. It's a miracle anything comes out of my eyes at all. Levent Efendi is losing patience with me and that hurts, but then I tell myself he's only a Turk. His revelation doesn't change a thing. If anything it makes things worse: even though he is one of us, he is really one of them. My mother says that he has sold out. It's he who ought to be ashamed for switching sides, not us for leaving. I walk past Amya's closed door; and, for all it means, I might as well have forgotten she lived or laughed or held me in her arms. Zotico's shadow was still fresh on the pavement when they closed the front door. There is no life there, only a cemetery silence. There is a black-and-white photograph of Athena in an album. It was taken in Istanbul before her disappearance. The edges are serrated. Her hair is piled on top of her head. She is wearing a long expensive coat, high heels. Two gloves rest like pale fish in the palm of one hand. Elegant and confident, there is nothing of the village girl in her. If it hadn't been for that photograph, I would have trouble remembering her face.

It is not yet five a.m. A February so frozen, gloves and coats are useless. Inside the house, we are trying to keep warm and fix our courage before it comes undone. There is no use trying because the tears come, the sniffles from upstairs as Mama packs. Baba drags a large chest across the bare wooden floor. 'Come,' he calls from the landing. 'I need your help.' Together they carry the chest downstairs. Everything has been sold, packed or made redundant, the trifles of another life. We are not gone, yet the house rings with absence, echoes each footfall and whisper with supernatural clarity. Already it feels like a dead body, too small, and in possession of an emptiness that is absolute. In the kitchen I sip warm milk. Electra dips bread into her bowl and makes a show of eating, though she has no appetite. We wait suspended in an air of expectation and vague fear. We regard each other with big, uncomprehending eyes. Outside, the streetlights are still spinning haloes in the frosty air. There is ice on the door stoop and we must be careful when stepping out. A steady wind sweeps the road and rattles the window in the living room. Baba said he would replace the glass, do something with the frame, anything to stop it from rattling like that. Now it is too late. One night when we are gone, the glass will fall and break on the pavement, a faint tinkle in the night, barely heard in dreams, our final salutation to the neighbourhood. But it won't matter to us. By then we will be far away. Breezes will sneak in and skitter across Mama's floors and find their way into the kitchen. They will settle in the hearth and wait for whoever comes after us. Cobwebs and silence will be tenants in upstairs corners where once we slept and the vigil light burned in the shrine. On the street, an unearthly presence broods where soon men will walk horses and donkeys to the country. The sound of goats' bells will not fill our ears. We won't be here to see this ritual that makes the fabric of our daily lives. When next it comes round, we will no longer play our part. It will simply go on without us. Grandmother arrives, downcast as the weather. 'Grandfather,' she announces, 'could not make it. He is not feeling well.' As usual, she seems sad. As we move about putting a final touch to things, she begins to cry. 'I am cursed,' she whimpers. 'All my children will leave this earth before I do. And I will stay behind to tend their graves.' With one hand she beats her breast, over and over, a white ball of flesh fluttering at her black bosom. I take the hand to stop it from harming itself. 'Don't,' my mother says, 'we don't need this right now. Not now.' Then Uncle Petro and Aunt Irene step into the living room. We stand round looking with startled, bleary wonder that this immensity could be happening. 'Timon and Evangelia are asleep,' Irene says. 'They will not accompany us to Captain Yakar's boat.' Exasperated, in a scornful voice, I say, 'I'll go wake them. I want to say goodbye.' 'Stay where you are. You're not going anywhere,' Irene says, blocking my way. Her eyes settle on her mother, sniffling at the opposite end of the room. She sits beside her like a hen warming her brood. I surrender without a fight, but will not forget. Soon after, Amya comes in and crumples beside her sister, hemming her in. She looks very old. 'Don't cry,' she pleads, softly. 'Why are you crying? Aren't you going as far as the city with them? Don't cry.' Uncle Haralambos holds up the doorframe. This early in the morning, he seems to be creaking out of the soil. No one has seen them since Athena died. Behind him the light struggles to divest itself of the horizon. Houses, laneways are distilled, struggling for lucidity. A light is on in Lelia's house. 'Another ten minutes,' says Uncle Petro, checking his battered wristwatch. 'Captain Yakar wants to leave on time today. The sea is black.' He has covered his balding head with a cloth cap, and looks his usual worrisome self. When the time comes, it happens quickly, in a blur of motion, now played way down slow, now speeded up, like a near-silent film, black and white. Sometimes

a sound intrudes; other times a colour. On the street a congregation of Greek and Turkish friends has gathered, a silent
flock that will flutter with us all the way to the harbour,
respecting the solemnity of the occasion, and washing our footprints with their tears. Ezet is among them. At one stage, in the
town square, before the school, he closes in and holds my hand
as if to protect me from the lashings of wind and rain. Here
Aunt Vasiliki, Uncle Yanni and Zoe join us. In the turmoil, I
am reminded of the funerals that go by our front door on the
way to the cemetery. Only this time there is no coffin to be
carried on the shoulders. The dead are walking of their own
accord to the boat that will carry them across the water. We
stand on the street, surrounded by luggage. Men step forward
to do their duty while their womenfolk cluster against walls and
in doorways, out of the icy blast. Baba turns the key in the lock
with finality, a click that is louder than it has a right to be, and
we are shut out for good. He hands the key to the man charged
with selling the house. As easily as that, we have given up our
rights to a life on Tenedos, in Turkey even. Nothing belongs to
us; even our lives are forfeit.

I am floating, circling Captain Yakar's boat. I am doing three-
hundred-and-sixty-degree turns round the boat. I am approx-
imately twenty feet away, bobbing in the water, recording everything like a camera. I don't know where the real me is, perhaps at
the bottom of the sea, waiting. High above the boat, the morning
has turned inside out. Water is flying from all directions. At the
prow, I stand with my back to the shore, between a known past
and an uncertain future. Behind me, people embrace, cry and
observe the rituals of farewell. 'Stay, don't go.' 'Why must you
go?' 'One day we too will take a ship and go from here.' 'What
will happen to us?' 'Stay, don't go . . . ' The sun rises. When they
reach us, its rays carry no warmth. 'Where are you? Come say

goodbye to your godmother,' my mother calls. 'Come here.'
She beckons. I see myself turn to perform my duty. I allow
myself to be embraced, enfolded by withered arms. Scaly hands
bedecked in rings caress my face as the frightening woman
clamps her lips to my forehead. 'Write,' she whispers. 'Don't
forget to write to me, dear child.' That's what Levent Efendi
said, too. 'Write, Dimitri. Don't forget to write and tell us what
this new country is like. Remember us.' And I have a flash. I see
myself a year or two from now, writing and posting a letter to
him. Weeks pass. And one day, the letter comes back unopened.
Written on the front, in red ink are the words: Address unknown.
So I was right: Tenedos did not exist. I break free from my
godmother and fly back to my perch at the prow. Grandfather
Dimitro appears beside me. He seems made of ice. 'You must
harden yourself for the ordeal to come,' he says. 'Make your
soul cold as the morning frost so that nothing, nothing, can
penetrate, or ever hurt you again.' I bury my face in his jacket.
Tenedos is calling. It scratches my back with its fingers, taps my
shoulder. More from shame than anything else, I let go of
Grandfather and turn. How can I abandon this place? How can
we? When I glance back it is already too late. We are outside the
harbour, out on the bandit sea. Spray whips the air as the boat
falls into valleys and surging troughs. When Captain Yakar sees
how frightened I am, he says, 'Don't worry, Dimitri, this boat is
made from Anatolian timber. It will last forever.' The camera
that was in the water is back in my head again, looking out
through my eyes. Colour has come back to the world and sound
burrows into my ears. It is freezing cold. Someone is being sick.
I race to see the sunlight lie down in the meadows, grow tall on
the backs of hills, cross over crags and orchards to lick roofs in
the village. Somewhere in that nub of houses, Timon and
Evangelia are sleeping, unaware. Byron. Where is he? As the
island is forsaken to the waves, I write my name on air and toss

it overboard. The colours grow dense, something scampers out, blots the sky. I thought I was awake, but I wasn't. When I truly wake, Tenedos is a barely remembered scent. 'At least now,' my father whispers, 'we won't be persecuted any more.' And many other words carved on the waves. 'At least now we'll have some money.' He wraps his arms round me and rests his chin on my shoulder. By the time we reach Istanbul, Tenedos is awash in myth, a never-ending summer. By the time we arrive in Melbourne, more than a week later, we have washed our hands clean of her. Throughout the ordeal, I remind myself that I will turn ten during our first week in Australia. I repeat it over and over, like a mantra, as if the words hold a magic potency capable of eradicating the past.

Turkey, Bozcaada (Tenedos)
2002

The past is not dead. It's not even past.

WILLIAM FAULKNER

THE CAR-LADEN FERRY drifts toward Bozcaada. I am with Sinan on the top deck. A young soldier in khakis sits inside the passenger cabin, an indication that an army base is still located on the island. Opposite him, an elderly woman wars with plastic bags as two boys run round, laughing. The Aegean is calm and still, the day already muggy. My thin white shirt flaps in the breeze that stirs the hair at my temples. I lean against the railing intent on not missing a thing. Inside stirs a hopeless joy at seeing the island again, and an overwhelming terror.

Perturbed by my prolonged silence, Sinan asks if I am all right. Since the words to answer him will not come, I produce the gestures that I hope encourage him to think that all is well. I don't think I make a convincing display of it, because he continues to study me with worried eyes.

'I thought you would be glad to see the island,' he says. His voice is soft and carefully modulated, as if he is casting it into unknown depths.

'I am. But I am also afraid. You understand . . . '

He hesitates. 'No, not really,' he declares, his English tinged with the soft lilt of a Turkish accent. And after considering his words: 'If you need anything, I am here. Don't worry.'

A comfortable silence falls as we immerse ourselves in the private course of our thoughts.

My heart goes out to Sinan. I feel guilty and weirdly triumphant for having involved him in this ill-advised trip. He's taken a day off work and sacrificed his weekend for the jittery emotions of a highly strung Greek he barely knows.

During the six-hour drive from Istanbul to Çanakkale, he would have realised that this was no mere sentimental trip for me. Nearing middle-age and desiring to lay the past to rest, I am on a somewhat desperate mission to reconnect with my Greek-Turkish heritage; however, nothing is that straightforward. Even as my rational mind wants to forgive Turkey for rejecting us, my heart screams out against such conciliatory gestures. Mixed into this is an obscure wish to give my mother the symbolic burial I feel she deserves now that she is no more. For the life of me, though, I do not know how Sinan, a man who was born the year after we left Turkey, fits into my paralysis of the soul. As Australians say, I did not know him from a bar of soap. Unable to believe that he, a Turk no less, was merely acting out of the kindness of his heart, I indulge in all manner of paranoid fantasies. One minute he is the kind and thoughtful friend, the next a government agent sent to spy on me. Only when I momentarily manage to douse my penchant for melodramatic scenarios, do I see him for what he is.

Cosmopolitan and gentlemanly, Sinan is an economist with a prominent Istanbul bank and an economics lecturer at one of the city's many universities. Tall, thin, with intelligently assessing eyes, he is the kind of man who holds himself with the quiet dignity and modesty I associate with the best of the Turkish people. I could not imagine him getting flustered at the bank or flying off the handle with one of his students, for instance. From sparkling head to well-shod toe, he is a modern Turk in every sense of the expression. Aside from his enlightened politics, I was amused to note, in the early days of our acquaintance, that he was averse to the national drink *rakı*, and preferred a strong cappuccino rather than Turkish coffee. I sense that for him these small defiances are acts of civil disobedience or protests against tradition, a way of signalling his class, education and illumination to the world; they proclaim

him a 'white Turk', not a 'black Turk'. Our slightly cautious
friendship is a very contemporary affair. It developed via an
exchange of emails and telephone conversations, in part,
because of his liberal outlook and social conscience. Until the
day I arrived in Istanbul, we had not met before. Though he is
younger than I am and gives every indication of being more of
a rationalist than a man given to impetuous emotion, knowing
him is unlike any relationship I have had in my adopted
country. For the first time in three decades, I do not have to
explain myself. I do not feel like a complete outsider. Despite
the fact that we belong to different tribes, he knows and understands implicitly. I do not have to put certain things into words.
There is a perception of a shared history, a desire to right wrongs,
and to draw two opposing shores together.

Needing the strength, I rest my hand on his bony shoulder.
He gazes at me quizzically and his thick, black eyebrows meet
over the bridge of his nose, reminding me of a darting sparrow's
wings.

I smile and turn away. Sunlight glitters skittishly on a sea so
dark and depthless, it could be drawn from a cup of wine. I wish
that I could drink from it and forget. The last time I had seen
these waters, it was a frozen winter's day, and I had been a
frightened child.

Despite the heat, I tremble and wonder at the wisdom of
returning home. As if they are the cries of gulls, I hear first my
father's voice, and then the voices of obscure others floating
toward me on the breeze: *Keep your mouth shut and you will be
all right. You don't know what Turks are capable of. Don't trust
them. Run!* I close my eyes to clear my head. When I open them,
Tenedos sits on the sea's edge.

At first I think it is a mirage. With each passing minute, as the
craft ploughs ponderously forward, the island gains in purple
mass. It grows dense and long beneath an almost transparent

sky, until it floats on the back of a thin white wave, a rusty bronze reality too solid to ignore. From this distance, Tenedos is visible end to end. I am struck by its modest size. It is not a very large place. One could hire a donkey or bicycle and see all there is in a day.

The fortress on the shore comes into view first. In stark contrast to the barren hill that crouches behind, its buttresses and crenellations catch the sunlight and cast an almost blinding alabaster light across the water. The boat surges forward. As it swings round and begins the slow drift toward the harbour, the shoreline and surrounding areas unfold like a series of screens, revealing the town by degrees. Every available space on this side of the island is dense with human habitation. New developments climb the foothills, one behind the other, and crown the denuded hilltops. Unattractive concrete boxes that are more suited to the outskirts of a major metropolis than the Aegean devour the lower ramparts immediately behind the original township. It looks as if it has not rained in years. In the middle of this overdevelopment, the familiar minaret of the Köprülü Mehmed Paşa mosque still links earth to sky.

I reach for my overnight bag. I stand on uncertain legs and descend the stairs to the main deck. The boat docks amid a plume of diesel fumes. Cars disembark first; three or four foot passengers trail off and vanish into the waiting streets. There are no tourists, save Sinan and I.

Sinan drives his car out. I am left alone, a solitary figure, too scared to go back and too frightened to step forward. I check that my mother's photograph is still in my breast pocket and step off the boat. I stand for a long time on the solid new concrete pier and survey from a safe distance the laneways that wend their way, as they always have, into the heart of the town. The tree-lined square seems familiar and yet utterly alien. No one rushes forward to greet me; there are no relatives left on the island to do so; only a handful of elderly neighbours who may or may not remember me.

When the heat becomes unbearable, I step forward, and follow that with another step, and then another. I tell myself, it's only land. It is only earth, stone and trees.

Sinan parks the car outside a café in the square. Thus, Mother, he and I venture into the beehive we once called our village. In minutes I am lost, confounded by the tangle of streets and byways.

Despite Sinan's assurances, I am not confident that the map in my head will untangle. We stop on a corner and I survey the stillness. The houses are built close together so that all that is visible overhead is a narrow strip of cloudless sky. A black bird flies past. A red kitten bravely ventures out of a doorway and coils softly at my feet. I had planned to walk past the fortress and veer to the right, toward the Cauldron District. This once familiar course would have led straight to Grandmother's hotel. She and Grandfather migrated to Australia a few years after we did, but I know that the house they lived in still serves the same function as it did when they were here. But I am unable to get my bearings. I feel a foolish panic. My throat tightens and dries. I look right to left, with no discernible results.

As I stand paralysed by indecision, it seems as if the world has shrunk and pressed in on me. The houses are more closely packed than my memory has them, and not as towering. Nor are the streets as big as the ones that live in my head. To the boy I had been, these alleys had been long and wide and full of promise. Now everything has shrunk. Gone are the distances of childhood. I am an Alice grown too big for the house, arms and legs poking out of every conceivable opening, waving about in streets unable, unwilling, to accommodate overgrown, clumsy extremities. If I choose I could stalk on my long legs from one end of the village to the other, a Gulliver, and go back to Istanbul on the evening ferry. The yawning lots, the derelict houses, the charred ruins, the ugly graffiti we had passed on our way have made me feel uneasy. They do not fit my picture of Tenedos. The shabbiness and modernity belong elsewhere, not here.

A rooster crows in another street. It makes a high, piercing cry. As if summoned by the call, a wave of nausea sweeps through me. My throat contracts and I almost retch on a doorstep. Sinan places a hand between my shoulder blades. As I lean on the wall, trying desperately to compose myself, I recall that this house had served as the backdrop for a photograph taken at a wedding celebration in 1967 or thereabouts. I see myself clearly, standing on the doorstep in scuffed shoes. On my head is a khaki beret tilted at a rakish angle and my legs are covered in dark pants that are too short at the ankles. My torso is clothed in a coat with three buttons and two deep pockets. My hands poke out of the sleeves like carved ivory. Twisted round the first button is a confection in honour of the festivities. As simple as that a map unfolds in my head, its secrets branching, fanning out in all directions until the twists and turns of the labyrinth spread out, mysterious no longer but subtly welcoming and knowable.

I straighten. 'It's this way,' I say, pointing at a corner house with wrought iron bars over the ground-floor windows and basement casements: Grandmother's hotel. It too has shrunk and appears the worse for wear, but there is no doubting the repository of memories that gaze from the upstairs windows, the games played in the inner courtyard, the quarrels with Timon on the stair. They could be Grandmother's tattered slippers on the wet porch.

It is October. The tourists have left and peace has been restored. Students are at their desks. It is easy to find a room. I fling my luggage on the bed and hit the streets again, eager to continue the search now that the compass is set aright. I have to keep going. A desperate urgency informs every step, every gesture and turn of the head. I fear that, should I stop to rest, the village might fade like Brigadoon, shy of the morning light.

Sinan insists on coming with me. 'I want to see everything with you,' he says. 'I want to see where you lived. I want to hear the stories.'

Coiled like a spring, I doubt my capacity for storytelling at this moment; nonetheless, together we walk to Aunt Vasiliki's house. It is a short stroll round the corner. Kiymet Sokak announces itself with a dainty blue plaque on a wall. A discreet arrow beneath the white lettering directs the eye into the narrow street. Number 1 Kiymet Sokak. Here, in a life so distant it might have been lived by someone else, had lived Aunt Vasiliki, Uncle Yanni and mandolin-strumming Zoe. And before them, my grandfather Dimitro. The house is closed for winter. The door is painted a deep English green, and dazzling white shutters close their eyes over the windows. As middle-class necessity dictates, the house is now being fed by electricity and a telephone. The walls have been rendered and painted a buttery yellow. What a charming house it is; loved after so long.

I cast my eyes round. As the peasants have been flushed out to make room for the moneyed classes, the substance of the streets has been altered to suit the new occupants' requirements. The robustness has been taken out and replaced with the essentials of a tasteful Istanbul suburb, like Bebek or Arnavutköy. The houses have been freshly painted and the shutters replaced. Those that boast an overhanging upper floor, in the Ottoman style, present an aquamarine or a burnt-brown brow to the spotless street. Flowering greenery climbs every wall. Antique stores and bed and breakfasts announce themselves. With the introduction of electric lights, cleanliness has come to the island. Even the ruinous old house across the street that had thrilled me as a boy has been restored to its former glory.

The next afternoon finds us travelling to what had been our country house. Sinan had offered to drive, but I chose to walk in honour of the times my family had travelled the distance from the village to the *dâm* under its own steam. The harvest is over and the roads mostly deserted. Occasional feral gusts slip from the surrounding sun-burnt hills. I spy a couple casually walking a road parallel to the one we follow, heading toward Ayazma. A solitary man ploughs the hard-baked earth round his bare vine stalks. The soil has the insistent gold of over-ripe pears. I put one foot in front of the other and pretend the sun is not beating down on my head. The nape of my neck is burned and I curse myself for not bringing a hat. The roadside is littered with rubbish. Plastic bags snag on thorny bushes and in the undergrowth.

We arrive as shadows stretch in the bronze last light of day. The first thing I see is the back of the chapel. Then comes the low structure of the *dâm*. We step off the road, onto the property. The garden is a riot of weeds and thistles the colour of burnt paprika. Neglected grapevines struggle out of the exhausted soil. Other than the generous spread of an almond tree, there is no greenery. As we silently walk about, I see that the cherry grove, the fig and the mulberry have ceased to exist. Gone too are the poplars that screened the house from the road. The earth has also claimed the olive trees and the old grave beneath them – I had discovered in recent years that my grandfather Dimitro was not buried there after all; it was the resting place of the original owner of the property.

The sinking sun paints the world an unreal copper. Oddly, the landscape reminds me of the Australian outback. Only this is meagre and compressed by comparison, utterly depleted. A newly built home looms on the next ridge, where Ali Berber's haunted ruin used to be. And across the road is a house that is a city slicker's idea of a peasant farm dwelling, a vulgar display with a huge satellite dish teetering on the roof. Sinan tells me that it belongs to a famous actress. The windows blink and wink in the afternoon light, making me feel watched, a trespasser.

Your kitchen, Mother, is shrouded in a darkness and silence that is infinite. It will never again fill with the aroma of baking bread and the sizzle of frying peppers. As I stand in the doorway, I see again the cheesecloth you used to hang from a hook to the right of the door. It resembled a pale lactating breast with its weight of fermenting, salted goat's milk for our cheese. And I remember Byron, our terrier, who sat at your feet, enchained by the promise of food. I hate to tell you that the chapel's dome has collapsed, and the interior is stripped of the gold and iconostasis. Nothing remains, only a shell, open to the sky.

Memories: how they crop up to torment us when we least expect them. They come like a thunderbolt and depart as quickly, taking no responsibility for the devastation they cause. As I try to stem the storm of memory, a donkey pokes his glossy head out of the kitchen window and looks at me with lambent eyes. For a minute I almost believe it is Train, waiting these many years for our return. Gazing at this donkey that is not, yet could be Train, I wonder about the mystery of time. Over thirty years separate the man who stands here now from the times our family shared in this house. Yet they feel as if they happened yesterday. No, they are happening still, right now, before my eyes. Is it possible that there exists an inner and outer time, running side by side, concurrently, each disregarding the other yet inextricably intertwined and co-dependent; each with its own rules that govern the everyday on the one hand, and our inner, subterranean lives on the other? Is that why the past is lodged in our minds on a grander scale than the diminutive present?

I gaze into the donkey's eyes. They are deep wells. It seems a portal has opened and I fall headlong into it. The past unleavens and superimposes itself over the present, creating a shifting, out-of-focus picture, blurred and fuzzy at the edges, like a badly aligned three-dimensional movie. There is Train, and there is you, Mother, coming out of the kitchen. You are wiping your hands on your apron, in that casual, slightly distracted manner you had of doing things. You are a fresh-faced young woman, and wafting behind you is the aroma of baking. Mint and parsley grow by the door; a bunch of oregano dries at the window. Slowly, the picture comes into focus and it is 1970 again, our last summer on the island. Yet I can see through you. The wall behind you is shattered, the window frame warped and buckling. The cracks are so violent they could be offering a glimpse to the underworld. A light-blue iron bed frame rests against the mellow stonework, almost obscured by the knee-high grass. I turn to take in the five wells on the property and the spring by the vegetable gardens – all dry now. I point out to Sinan that a stranger seeing this for the first time would not know that water had once been plentiful, that it had been a modest kind of hellish paradise for us.

Rain rattles on the roof of the hotel. It is dark and windy out. The weather has turned. As I write in my journal, Sinan rests against the headboard of his bed, reading. He too has been silent and thoughtful since our return from the country; we barely uttered a word over our dinner at a seaside restaurant. I have been feeling withdrawn and melancholy, more content to remain with my thoughts than to engage with the world. We are due to leave the island tomorrow on the noon ferry. I am not ready to part ways so soon. But there is no alternative; Sinan has to return to work at the bank on Monday. And I am reluctant to remain on my own, without a buffer.

'I am so sorry,' he says, unexpectedly looking up from his

book. 'I feel terrible.' He draws up his knees and leans forward. 'I had no idea any of this happened, none of it. I mean it is horrible what they did. To make people leave their homes . . . ' He shakes his head and opens his hands helplessly.

I am not sure if he is being disingenuous or is genuinely ignorant of the facts. How could there be such a disconnection between past and present? Am I honestly expected to believe that an educated man can go through university and not know what his country had done to us? Nonetheless, I say, 'There is no need to apologise. It's not your fault. You weren't even born when it happened. The fact that you are here now, listening and observing, being a witness, means more to me than a thousand apologies. And for that I am grateful.'

I realise that I have done Sinan a great injustice. Immersed in my reservoir of barely acknowledged resentment and anger, fear and despair, love and hate, he has ceased to be himself and become a symbol. Sinan represents his people, his nation, Turkey, and everything that entails. The irrational ten-year-old that wars inside me, with all the yearning and selfish demands of a child, needs the motherland to understand, embrace, and take him back unequivocally. And he is looking to Sinan to accomplish all of that.

Meanwhile, Sinan is still speaking.

'The problem is not with the Turkish and Greek people. Politics is the problem,' he states. 'We saw this after the nineteen ninety-nine earthquakes. While normal people from both sides rushed to help each other, politicians were arguing. They couldn't decide what to do. Instead of helping, they got in the way. It's always been this way.'

I nod. 'The wrong people always end up going into politics,' I reply, morose. 'They are not interested in people or the cause they have sworn to uphold. They're only interested in power and what they can get for themselves. Even the ones that start off with good intentions are eventually compromised. They ought to be made to fight the wars they start, the reprehensible cretins.'

Sinan laughs and I am glad to see his handsome face light up. 'Maybe it is the nature of the job.' He lies down and pulls the bedclothes over his shoulders.

In the morning there is a nip in the air, but it is clear of rain. As we pack our luggage into the car, the air smells of winter's approach. After breakfast we cut across town to the church. It is Sunday, a good time to catch up with the Greeks that remain on the island. Together, Greek and Turk, Sinan and I descend the familiar fifteen steps to the courtyard and stand at the entrance. The empty yard smells of incense, damp roses and oleander. The service has started.

For the first time since we have met, Sinan appears uncertain. 'Should I come inside?' he asks, hesitating.

Though I do not feel it, I am more cavalier than he. 'Sure. Why not?' I respond. 'Who's to know you're not Greek? Just don't say anything, and look reverential. What are they going to do? Throw you out?'

The truth of the matter is that I need him to be with me, because I feel as uncertain as he does. I am about to confront people I have not seen in three decades. In all my imaginings, I can not conceive what manner of reception I might get, or if they will even remember me. And if they did somehow recall who I am, I have no idea what to say to them. My Greek is almost as bad as my Turkish; words fail me in more ways than one. Sinan is more than my guide and interpreter. He has become a barrier against harm. I have been experiencing everything these last few days through him. He is my sieve, straining and refining varied sensations for my consumption.

We step inside the church. The low hum of the priest's

chanting enfolds us as surely as the overwhelming scent of incense. The interior is a faded jewellery box with the music slowly, inevitably, winding down. The reasons for this are immediately obvious. I had expected to see the island's entire Greek population inside, a throng worshipping on this holy day. But there are only two worshippers. An old man hunched in a pew at the front. With his head bowed, he seems as decrepit and in need of scaffolding as the collapsed belfry outside. The other, an elderly woman, sits like a ramrod in a stiff-backed pew. Her covered head is elevated and her lips part slightly to catch the priest's precious utterance, sustenance for the week ahead.

While Sinan claims a seat beside the door, I make my way to the middle of the floor. Feeling fraudulent and somewhat trans-parent, I light a candle and place a chaste kiss on the icon of the Virgin and Christ. I perform these acts not because they have any significance for me, but because it seems like the right thing to do. I think that reenacting the old rituals will somehow evoke the past and help me to step back, to understand what happened, where we went wrong, and how to rectify the situation. For all that, the only thing that happens is that my hands tremble and I feel as if I am walking on wooden legs. I totter back and take a seat beside my saviour.

I don't know how long we sit there. The general air of neglect becomes oppressive, suffocating. The priest and his elderly female assistant drone on interminably, and all the while I feel as if they are drifting further and further away on a cloud. I lift my eyes to the vaulted ceiling. Peeling paint and cracks festoon the dome. The fresco depicting Christ is tarnished and covered with soot, the gold leaf barely discernible. As I scrutinise the faded glory of this once-treasured place, I recall that religion had not played a great role in our lives. Mixing paganism with Christianity, the islanders had always displayed a grudging respect for the divinity and hardly refrained from uttering blasphemies against their maker and his earthly representatives when things did not go their way. Most likely the remaining Greeks couldn't give a fig about the liturgy. Still, the priest persists in coming every Sunday by boat from nearby Gökceada, and going back again when his duties to the diminishing flock are fulfilled.

I pat Sinan's hand. 'Let's go,' I say. 'I've seen enough, if you have.'

'Is that you, Dimitro?' Her words merge like the waters of a stream with other conversations, spoken long ago.

Our house. Sinan and I have been standing in front of it for several minutes, attracting the attention of neighbouring women. A short walk from the church, the building came into view before I had time to prepare myself. As we approach, I make a point of showing inordinate interest in the dwellings and alleys along the way, pointing at this and that, and filling in the gaps for Sinan as best I can. The same. Everything still the same. Yet I don't have the courage to scrutinise the one thing that has indeed changed – the house my sister Electra and I had been born in; the house my mother and father had locked up and abandoned. When I can no longer postpone the inevitable, I settle my eyes on its bruised face, its lopsided grin. Immediately it is obvious that it has remained unoccupied since our departure. The roof has caved in and the northeast wall peeled away so that the guts and skeleton of the upper storey are revealed to public scrutiny. The staircase is visible, as is a segment of the first-floor landing and the two bedrooms. Yellow newspapers and filthy rags have been stuffed into window casements where the glass has fallen out.

I touch the rusted padlock that secures the entrance. Then I press my face against the grimy window and peer in. There is nothing to see except chaos and ruin: rotten beams, chunks of plaster, and powdery sky. The wall between the living room and kitchen has fallen; whether by intent or neglect it is difficult to fathom. Yet the mezzanine remains, ascending to an upper level on the verge of disintegration.

Next door, Amya's house is in better condition and appears to be occupied.

I am ready to leave and never come back. I turn to Sinan. He is exchanging words with an elderly woman across the street. She is covered.

I approach them. 'Pagona used to live here,' I offer, pointing at the double-storey house behind them.

'You remember her?' the woman cries, delighted. The pale circle of her face is surrounded by a black headscarf. 'Well, well. Fancy that.' She chuckles and claps her hands. 'No, Pagona died long ago,' she replies, when I ask after our neighbour. 'A Greek journalist lives here now and I keep an eye on the house when she's away.'

'Pagona used to come home late at night,' I reminisce, 'after washing bottles at the winery. We would hear her key turn in the rusty lock. It made a dreadful racket. I was terrified because I thought it was a giant, chewing children's bones. I thought she was a witch.'

Sinan translates for the woman's benefit, and they laugh.

The woman touches my elbow. 'Who, Pagona?' she screams. 'She was a saint. A better woman never lived.'

They laugh again. She covers her mouth and shakes her head as if the memory is fresh as mint in her mind, too. I join them. It feels like I have not laughed for eons. The muscles in my face almost ache with the effort. And that's when I hear the other woman's voice. At first I am not sure if I really hear it or if it resides purely in my head.

'Is that you, Dimitro?' she says from behind me. She speaks Turkish. Nevertheless, she pronounces my name in Greek. Our little group turns to stare at her, a long-faced, fair-skinned woman approaching sixty. She too is covered, wearing a taupe headscarf and ankle-length coat.

'Ayşe, do you know these people?' asks the peasant woman. 'This one used to live in the house next to yours.' She points at me.

The new arrival ignores the woman. 'Of course it's you,' she continues, staring at me. 'I'd recognise you anywhere. You're the spitting image of your mother and father.' She reaches up and unashamedly clasps my face in her hands. 'It's as though they are living in the same body at the same time,' she adds, looking deeply into my eyes.

She seems vaguely familiar, but I cannot place her. I study her with the bemused curiosity of a scientist who has encountered a species thought to be long extinct in a remote forest. She is shorter than me and I have to tilt my head down to address her.

'I am sorry, Aunt,' I reply in halting Turkish. I have unconsciously reverted to our old nomenclatures. 'I think I recognise your face, but . . . It's not possible . . . ' I shake my head, trying to clear the fog that is gathering. I am bewildered and yet my heart has quickened, as if a part of me knows that something momentous is about to happen.

She pulls me aside. 'It's me,' she whispers in broken Greek. 'It's Athena. Don't you remember me?'

I sit in Amya's front room. Everything is clean and gleaming, right down to the crooked broken boards on the floor and the rose-patterned plastic that covers the table beneath my fingers. Athena is out of the room, fixing me a drink. Before inviting me inside, she had asked Sinan to go to the harbour and wait for me. It is a testament to her authority that, after silently communicating with me, Sinan had left without a word.

Athena returns with a glass of cherry sherbet.

'Drink,' she orders, placing it in front of me. 'You've had a shock. You'll be all right in a minute.'

She has a very direct way of speaking and I do as she asks without argument. I am more interested in the room, which seems a museum piece from my childhood, loved and cherished, like the wrinkled face of a grandmother. There are cracks in the ceiling and the window is warped; nevertheless, none of it matters.

'How are you feeling now?' she asks.

We have precious little time together. Even though I am conscious of the passing minutes, I cannot reply. Finally, I say, 'Athena, I thought you were dead.'

Instead of answering, she says, 'It's so long since anyone called me Athena I don't know how to respond or even if I recognise myself in that name. I think I would prefer it if you call me Ayşe.'

I bow in deference to her request and wait for her to go on.

Some minutes pass before she speaks again. 'You're not the only one who thinks I am dead.' A cloud falls across her face, dimming her still-captivating, deep-set eyes.

'What happened?' I persist. 'Your mother and father told us you'd been murdered. They said they found your body in a shallow grave, and later they buried you in Istanbul.' Everything is coming out in a rush. I apologise. Nonetheless, I can not help myself. 'This must be hard for you to talk about, but I must know. You don't know the impact your disappearance had on my life.'

'No,' she says, holding up a hand. 'I don't mind talking about it, not at all. It's almost a relief, actually. It happened so long ago.' Her voice breaks. She closes her eyes and buries her face in her hands. When she lifts her head again, I see that she has been weeping. 'Is that what they told you? What a dreadful thing to tell a child! There are different versions, of course.' She cups her chin in both hands and gazes into my eyes. She breathes out. When she speaks again, her voice is calm, as if she has rehearsed the moment many times. 'I won't bore you with them. As you can see, my dear second cousin, I am very much alive. I was made to disappear. The Turks didn't kill me; the Greeks did. If they told you otherwise, they lied. My parents, they are the ones who killed me. I shamed them and they buried me without a backward glance.' She stops. A violent, bitter note crept into her voice toward the end. She regains control of herself and continues.

'Why? It's the age-old story. I fell in love with a Turkish man. I wasn't the first. The island is full of stories like that. Nothing unique about it. One poor couple drowned themselves so that they wouldn't be parted. To be fair, what made my situation intolerable was that I became pregnant before we married. You can imagine what the consequences of that would be. It's doubly worse if it's a Christian and a Muslim together. I don't know what it's like where you come from, but here when you do something like that you're making a stand. You are drawing a line on the ground. You have to be brave and see it through because there is no turning back.' She speaks in a rush and stops to catch her breath. 'As you can imagine, it was not easy for a Greek woman to assimilate into Turkish village life. It's still not an easy thing to accomplish; I can vouch for that. I thank Allah for my husband and his parents. I could not have done it without them.'

Athena shakes her head. Then she clears her throat and goes on. 'Do you know what it feels like to be cut off from your mother and father, for your siblings to go on living and not know what happened to their sister?

'The first years were the hardest. The isolation almost killed me. If it hadn't been for my new faith I think I would have killed myself, may Allah forgive me for even thinking it.'

I almost expect her to cross herself in the Greek Orthodox fashion. But her hands remain in her lap.

'When I found out I was pregnant,' she continues, 'my parents were understandably horrified. They packed me off to Istanbul for an abortion. My sister Penelope and her husband were going to organise everything. But I didn't want to do it. I'm not that sort. I ran away and joined Murat. I converted to Islam and we married. When the baby arrived, I ceased to exist for my family. As time passed, I came to see myself in the eyes of my husband and in the eyes of the two children he gave me. I began to see that there is another life – that I could regain some of what had been stolen from me.'

I think about how quiet she had been when we lived side by side. And here she was, a rebel in the making. I am filled with admiration for her.

'How did you end up back here?' I ask.

'Oh, we don't live on the island,' she replies, waving aside the suggestion as though it were preposterous. 'We only come for the harvest and then go back. I'm about to close up the house and return to the mainland. Murat went back yesterday because he has work,' she finishes off.

I ask when she purchased the house.

'We came here nine years ago for work. It was the first time I'd dared to come back after my expulsion.' She laughs weakly. 'Such was my fear and humiliation I thought that the Greeks would spit on me and throw stones. But they don't care, or if they do they're smart enough to keep it to themselves. Through word of mouth, I learned that my mother and father had died without a will. The house and two vineyards had not been sold and they remained in my father's name. As the only child still living in Turkey, I was entitled to them. I came forward and declared myself. They gave me everything. Ironic, isn't it, after the lengths they went to shut me out?'

I smile ineffectually. 'Are you happy?'

'Murat is a good man, if that's what you mean. And I love my children. They are smart young men, both of them in business.'

Glad as I am to see her, one thing bothers me. 'You are covered,' I point out, indicating her headscarf. 'I remember you saying you wouldn't be seen dead in one of those things. It would be like being a ghost. Those were your words.'

'And you remember them,' she replies, smiling. 'The things we say when we are young. And what about you, don't you believe in anything?'

'I mean no disrespect,' I reply, 'but I believe religion is fairy-tales for adults who are incapable of taking responsibility for their own lives. Rather than having the courage and conviction to be honourable, ethical human beings out of their own volition they create a policeman in the sky to make laws and mete out punishment should they stray too far from the straight and narrow. To me, they are exchanging free will for life-long tyranny.' I am quite worked up and have to force myself to stop.

She laughs as if I were a babbling fool. 'You wouldn't say that if you had faith. You are speaking with your brain and not with your heart. Allah, and even Theos, lives in the heart.' She touches her breast and the gold band that encircles her finger sparks.

'I am sorry, but I cannot respect any religion or political creed that treats half its citizens as second-class.' I wish we could get off the subject. It does not feel right to lecture her, and all the convictions that seem so right in Australia ring hollow here. 'If you weren't inferior to the men in your life, you would not be covered,' I finish off rather lamely.

'This,' she says, touching the scarf at her throat, 'is a symbol of my devotion to Allah.'

'Then why don't the men wear them, too?'

'Because they grow a beard.'

'And wear jeans and short-sleeved t-shirts. Can't you see it's hypocrisy? The scarf is only the surface symbol of a deeper female oppression that runs through Islam. Turkey is going further down that path every year. The secular democracy that Atatürk established is in danger. Do you want Koranic law to be imposed on the country?'

Her attention drifts out of the window. I see from her expression that she too would rather change the subject.

'Let me make tea. Then we can continue.' She stands and catches me checking the time. 'Don't worry; I am keeping an eye on the clock.' She indicates behind me where an old clunker loudly ticks away the minutes.

When she returns with two glasses of steaming tea, she seems unperturbed by my outburst. Plump and rosy-cheeked, I can not imagine her being thrown by anything a Westerner like me might have to say about the way she chooses to live.

She sits opposite me and places a sugar cube in her glass. 'Tell me,' she asks, stirring her tea, 'how is your family?'

'My father and sister are well. I am sure they will be surprised to learn that you are alive. Unfortunately, my mother died of breast cancer a long time ago.'

Athena places the silver spoon beside her glass and covers her mouth with trembling fingers. Her eyes fill with sudden tears. 'I am very sorry to hear that,' she says, stricken, 'more than I can say. Poor woman. Was it a long illness?'

I do not want to talk about my mother's illness and her long decline. After all these years, it is still a bruising subject. But I owe it to Athena after the grilling I have given her. 'I'm afraid so . . . ' I respond. And to change the subject, I add, 'I was going to bury this here.'

I pull out the photograph of my mother and place it on the table between us.

Athena picks it up. 'She is very young,' she observes, a sad smile crossing her lips. She glances at me and that dazzling smile lights up her face. 'We were all so very young then.' She studies the picture and floats away on the memories it evokes. When she returns to the room, something appears to have shifted inside her. 'This is what she looked like when she came back from Istanbul, round about nineteen fifty-nine it must have been. I'd forgotten how pretty she was. No wonder she broke hearts everywhere she went. I used to be very jealous of her, you know.' She smiles ruefully and shakes her head. 'The vanity . . . '

She slides the photograph across the table to me. I pick it up and return it to my pocket. Her difficult-to-read eyes look into mine for some minutes and when she speaks again her voice is cautious, tender.

'If you ask me,' she offers, 'I don't believe your mother wants to be buried on the island. Istanbul was her city. That's where she left her heart, in more ways than one.' And then, after another pause: 'You see we're not so very different, your mother and I.'

I seize the moment. 'What do you know about her, Ayşe?' I lean forward hungrily.

'What do you mean?' she says, pulling back as though startled. Her previous confiding manner evaporates and she becomes wary.

'There are so many questions in her life,' I offer. 'So many mysterious things that don't add up . . . '

She pushes back her chair and stands up. 'Let sleeping dogs lie,' she says.

I lean forward and grab her hand. 'I can't let sleeping dogs lie because I believe one of them may be lying in the cemetery,' I reply.

'What do you mean?' she says, shocked.

'Ayşe, I used to fantasise that I had an older brother. When I was a kid, I made up stories about him. They were so vivid,

I remember them as though they were real. I have these recollections of my mother taking me to his grave. Her beating me because I told my father about it. Why did I make up these stories? Where did they come from?'

Athena sits again. She crosses her arms and for a long time her eyes remain distant, almost hostile. I feel her weighing me up ruthlessly and deliberately. She must have found a degree of resilience because she finally says, 'Why do you think it was a fantasy?' She gives a curious smile, as if she can not believe I had been taken in by a clever ruse.

I almost shout. 'What else could it be?' Then I soften my voice and continue. 'I've asked my grandmother and my father. They deny there was another child. Even my mother told me it was a dream; that it never happened. It was obviously the fantasy of a lonely boy. I made him up. I was the first child and Electra the second. It's just the two of us.'

I found myself almost believing what I was saying.

Athena draws a deep breath. 'Of course your grandmother and father deny his existence,' she replies. 'They have no choice. Dimitri, there was another child. You did have an older brother. That is the truth and you must believe me.' She emphasises each word, dropping the syllables deliberately on the table so that they sit irrefutably before me.

I can see that this is not easy for her. Nonetheless, I persist. 'Then, I don't understand,' I remark, running a hand across my brow. 'Why would a father deny his own son?'

She shrugs to make light of what she suggests next. 'Perhaps because the baby wasn't his. Maybe your father doesn't know about his existence. I don't know. It's conjecture. The past is murky. A lot of things happened during the early years of your parents' marriage that only a husband and wife can know. I can tell you this, though. When your mother lived in Istanbul, she fell for a young man. His parents used to visit the house where she worked. They saw a lot of each other. He was Armenian, which caused a great deal of consternation in the family. It would not do, you see, to marry a non-Greek.' She gives a wry laugh. 'You see we were as prejudiced as everybody else.' She pauses for a time, seemingly weighed down by the years and the folly of man. Then she sips her tea and goes on. 'I can't remember if he was a young doctor or the son of an industrialist. In any case, despite the fact that they belonged to a different class and ethnic group, he loved her and she him. While your mother was still in Istanbul, there was talk of an engagement.' She points at my shirt pocket. 'He was in the photograph you have there. Your mother obviously cut him out. That's why the photograph is cropped round her body. He was a handsome, dark-haired man with a pencil-thin moustache, as was the fashion.

'Then, quite suddenly, your grandmother brought Galatea back to the island and married her off to your father. I mean she was forced. There was no option. No negotiation. It was a done deal and your mother had to live with it. Needless to say, it was not a happy union. Your mother did not say anything, but it was obvious that she pined for the other man and for the city life. There was no pleasing her, no matter what your poor father did. They argued; they fought. The normal stuff.' I was about to interrupt and tell her that a beating is not 'normal stuff'. She holds up her hand. 'You haven't long to go. If you want to hear this, you must listen.'

She seems to collect her thoughts from some deep, untapped source and then continues. 'The first baby arrived and they called him Dimitro, after your paternal grandfather. But he was weak and not blessed with a long life. He died after two or three weeks. I still recall where he is buried,' she adds.

'So do I,' I interject. 'But I can't find the grave. The cemetery is a mess. No one looks after it any more.'

'Be that as it may, there is a little body in an unmarked grave and it belongs to your brother.'

'Why doesn't Father acknowledge him?'

She makes a helpless gesture. 'There was talk that the boy was not your father's, if you know what I mean.' She bows her head. 'I am sorry if that offends. You asked and I am telling you what I know. The whole thing happened while your father was away on a fishing trip. Then he returned, and nine months later, you arrived.' She smiles, leans across to pat my hand. 'Both your parents loved you very much. They would have walked over broken glass for you . . .'

She glances at the clock and continues with urgency.

'For a time things seemed to settle down. The arguments were not as frequent. We could hear them through the walls you know. Then Galatea became pregnant again and the world turned upside down. She asked my mother to help her abort the baby. She sat here, in this room, and told my mother that she couldn't bear to have another child by your father. That's when we realised she still loved the other man. She resented your father enough to want to destroy the life he had caused to take root inside her. Of course, my mother refused to help. She even broke a confidence and told your grandmother. But that wouldn't stop your mother. Galatea was a hurricane when she got going. When your father was at sea, she killed the baby.' Athena's voice cracks. Her hands shake. I want to enfold them in mine, but I do not dare. 'Allah forgive her. It's a miracle that Electra is with us today.'

'Why didn't she do the same to Electra, or me for that matter?' I ask. I can barely believe what I am hearing. Yet it makes lunatic sense. Every utterance falls into place easily, elegantly even, the pieces of a jigsaw.

Athena shrugs. 'I don't know,' she replies, 'except to say that by the time your sister arrived your mother's conscience was starting to bother her. She was convinced that one way or another God would find a way to punish her. She died of cancer, you say? I can imagine how she interpreted that.'

'Did my father know this?'

Athena tilts back her head and clicks her tongue. 'No,' she says. 'I am convinced your father thought they were having a run of bad luck, if he even knew of the pregnancy. He was a simple man, completely uneducated, and away most of the time. It would have been easy to hide things from him.'

She comes to the end of the story and falls silent.

If what she claims is true, the people closest to me had lied to the child I had been. They claimed that Athena had been killed and her body dumped. And yet here she is, alive and by all accounts happy. Amya and Uncle Haralambos had betrayed my childish trust: their lie had spawned a thousand pernicious actions of which I was ashamed. For all I knew, my parents were in on it, too. They must have been. They lived in each other's pockets. Whether they meant to or not, their words had poisoned my life.

As if she can read my mind, Athena says, 'Don't judge them too harshly. I am sure that they suffered too. You can not kill your own flesh and blood and not feel it in the deepest part of your being. Your mother and my mother had to live with that for the rest of their days.' She reaches across the table and takes my hands. I am too petrified to nod, too choked up to speak.

'Come,' she says, placing her palms on the table and pushing herself up with a grunt. 'It is time.' In that instant I see that she must be a mother whose word can not be denied. I am glad to see it, and that inordinate pride I felt for her earlier wells up in me again. I stand up and force my face to smile.

'I would like to give you a hug and a kiss,' I say, standing before her. 'But I think maybe I am not allowed.'

'You may not,' she answers, smiling shyly. 'It is not permitted.

I can allow you this . . . ' She extends a small hand. I take it in mine. I hold it for a time and search her face for a lost world that had never really existed.

'I hope to see you again,' I say, 'Athena.'

She casts her eyes modestly to the floor, allowing my indulgence to pass. '*Inşallah*, next time you visit the island my husband and I will be here,' she replies.

I turn to leave.

'Dimitri,' she calls. 'Let me tell you something.' I turn to face her. 'You and I,' she says. 'We are caught in the crossfire. We are Greek and Turk at the same time. We are like a person who loves two people at the same time. Let us share in the *ouzo* and the *rakı*.' She realises what she has said and smothers a laugh with her hand. 'Not that I touch the stuff, mind you.'

Without uttering a word, I turn and leave the house. From the Dadaoğlu house, I walk downhill to Republic Street and from there to the water. I reach the harbour in less than fifteen minutes to find Sinan pacing the pier.

He is obviously relieved to see me. 'Ah, you have arrived,' he says, dashing forward with an anxious frown. 'I was starting to worry.'

'No need,' I reply, hooking my hand through his elbow. 'I am here. Let's go.'

We board the ferry. Sinan climbs to the upper deck, while I sit inside the car. I can not bear to look back as the island falls once again into the fathomless horizon. As the ferry draws away from the pier, I sit with my back turned and my hands buried in the soil I had collected yesterday from our country property to fill my pockets. In my shirt pocket, I feel the weight of the small white stone picked from the chapel ruins.

In legend and folklore, it is said that vampires must sleep on native soil to gain maximum benefit from the sleep of unrest. Some line their boots with it so that the mother of creation can sing from the soles of their feet up. Then and only then can they ease the burden of yearning for that which was lost in the quest for immortality. Since we were islanders, it was also said that a vampire could not cross running water unless he had a supply of native soil about his person. Even then he would be liable to experience listlessness and vertigo, disorientation and possibly even the true death.

Though I sit in the full glare of the sun, I know how vampires must have felt. Through the thin fabric of my clothing, the combined alchemy of stone and soil penetrate my skin and work into my bloodstream, rejuvenating, strengthening, and quietly poisoning a part of my being, too.

I cast a final glance at the island, purple as a plum and lumpy as a gourd. There on the jetty stands the ten-year-old boy in scruffy shoes and eyebrows downy as kitten fur. He is unmoving, rigid. He smiles. His teeth are mirrors, and when he plunges into the sea, his outstretched arms anchor his body to the ocean floor. In the moment before his body arches toward the water, an exquisite image of a woman with dark, streaming hair rises from the depths to drag him down. When the tops of their heads meet, there is barely a ripple on the surface, the worlds part, the boy is absorbed and the iron grille of the sea closes over.

On a suffocating autumn evening, I leave my air-conditioned hotel and take to the streets of Istanbul. Even though I am high up in Beyoğlu, the heat is stifling. Taksim Square and Independence Street are a sea of people on the promenade, surging into the narrow boulevard, cascading down the steep side streets. The rising aroma of grilled food is like a tent overhead; held up by sprigs of lancing Turkish pop music. There is laughter and a sound that is like the buzzing of bees but is in fact people speaking and laughing all at once.

I wonder if it had been this lively in the 1950s, when my mother lived nearby. Earlier I had dined with Sinan, our farewell. When he dropped me off in the narrow street outside the Pera Palas Hotel, I held him in my arms and whispered in his ear, 'Goodbye, little brother. See you next time.' For that is what he has become. My lost sibling, younger and, in some ways, older than me. Despite the great distances that separate us, I know that I have found a kindred spirit. 'Yes, see you,' he replied, kissing me on both cheeks. I do not know how long it will be before I see him again. Nevertheless, an unbreakable bond exists between us. In ways that neither one of us can fathom, it is as if we have always known each other and have been waiting for this juncture in our lives to meet again.

After he leaves and the crowds evaporate, I walk from Taksim Square the length of Tarlabaşı Street, through the tangle of dark alleys, to the Golden Horn. In the still, clear air I want to have the city to myself. To listen as its pulse slows. At one point, I become aware that I am in the district where my mother lived and worked for two years. Further down the hill, closer to the water, then, should be a more imposing nineteenth-century residence. In the 1930s, my maternal grandmother had worked there as a maid for a Greek merchant.

There is hardly anyone out, even fewer cars. Yet the streets are haunted by so many periods, ages, sighing as the buildings cool and stretch, and the vacant lots turn over in their sleep. The magical qualities of this half-half city are in the seven marble hills, in the gait and lope of streets, in the purple coils of morning glory. They're in the gleam of dark hair caught under amber light, in the shape of a nose and the turn of an ear and jaw, in the relaxed limbs. In the rubbish heaped beside a doorway. It's all there; coming at you, age upon age, crumbled dream upon crumbled dream.

And that's when I see her, coming toward me.

Her fawn handbag sways at her elbow, chestnut hair curls over her lobes, a suggestion of earrings glitters palely in the light. She looks barely twenty. She has the same quizzical brow and unwavering gaze that pinned you down like a butterfly on green velvet, and she walks casually on the sidewalk, like the poet Orhan Veli's coquette in 'I am Listening to Istanbul'. And yet, unlike Veli's, my eyes are open. Any minute now, I expect a rose to fall from her hand.

My immediate impression is that she belongs here, un-equivocally. I know that she had always felt out of place on Bozcaada. But here, she breathes a rarefied air. There's manna on her tongue. It is in her walk, the way she places one foot before the other as she comes closer. In the way her long coat, irrespective of the warmth, drapes her body. She angles her head slightly to the right and smiles.

'It is you,' she says. 'I wasn't sure at first. But it is you.'

I remain wordless. She turns and we walk down the hill, towards the water, mother and son, in silent solidarity. We don't need any evidence, even though she, the mother, is younger than the son. And I, the son, now a grown man, am almost twenty years her elder, the woman whose body had been, in another time, my carriage to the world.

As she turns into this street and follows that alleyway, a labyrinth, she rails about the fact that there are no *simit* sellers at this time of the night. 'You used to love them so,' she says. 'Remember?' I nod, fighting back the tears.

That the stalls in the Flower Market are closed bothers her even more. 'You can live without food,' she says. 'But the smell of blooms and leaves is majestic.' I don't have the heart to tell her that the Flower Market no longer sells flowers. She never spoke like this when alive. I think that perhaps I am seeing and hearing the other her, the woman she might have been had she remained in Istanbul and never come back to the island.

That's how it really was. My body becomes legs that follow, eyes that dare not blink, and ears that resound with the roar of the sea. Finally, on a steep cobbled street that washes its feet in the Horn, she stops before a building unaffected by the general decline of the district. The house has a dove-grey door with a brass knocker, a graceful hand with a pommel in its grasp. When I look directly at the number on the door it evaporates, like milk in water. When I glance away, it coalesces again in the corner of my eye.

From her bag, the girl that is not yet my mother retrieves a large, old-fashioned key, beautifully crafted, and soundlessly slides it into the lock. Inside, on a low table, I see that a kerosene lamp burns. The corridor stretches into darkness on one side while the first few steps of a staircase climb to the upper storeys on the other.

With her back to me, she says, 'Don't live in the past. No good can come of it.'

'It's too late, Mama,' I respond.

'It was inevitable.' She turns and looks into my eyes. 'I see that I can't help you after all. I thought I might be able to. But you are on your own and you must decide what to do and where to go from here.'

The door closes gently. In the rectangular glass above, I see the light retreat into the house. I am left standing on the street, feeling like Montgomery Clift rejected by Olivia De Havilland at the end of *The Heiress*. If I have dreamed this, while walking the streets of Istanbul, the subconscious of lives aborted, past and present, brushing by me in the dark, what makes it so real? I check to see if by chance 'a white moon is rising above the pistachio tree'. But, unlike Veli's eyes, mine are open.

Much later, I find myself on the first of the bridges that link the new city to the old. I can not recollect having walked here. A soft rain falls, tickling my ears and running down the back of my neck. It is late. The fishermen that line the bridge in daylight have gone home for the night. An occasional car swishes by behind me on the wet road. High on the hill, the Galata Tower stands sentinel over my dreams, and on the opposite shore the New Mosque and the Spice Bazaar shimmer in the misty light.

I search the turbulent depths below me. At this point, the Golden Horn joins the waters of the Bosphorus. They come together in a clash of wills. I remove your photograph from my pocket, Mother. I place a kiss on your lips and let it fly into the darkness. I stride away before the swirling water closes over your head. The most beautiful word in the Turkish language is also the saddest: *Elveda*. It means farewell. This now I say to you. *Elveda*.

ACKNOWLEDGEMENTS

The author wishes to thank the following for support and advice during the writing of this book: Effie Kakmi, Leigh Hobbs, Ahmet Cimenoğlu, Moris (Musa) Farhi, Ivor Indyk, Oya Kural, Ersin Ciğerli, Binnur Karaevli, Katina and Manolis Zafiris, Azhar Nik and John Kemp, Phillip Batty, Ebru Hilal Kolçak and Alper Demir, Hatice and Vecihi Başarin, Hatice Gök, Virginia Bernard, Barnaby Rogerson and Rose Baring, Cameron Rogers and The Peter Blazey Fellowship.

This is a true story; some names have been changed. Some events have been chronologically rearranged for dramatic purposes; in two instances, two people have been fused into one. A fictional episode has been inserted into part three to facilitate the revelation of factual information gained over a period of years from different individuals, in a manner that makes dramatic sense and hopefully provides a satisfactory conclusion for the reader.

ELAND

61 Exmouth Market, London EC1R 4QL
Fax: 020 7833 4434
Email: info@travelbooks.co.uk

Eland was started in 1982 to revive great travel books
that had fallen out of print. Although the list has diversified
into biography and fiction, it is united by a quest to define the
spirit of place. These are books for travellers, and for readers who aspire
to explore the world but who are also content to travel in their own
minds.

Eland books open out our understanding of other
cultures, interpret the unknown and reveal different environments
as well as celebrating the humour and occasional horrors of travel. We
take immense trouble to select only the most readable
books and therefore many readers collect the entire series.

All our books are printed on fine, pliable, cream-coloured paper.
Most are still gathered in sections by our printer and sewn as well
as glued, almost unheard of for a paperback book these days.
This gives larger margins in the gutter, as well as
making the books stronger.

You will find a very brief description of all our books on the
following pages. Extracts from each and every one of them can be
read on our website, at www.travelbooks.co.uk. If you would
like a free copy of our catalogue, please fax, email
or write to us (details above).

ELAND

'One of the very best travel lists' WILLIAM DALRYMPLE

Memoirs of a Bengal Civilian
JOHN BEAMES
*Sketches of nineteenth-century India
painted with the richness of Dickens*

Jigsaw
SYBILLE BEDFORD
*An intensely remembered autobiographical
novel about an inter-war childhood*

A Visit to Don Otavio
SYBILLE BEDFORD
*The hell of travel and the Eden of arrival
in post-war Mexico*

Journey into the Mind's Eye
LESLEY BLANCH
*An obsessive love affair with Russia and
one particular Russian*

Japanese Chronicles
NICOLAS BOUVIER
*Three decades of intimate experiences
throughout Japan*

The Way of the World
NICOLAS BOUVIER
Two men in a car from Serbia to Afghanistan

Persia: through writers' eyes
ED. DAVID BLOW
*Guidebooks for the mind: a selection
of the best travel writing on Iran*

The Devil Drives
FAWN BRODIE
*Biography of Sir Richard Burton,
explorer, linguist and pornographer*

Turkish Letters
OGIER DE BUSBECQ
*Eyewitness history at its best:
Istanbul during the reign of Suleyman
the Magnificent*

My Early Life
WINSTON CHURCHILL
*From North-West Frontier to Boer War
by the age of twenty-five*

Sicily: through writers' eyes
ED. HORATIO CLARE
*Guidebooks for the mind: a selection
of the best travel writing on Sicily*

A Square of Sky
JANINA DAVID
*A Jewish childhood in the Warsaw
ghetto and hiding from the Nazis*

Chantemesle
ROBIN FEDDEN
*A lyrical evocation of childhood
in Normandy*

Croatia: through writers' eyes
ED. FRANKOPAN, GOODING & LAVINGTON
*Guidebooks for the mind: a selection
of the best travel writing on Croatia*

Viva Mexico!
CHARLES FLANDRAU
A traveller's account of life in Mexico

Travels with Myself and Another
MARTHA GELLHORN
*Five journeys from hell by a great
war correspondent*

The Weather in Africa
MARTHA GELLHORN
*Three novellas set amongst the
white settlers of East Africa*

The Last Leopard
DAVID GILMOUR
*The biography of Giuseppe di Lampedusa,
author of* The Leopard

Walled Gardens
ANNABEL GOFF
An Anglo-Irish childhood

Africa Dances
GEOFFREY GORER
*The magic of indigenous culture
and the banality of colonisation*

92 Acharnon Street
JOHN LUCAS
A gritty portrait of Greece as the Greeks would recognise it, seen through the eyes of a poet

Egypt: through writers' eyes
ED. MANLEY & ABDEL-HAKIM
Guidebooks for the mind: a selection of the best travel writing on Egypt

Among the Faithful
DAHRIS MARTIN
An American woman living in the holy city of Kairouan, Tunisia in the 1920s

Lords of the Atlas
GAVIN MAXWELL
The rise and fall of Morocco's infamous Glaoua family, 1893-1956

A Reed Shaken by the Wind
GAVIN MAXWELL
Travels among the threatened Marsh Arabs of southern Iraq

A Year in Marrakesh
PETER MAYNE
Back-street life in Morocco in the 1950s

Sultan in Oman
JAN MORRIS
An historic journey through the still-medieval state of Oman in the 1950s

Hopeful Monsters
NICHOLAS MOSLEY
Love at the birth of the atomic age

The Caravan Moves On
IRFAN ORGA
Life with the nomads of central Turkey

Portrait of a Turkish Family
IRFAN ORGA
The decline of a prosperous Ottoman family in the new Republic

Sweet Waters
HAROLD NICHOLSON
An Istanbul thriller

The Undefeated
GEORGE PALOCZI-HORVATH
Fighting injustice in communist Hungary

Travels into the Interior of Africa
MUNGO PARK
The first – and still the best – European record of west-African exploration

Lighthouse
TONY PARKER
Britain's lighthouse-keepers, in their own words

The People of Providence
TONY PARKER
A London housing estate and some of its inhabitants

Begums, Thugs & White Mughals
FANNY PARKES
William Dalrymple edits and introduces his favourite Indian travel book

The Last Time I Saw Paris
ELLIOT PAUL
One street, its loves and loathings, set against the passionate politics of inter-war Paris

Rites
VICTOR PERERA
A Jewish childhood in Guatemala

A Cure for Serpents
THE DUKE OF PIRAJNO
An Italian doctor and his Bedouin patients, Libyan sheikhs and Tuareg mistress in the 1920s

Nunaga
DUNCAN PRYDE
Ten years among the Eskimos: hunting, fur-trading and heroic dog-treks

Ask Sir James
MICHAELA REID
The life of Sir James Reid,
personal physician to Queen Victoria

A Funny Old Quist
EVAN ROGERS
A gamekeeper's passionate evocation
of a now-vanished English rural lifestyle

Meetings with Remarkable Muslims
ED. ROGERSON & BARING
A collection of contemporary travel
writing that celebrates cultural difference
and the Islamic world

Marrakesh: through writers' eyes
ED. ROGERSON & LAVINGTON
Guidebooks for the mind: a selection
of the best travel writing on Marrakesh

Turkish Aegean: through writers' eyes
ED. RUPERT SCOTT
Guidebooks for the mind: a selection
of the best travel writing on Turkey

Valse des Fleurs
SACHEVERELL SITWELL
A day in St Petersburg in 1868

Living Poor
MORITZ THOMSEN
An American's encounter with
poverty in Ecuador

Hermit of Peking
HUGH TREVOR-ROPER
The hidden life of the scholar
Sir Edmund Backhouse

The Law
ROGER VAILLAND
The harsh game of life played in
the taverns of southern Italy

Bangkok
ALEC WAUGH
The story of a city

The Road to Nab End
WILLIAM WOODRUFF
The best selling story of poverty and
survival in a Lancashire mill town

The Village in the Jungle
LEONARD WOOLF
A dark novel of native villagers struggling
to survive in colonial Ceylon

Death's Other Kingdom
GAMEL WOOLSEY
The tragic arrival of civil war in an
Andalucian village in 1936

The Ginger Tree
OSWALD WYND
A Scotswoman's love and survival
in early twentieth-century Japan

Poetry of Place series

London: Poetry of Place
ED. BARING & ROGERSON
A poetry collection like the city itself, full of
grief, irony and delight

Andalus: Poetry of Place
ED. TED GORTON
Moorish songs of love and wine

Venice: Poetry of Place
ED. HETTY MEYRIC HUGHES
Eavesdrop on the first remembered glimpses
of the city, and meditations on her history

Desert Air: Poetry of Place
ED. MUNRO & ROGERSON
On Arabia, deserts and the Orient of
the imagination

Istanbul: Poetry of Place
ED. ATES ORGA
Poetry from her long history, from paupers to
sultans, natives and visitors alike

The Ruins of Time
ED. ANTHONY THWAITE
Sized to fit any purse or pocket, this is just the
book to complement a picnic amongst the
ruins of time